THE TREASURE OF PARAGON BOOK 8

tHE DRAGONS Of PARAGON

USA TODAY BESTSELLING AUTHOR
GENEVIEVE JACK

The Dragons of Paragon: The Treasure of Paragon, Book 8

Copyright © Genevieve Jack 2021

Published by Carpe Luna Ltd, Bloomington, IL 61704

First Edition: August 2021

eISBN: 978-1-940675-66-4

Paperback: 978-1-940675-73-2

v 2.3

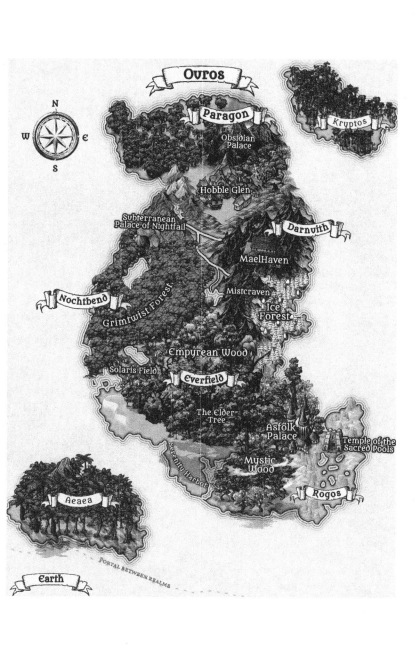

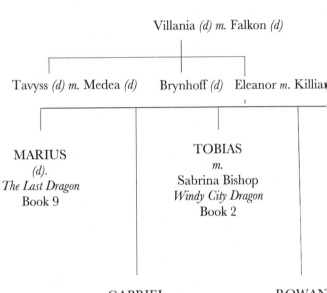

Villania *(d) m.* Falkon *(d)*

Tavyss *(d) m.* Medea *(d)*   Brynhoff *(d)*   Eleanor *m.* Killian

MARIUS
(d).
The Last Dragon
Book 9

TOBIAS
m.
Sabrina Bishop
Windy City Dragon
Book 2

GABRIEL
m.
Raven Tanglewood
The Dragon of New Orleans
Book 1

ROWAN
m.
Nick Grands
Manhattan Dr
Book 3

The Treasure of Paragon

FAMILY TREE

EXANDER
m.
Maiara
Dragon of Sedona
Book 4

XAVIER
m.
Avery Tanglewood
Highland Dragon
Book 6

COLIN
*The Dragons of
Paragon*
Book 8

NATHANIEL
m.
Clarissa Black
*The Dragon of Cecil
Court*
Book 5

SYLAS
m.
Dianthe
Hidden Dragon
Book 7

AUTHOR'S NOTE

Dear Reader,

Love is the truest magic and the most fulfilling fantasy. Thank you for coming along on this journey as I share the tale of the Treasure of Paragon, nine exiled royal dragon shifters destined to find love and their way home.

There are three things you can expect from a Genevieve Jack novel: magic will play a key role, unexpected twists are the norm, and love will conquer all.

The Treasure of Paragon Reading Order

The Dragon of New Orleans, Book 1
Windy City Dragon, Book 2,
Manhattan Dragon, Book 3
The Dragon of Sedona, Book 4
The Dragon of Cecil Court, Book 5
Highland Dragon, Book 6
Hidden Dragon, Book 7
The Dragons of Paragon, Book 8
The Last Dragon, Book 9

Keep in touch to stay in the know about new releases, sales, and giveaways.

Join my VIP reader group
Sign up for my newsletter

Now, let's spread our wings (or at least our pages) and escape together!

Genevieve Jack

ABOUT THE BOOK

A clash of kingdoms.

Colin's dragon has its jeweled heart set on Leena, but she's a distraction he doesn't need. The stars have aligned, and it's time for the Defenders of the Goddess to take back the throne of Paragon or be crushed under the evil empress's heel. Colin, along with his siblings, is at the center of it all, so why can't he stop his dragon's obsession?

A war of hearts.

Elf scribe Leena made a vow to the goddess and her people—and she doesn't intend to break it. Still, there's only so much temptation any woman can bear. War threatens Rogos. As much as Leena would like to avoid her feelings for Colin, she's key to helping him and the resistance defend her land against Paragon.

A final chance.

As the world unravels around them, Colin and Leena must come to terms with what's truly important. How far will Colin go in his quest for the kingdom? And can Leena resist the comfort of his embrace in what could be their final days?

CHAPTER ONE

Titan Beach
Aeaea Island
Year of the Goddess: ‚βιθ, Capricorn 2nd

I, *Leena of Niven, scribe of the Order of the Sacred Pools,*
continue to document the events unfolding on the island
of Aeaea as the Defenders of the Goddess make strides in the
effort to liberate Paragon from Empress Eleanor and end her
tyrannical expanse of power in Ouros. In recent weeks,
Dianthe of Everfield and Sylas of Paragon successfully
obtained the five orbs left behind by Medea for those prophe-
sied to challenge the empress.

As detailed in the scroll of Daluk, each orb held a frag-
ment of a key to the hiding place of the golden grimoire, a
book of spells foretold to carry the secret to Eleanor's undo-
ing. It is widely believed that the book holds the magic of the
gods themselves within its pages, and anyone strong enough
to wield it will be powerful enough to reign over all of Ouros.

Last night, Charlie, the daughter of Gabriel and Raven,
passed her hand through each of the enchanted orbs and

obtained the fragments sealed inside. All five had already proven impervious to the goddess's tears, dragon fire, and all manner of blade and claw. The fact that the child was able to retrieve each of the objects effortlessly proves Medea's magic is as relevant to the cause today as it was during her time as queen of Darnuith.

Once the key was assembled, it proved to be an elven crypt key, which means the golden grimoire is likely hidden somewhere in Rogos in an elf's tomb. Daluk's writings are intentionally vague. The location of the crypt and the code to set the key remain a mystery. As Daluk has passed on to the eternal forest, the scribe's scrolls are the only clues to the grimoire's whereabouts.

There is another message hidden by enchantment beneath Daluk's writings, and it is my belief that the palimpsest holds the answers to obtaining the grimoire. However, no elf or witch magic—not even that of the three sisters—has been able to break the spell concealing it. Worse, before her death, Aborella claimed the only way to read the message was by focusing the three sisters' magic using the tanglewood tree, which was unfortunately destroyed by fire in the earthly realm centuries ago.

Unless another solution presents itself soon, the Defenders of the Goddess will find themselves in the position of having to move forward without the grimoire. The circumstances couldn't be more dire as, just days ago, Everfield fell to Paragon. The Obsidian Guard now occupies what was once the Empyrean Wood and therefore controls trade routes between Nochtbend and the rest of Ouros.

Colin, leader of the resistance, trains daily with his brother warriors, readying for war, but with Eleanor's ever-increasing magic and army of immortal dragons, the resis-

tance will need far more help if they are to have any hope of defeating Paragon.

"THEY'RE FUN TO WATCH, AREN'T THEY?" DIANTHE asked, interrupting Leena's writing.

Leena stopped her scrawl, the metalwork quill she used poised over the parchment. The finely crafted writing implement looked like a feather but was far more sophisticated. Enchanted to never run out of ink, it was the hallmark of her position as a scribe, as was the enchanted parchment she used that never ran out of room to write. "I'm documenting what's happening here. Even with the aid of the holiest of sacred pools, no scribe can see Aeaea. I'm the only one who can record these events for the sacred library."

Dianthe sat beside her, her wings fluttering as she balanced on the boulder and crossed her legs. The fairy's long, lithe limbs were not unlike an elf's, but she moved with a supernatural grace Leena had always admired.

"You know, you can both appreciate the view and write about it," she said, flashing Leena an impish smile.

Leena raised her eyes, and they instantly locked on Colin. Although he was only one of several shirtless masses of muscle performing exercises on the beach, he might as well be moving through his routine alone for how much she noticed the others. Maybe it was his size; he had at least a hundred pounds on his twin, Dianthe's mate Sylas, and was as large, if not larger, than Gabriel. Golden skin glinted with sweat, his muscles bunching and rippling with his movement.

Colin pivoted, shouting instructions to the other dragons. They all paired up and started to spar. Sylas and Colin exchanged punches and blocks faster than her eye could follow. Their almost identical garnet rings flashed in the sunlight as their heavily muscled forearms connected again and again.

The dragons always trained with their wings out. Colin's were leathery and dark red, almost black, with a lethal-looking hooked talon at each apex. He wielded those massive claws like the weapons they were, hooking into the talons in Sylas's lighter-colored wings to hold him in place before landing a strike into his brother's side.

Everything about Colin designated him as their leader, from the way he carried himself to the confident gleam in his gray eyes that always reminded her of burnished steel. And then there was his arm. Wavelike furrows ran from wrist to neck. She'd watched him snatch the purple orb from the bottom of a sacred pool at superspeed with that arm. It was incredibly brave and equally stupid. The goddess's tears had burned away his flesh, and he'd fallen on the sand, writhing in agony. She'd tended his wounds following that ordeal. Although he'd healed, the skin of his arm—his right foreleg in dragon form—was permanently scarred.

Those scars were a symbol of his limitless bravery. A sign of his unreasonable ability to endure pain.

Yes, any opponent should fear what that arm represented. It was proof that Colin would be the last to give in and he'd never give up. Even if the resistance never found the grimoire, Eleanor would be a fool to underestimate him.

"Blink, Leena," Dianthe said. "Breathe."

She started, her head snapping around to look at the fairy. "I, uh…" Had she lost herself staring at Colin again? Her cheeks blazed.

Dianthe's teasing expression softened, and she placed a hand on her arm. "Please don't be embarrassed. It's the rare woman who can claim immunity to a dragon's charms. I've been married to Sylas for decades, and it still makes me feel like a flower in the sun every time he looks in my direction."

Leena licked her lips. Maybe it was normal what she was feeling, even though she was a scribe. She pressed her hand into her stomach. "When I look at Colin, it feels as if I've jumped off a high place."

Dianthe's brows edged toward each other, her dark skin wrinkling between her eyes. "Just Colin? Or all the dragons?"

Leena's face was hot again, and she scratched behind her ear. "Just Colin. It must be because I know him best. I'm sure that is common for females."

The fairy brushed a hand over one of her arms as if dusting away something that wasn't there. "That depends. Can I ask you a personal question, female-to-female?"

Leena nodded. Desperate to do something with her nervous energy, she returned her quill to its box and began rolling the scroll carefully in her lap.

"Do you have much experience with males?"

She chewed her lip, then twitched a nervous smile. "No. Of course not. I'm a scribe."

"Not even from before you became a scribe?" Dianthe's voice was soft and supportive, without a trace of judgment.

Leena felt she could tell the fairy anything and she'd keep it in the strictest confidence. So she told the truth. "I grew up in the temple, so there is no before."

Dianthe tensed beside her, only for a fraction of a second, and then she uncrossed her legs and hugged her knees. "Is that common among your kind?"

"No." Leena smiled. Now they were in territory she

didn't care to talk about, no matter how much she knew she could trust Dianthe. Her brow furrowed. "I had special circumstances." She made her answer curt enough that she was sure her friend wouldn't push it.

A long silence stretched between them, punctuated only by the grunts of the warriors practicing in front of them. Leena slid her scroll and the box with her quill into her satchel. She should go back to her tent.

"It's just..." Dianthe nudged her arm before she could climb off the stone. "...I wonder why that's allowed. I mean, your special situation."

"Hmm?" Leena didn't understand what she was getting at.

Dianthe folded her arms across her middle. "Don't get me wrong, I've always had a deep respect for scribes and the sacrifice all of you make for your beliefs. I wonder, though, how one can give something up before they even know what it is they're giving up. Aren't there... things you're curious about?" Her eyes darted to Colin but didn't linger.

All at once, Leena's skin tightened. She'd been too obvious in her observation of Colin. Dianthe could see right through her to that strange thing he produced in her. Her heart thumped in her chest. "I... It would be inappropriate."

Dianthe sighed. "Of course. It's against the rules."

"Not strictly," Leena admitted. "The Quanling—our superior as female scribes—takes a vow of celibacy, but scribes such as I only take an oath to devote our lives to recording the history of Ouros. That oath is incompatible with marriage, mating, or children as those things would distract us from our calling, but... technically... other things are not prohibited as long as they don't pull us away from our work."

The fairy's smile widened, one corner of her red lips

twitching with amusement Leena wasn't sure she followed. "Do some scribes often indulge in these other things?"

Leena scoffed. "Honestly, no. None of us would have the opportunity. We rarely leave the temple or encounter anyone outside the order. Even among our kind, males and females live their lives in separate wings of the temple. We rarely cross paths."

"Hmm." Dianthe drummed her fingers on her knee. "So you are in a unique position then to... broaden your horizons."

The innuendo landed in the pit of Leena's stomach, and her eyes flicked up to Colin of their own accord, her heart pounding harder at the mere idea of experimentation with the golden mountain of shimmering muscle who at that very moment was throwing Sylas to the sand. "Until I become Quanling," she said absently.

"Is that something you want to do?"

Leena took a deep breath and turned back toward Dianthe. "It's all I've ever worked for. If all goes well, I'll replace my Quanling, Marjory, next year when she retires."

"In a year! But you're so young!"

Leena wasn't sure why Dianthe seemed horrified by the idea, but her smile had flipped at her admission. "I started in the order at a young age. I meet all the requirements."

Wings fluttering, Dianthe turned her face toward the sun and closed her eyes, seeming to absorb the heat. "Well then, if you have any curiosity about... other things... I guess now would be your chance to get it out of your system."

Palms sweaty, Leena checked that Dianthe's eyes were closed before taking another lingering look at Colin. A thought she'd long suppressed wormed its way to the surface of her mind. Was she attracted to him? Did she want to experiment with the things she would one day swear to leave behind? She shook her head. The very thought was folly.

Absolutely this was the right time to leave, to slip back to her tent before things became even more confusing. She pushed off the rock and looped her satchel over her head so that the strap fell across her body, adjusting it on her shoulder. But before she could exchange parting words with Dianthe, the three sisters strode onto the beach.

The three women were a formidable sight. Raven, with her long black hair and striking blue eyes, exuded raw power, even with baby Charlie in her arms. Avery, who had almost identical features as Raven but a curvier build, was never without her sword, and Leena had witnessed her brandish that iron better than any man. Clarissa with her platinum hair and dark roots always struck her as the most unpredictable. The woman was friendly, though occasionally irreverent, and wielded her power in the most unexpected way, through song. Together, the three commanded attention. Immediately, the dragons stopped practicing and looked their way.

In Raven's arms, Charlie, who seemed to have grown an inch overnight, pointed to Gabriel and squealed, "Da, Da, Da!" Avery and Clarissa hung back a few steps behind their sister. Strange. It looked almost as if they were dreading what was about to happen.

Raven raised her chin. "Everyone, if you'll gather around, we have some news."

CHAPTER TWO

Colin wiped the sweat from his eyes, lengthening one arm across his chest while extending his opposing wing to increase the stretch. He moved in closer, curious about what Raven had to say. She looked serious, and it was never a good sign when a powerful witch like her was serious.

"What's going on?" he asked as the others filed around him. He noticed Leena at the edge of the crowd of dragons, near Dianthe. He always noticed Leena. His inner dragon seemed to have become a compass that pointed toward her rather than north. He forced himself not to look at her and instead focused on Raven as Gabriel lifted Charlie from her arms.

"Last night, when we spoke about how Aborella died and what she shared in her last moments, it's possible some vital information was overlooked," Raven said.

Out of the corner of his eye, he saw Dianthe fidget with her hair, her eyes darting toward the sky as if this wasn't exactly news to her. He narrowed his eyes on Raven. "What kind of information?"

Avery cleared her throat. "Aborella seemed to think that part of the tanglewood tree remains somewhere in our parents' bar—the Three Sisters—in the Earth realm."

"Do you mean to tell me that, where you are from, your parents own a tavern called the Three Sisters?" Sylas grimaced, a low growl rumbling from his chest. "Prophetic, wouldn't you say? Why didn't you mention this last night? We were under the impression we'd have to find a way to do this without the book. Why would you hide something like this?"

"Easy, Sylas." Colin placed a hand on his twin's chest, although he could understand his brother's unease. When Sylas and his mate had returned from their journey to find the orbs and Dianthe and Avery had shared how Aborella had died at Avery's hand, they were all led to believe that all hope of translating the scroll was likely lost, burned with the tanglewood tree. This news meant that someone was holding back information during their debrief—information that could change everything.

"I needed time to process what she told me. It didn't exactly make sense," Avery said defensively.

Sidling up to her sister, Clarissa shot Sylas a look hard enough to have been a physical push. "Let's not get our hopes up, okay? Aborella wasn't always honest, and even if what she said is true, if any part of the tree is there, it will be complicated for us to find."

"What's so complicated about it?" Colin had a bad feeling about this.

"We know for sure that most of the tree was used as fuel to burn my ancestor, Circe—Medea's sister—at the stake," Raven said. "Aborella wasn't specific about what she saw. If any part of the tree survived, it's been hidden for over three hundred years. For all we know, it could be sealed into a wall or rotting under the floorboards. It won't be easy to find, and it means returning to New Orleans, where we're vulnerable. The entire reason we came here to Aeaea was to escape the possibility that Hera or Eleanor was tracking us. She did once with Scoria. She can do it again."

Gabriel's eyes blazed red with his suspicion. "Could be a trap. Aborella was bound to Eleanor. This all might be a ploy to lure us off the island."

Avery dug her toe in the sand. "I don't think it was a ploy. I can't prove it, but if you were there—"

"I agree with Avery," Dianthe said. "I think Aborella was telling the truth."

Colin bristled. His siblings and their mates had fled Earth for good reason. Eleanor could track them if they left Aeaea where Circe's celestial protection shielded them from Eleanor's blood magic. Eleanor wanted Charlie dead. The prophecy said that the child would be her undoing and the end of Paragon as they knew it. The empress had broken through Nathaniel's strongest wards to try to murder the babe. If it weren't for Aborella's warning, the child might not have made it out alive.

"Ye won't be goin' alone, that's fir sure," Xavier said, crossing his arms over his bare chest and staring at Avery as if willing her to fight him on that point.

Nathaniel seemed equally peeved by the idea. He reached a hand toward his hip, most likely reaching for his pipe, then seemed to realize he wasn't wearing his usual suit and crossed his arms, echoing Xavier's stance. "Definitely not going alone," he said, his British accent growing stronger with his anger. "You'll need my magic to travel safely to New Orleans. Public transportation would be suicide."

Gabriel grunted. "Our home in New Orleans has the

strongest blood ward I've ever encountered, thanks to Raven. We'll be safe, at least while we are within its walls."

Contemplating the news, Colin ran a hand along his scarred arm, hating that there wasn't a better alternative. As the leader of the Defenders of the Goddess, he knew the others were waiting for his blessing, but it was risky sending the three sisters back into the earthly realm. Strategically, the resistance needed their magic if they were to have any hope of defeating Eleanor, and personally, he would never forgive himself if something happened to one of his siblings or their mates. But the promise of the grimoire was enough bait to get him to bite. It was their best and truest hope of salvation.

"If there's a chance the key to finding the grimoire is on Earth, we have to try," he said. "Raven, Avery, Clarissa, Gabriel, Xavier, and Nathaniel will go. Between the six of you, you should be strong enough to keep one another safe."

"Seven," Raven said. "We're not going anywhere without Charlie."

Colin growled. "It isn't safe—"

Raven's eyes flared, and the ground rumbled beneath his feet. "She's safe where her mother and father are."

He wasn't going to fight with that. Coming between a witch and her daughter was far beyond his pay grade. A quick glance at Gabriel confirmed he didn't have a problem with it. If his brother thought the best course of action was taking the child, Colin wouldn't force the issue. "Fine. The seven of you will go, find the piece of the tree, and return here."

A murmur passed through the others.

Raven gave him a curt nod. "We'll try our best to be quick about it."

"Excellent." Colin knew he was being hopelessly optimistic, but he felt good about this move. "With any luck, you'll find the tree and we'll have the enchantment on that scroll cracked before things heat up any more on Ouros. We need to know the content of Medea's message."

The group dispersed, and Colin allowed himself the pleasure of glancing in Leena's direction, but she wasn't there. He caught the back of her dark copper braid as she disappeared into the jungle in the direction of her tent. *Odd.* Almost like she was running away.

CHAPTER THREE

L eena hadn't come to dinner, and Colin was tempted to go find her.

Funny thing, temptation. As the youngest heir to the throne of Paragon, Colin had plenty of experience with it *and* the disappointment that followed when acting on that temptation led to disaster.

When he was seven, he'd been tempted to skip lessons and play in the garden with the cook's son. How he loved their games. It was the most fun he'd ever had until they were caught.

That was his first lesson that having a royal title wouldn't buy him an ounce of sympathy. They'd both been returned to the palace, where he was whipped by his father, Killian. Dragons were immortal and healed quickly, but a switch against one's backside hurt, nonetheless. The sting was permanently branded on his memory.

Worse, he'd had to watch as his friend received the same from the cook. There was no mercy in those blows, and Colin had witnessed the twinkle of something innocent and pure extinguish from his playmate's eyes with every strike.

The punishment was enough to permanently end their young kinship. The cook, after all, must have feared that his son would cost him his job in the palace. Colin rarely saw the boy after that.

When Colin was fourteen, during one of the family's many royal balls, he'd been tempted to lead a Highborn's daughter out into the same garden for a different sort of play. Perhaps it was a testament to how hormonally distracted he was that he thought things had changed, that being last in the birth order would allow him more freedom to do as he pleased. After all, he never expected to be king. At any rate, his choice of destination could only be chalked up to youthful senselessness. It was arguably the worst hiding spot in the palace.

Surprisingly, when Colin was caught with his hand up her dress, Killian didn't punish him. Instead, he was given a long lecture on the realities of his royal responsibilities. Although the girl might be a temporary distraction, she was not marriage material, and therefore he must be careful not to attach himself. No political gains could be had by the match, after all.

Later, Colin noticed the girl's eyes refused to meet his, and his heart broke at the loss of something—he wasn't sure what—that never had a chance to become.

At twenty and as a fully grown dragon, Colin was tempted to pummel Marius in the pits. All his life, he'd been warned that the younger heirs must never win against their eldest brother. As the one destined to take the throne opposite his sister, Rowan, Marius must always be presented as the strongest and the smartest of the royal clan. Truthfully, Colin thought he was nothing but the haughtiest. But the night Colin gave in to temptation and knocked him on his pompous ass, he was disqualified, accused of cheating, and banned from the pits for an entire season.

And finally, three hundred years ago, a new temptation caught his fancy. It happened after Colin witnessed his uncle Brynhoff murder Marius in the Great Mountain Hall of the Obsidian Palace. Everything changed after that. Scattered to the winds, he and his siblings were suddenly free of any whim other than their own. Oh, he'd followed Nathaniel for a time and then settled in Romania for a few decades, but when temptation struck again, he disobeyed his mother's warnings and returned to Paragon.

That was when he'd learned what she'd done. That was when he'd been tempted to destroy her and his wicked uncle too. It took centuries to build a solid network of resistors across the five kingdoms, and when he caught up with Sylas on the island of Aeaea, he allowed himself to give in to temptation once more and dream of vengeance. He vowed to bring their mother and uncle to justice.

If history was any sort of teacher, he should expect to fail at this too. He was prepared to fail. Prepared for disappointment. But he'd never give up on the Defenders of the Goddess. Not until either he or Eleanor was dead.

After all that, he should be an expert at dealing with temptation. But he found himself experiencing a different sort than he'd ever experienced before. His dragon wanted Leena. Wanted her like he'd never wanted anyone, like a bird longs for the sky. Unfortunately, his feelings for her were doomed to be unrequited.

Leena was a scribe, part of a religious order that took a vow to devote their lives to chronicling the history of Ouros. He'd been lucky even to have these weeks alone with her. Normally the scribes never left the temple. Leena might have spent her entire life gazing into a pool of tears and chronicling what she saw in its reflection if he hadn't ended up at the temple library and employed her help in researching ways to stop Eleanor.

But she was here now, on Aeaea, at least until the three sisters translated Medea's scroll. She'd been assigned to protect it, and he knew she'd guard it with her life until it was safely returned to the temple library.

So when she didn't come to dinner, he simply had to know why, and although on some level he understood she must want to be alone, he couldn't resist the temptation to seek her out. He found her on the beach, watching the suns set over the horizon, the sky painted with turquoise and amethyst in a fantastic display of color that was unique to Aeaea.

"Good news about the three sisters." He cleared his throat and watched her dark copper braid slide off her shoulder as she turned her head to look at him. Her violet eyes sparked as if they were ignited by the sunset behind her. Fragments of the same color purple that streaked the sky flecked her irises, almost as if the heavens had leaked into her. It left him breathless.

"Colin! You startled me. I thought you were at supper?"

"I was. You weren't. I was worried." He searched her face. "The sisters and their mates send their goodbyes. They left right after the meal."

Leena adjusted the neck of her robe and stepped closer to him. Mountain help him, a whisper of blackcurrants and wild primrose wafted through his senses, sending his inner dragon into a frenzy. He schooled his features and tried not to breathe.

"I wasn't hungry." She toyed with her collar again. "I was thinking about what Raven said. If they find the tree, they'll translate the scroll."

"Exactly what we've been waiting for. This could be the break we need."

The corners of her mouth lifted into a shallow smile that didn't quite reach her eyes. She turned her attention to a shell in the sand. "It is great news. How long do you think it will take?"

He sighed. "Days. Weeks. Who knows? This island was created to be a prison for Circe. That means the only way off is by ship to Crete. They can't simply open a portal between realms as they could if they were in Paragon. Once on Crete, Nathaniel can help them travel by magic, but I'm not sure how far or how fast. And once they're there, they'll have to find the tree—what's left of it anyway. Even if I could estimate how long all that would take, time flows differently on Earth. Makes it impossible to guess when they'll return."

She sighed and turned away from him, back toward the sea, looking almost saddened. It didn't make sense. She should have been ecstatic. She'd repeatedly mentioned her desire to return to Rogos. "Are you disappointed it won't happen faster?"

Her brows knit as she answered him. "Not exactly."

"Then what is it?"

"I shouldn't have come here. I shouldn't have left the temple."

"What are you talking about? Do you even realize how much you've helped us?" Perhaps it was ill-advised to move closer to her, but he took her by the shoulders, wanting to make her believe that every word he spoke was true. "I would have never found the first orb without your help... or the scroll. You are the reason we have a fighting chance against Eleanor. We needed you, Leena. We still need you."

A low, feeble sound came from deep in her throat, and

she shook her head. "You don't understand, Colin. I took an oath to devote myself to the goddess. Being here has distracted me from my calling."

Was that a tear in the corner of her eye? Colin frowned. Why was this affecting her so strongly? "Leena," he said softly, "we are called the Defenders of the Goddess for a reason. We've learned that Eleanor's ultimate goal is to kill the goddess and take her place. While I have my reservations about whether that's possible, she's a threat to everything the goddess created and a threat to Ouros. How is it that you believe you're not devoting yourself to the goddess when everything you've done these past weeks has helped us take a giant leap forward in defending her and the traditions she set in place?"

"It's not that what you're doing isn't important. I know I've helped, and I know... You're going to change the world, Colin." She lifted her gaze to his, and her tears made the violet color of her eyes go electric with inner light. "It's just... It's just..."

He lowered his voice to a soothing whisper and swept his thumb under her eye. It came away wet. His chest sank with a deep protective instinct. What was hurting her? How could he stop it? "You can tell me anything, Leena. I'm on your side. Are you homesick? Are you afraid you're missing something in Rogos?"

"No." The word pinched off in her throat, her gaze darting sideways as if she couldn't bear to look directly at him. "I... I fear that I have enjoyed my time here a bit too much."

He had to consciously stop his fingers from digging into her shoulders as his dragon rushed to the underside of his skin. Had he heard her correctly? Was he reading too much into her words to think she was talking about him... *Them*?

He swallowed the thickness in his throat, aching for her to elaborate. "I've enjoyed having you here too."

"I... I never thought I'd feel like this, like I've tasted the corner of life and suddenly want to consume the whole thing." She backed away from him, and he let her go. "My whole life, I've watched the world go by in a pool of the goddess's tears. I've seen our world from every angle. Every kingdom. I thought I had everything. I thought I knew Ouros better than anyone. But... but..."

"But life is more than a reflection of someone else's experiences." He finished her sentence using the softest voice he could muster, but she flinched anyway and looked at him as if he'd injured her. "I'm sorry. I take it back. That was rude of me. I didn't mean to put words in your mouth."

"No. You're right." She wiped the tears from her cheeks. "I never realized how much I was missing. The food here. The freedom." Her gaze met his and held it. "The people."

His skin tingled with the need to touch her, but he kept his hands by his side. They were in uncharted territory. On his end, he felt himself drawn to her by some sort of magnetism or gravity. It almost hurt to deny it. And in her eyes, he thought he saw a similar sentiment. But he reminded himself that she was an innocent, an inexperienced scribe. She couldn't know what it did to him for her to hold his stare. She couldn't know how much he wanted her.

"Dianthe made me realize today that this may be my last and only opportunity to... sample life before I return to the temple for good. I'm on a path to becoming Quanling—"

He cleared his throat. "If there's anything you'd like to try before you go back, I'll make it happen." He shifted his gaze to the sea to break the tension. "Then, when you go back to the temple, you'll have the memories of your time here. It will make your descriptions in the scrolls even more vivid and give you enough memories to last a lifetime." How painful it was to think about her going back. How he wished there was a chance he could make her his. But he wasn't a predator. No matter how much he wanted her, there would be no honor in trying to seduce a scribe.

He was surprised when her hand landed on the bare skin of his arm. Her fingers were long and tapered. Elves in general were shaped narrower and leaner than dragons. *Lithe* would be the word for the people of Rogos. Leena radiated grace and beauty.

Never had a simple touch turned him inside out as hers did. His brow furrowed. "What do you want, Leena?"

Her eyes narrowed, and she licked her lips. When she spoke, her voice was low, as if she feared someone might hear them. "There's something I'd like to try, something I could never do in the temple and may never have the chance to do again."

Colin held absolutely still. "What's that?"

She closed the space between them. Both her hands moved to his chest, her touch a brand through the thin material of his tunic. The tips of her nails scraped over his shoulders, into the short hair at the base of his skull. He forced himself to swallow, and the sound of it blared exceptionally loud in his ears, the pounding of his heart a background rhythm that grew louder with her nearness.

And then she kissed him.

Colin was no stranger to temptation. He locked his hands at his sides, his mind reeling with the feel of her mouth on his, her floral scent invading his space, a welcome and intoxicating storm of his senses. He tentatively returned the kiss, completely lost to the moment. Her lips parted, and there was no denying his need. His inner dragon took over, and his hands lifted of their own accord.

One hand fisted the back of her dark copper hair, and the other banded her waist, clutching her against his body. He invaded her mouth, stroked along her tongue. *Mine,* his inner dragon bellowed inside his head.

Desire clamped him like a vise. He needed her. Needed to be in her, deep. Under her skin. To mark her as *his.*

Leena welcomed his response with a moan, opening wider for him. Her nails scraped along his back, under his wings. He wanted nothing more than to remove his shirt, but no way would he break the kiss to do so. Instead, he endeavored to show her with his mouth exactly what those nails did to him. His trill rumbled in his chest.

She froze. He pulled her closer, but she shoved her hands against his chest and another sliver of space appeared between them. "That sound..."

"My inner dragon."

"Your mating trill."

He nodded. "Be mine, Leena. Don't go back to the temple." It was out of his mouth before he could question his sanity.

All the color drained from her face, and she pushed him away. "No. I can't. I'm so sorry. Oh dear goddess, this was a mistake."

"What? No—"

"Colin, I can't."

The words crushed his soul as completely as if a tsunami had risen from the sea and flattened him to the beach. Cool air rushed between their bodies. It might as well have been a bucket of ice. He stared, stunned silent, as she turned on her heel and ran.

CHAPTER FOUR

New Orleans, LA

R aven blinked into existence on a sidewalk in the Garden District of New Orleans, her sisters' hands sweaty in her own. Even their mates looked beat. They'd sailed to Crete and hadn't wasted a breath before using a series of portals to reach Louisiana. Dragon magic or not, three hops across thousands of miles drained a person.

"Please tell me this is it," Nathaniel said, eyeing the Greek Revival home that stood to his left, set well back from the sidewalk and behind a wrought-iron fence. "I don't think I can do it again."

"Aye. Feels like someone's squeezed me 'bout the middle like a lemon," Xavier added. Even his kilt seemed to hang crookedly, the fabric itself drained of color like the rest of him. Avery leaned heavily into the Scot's side, and it was unclear who was holding up whom.

"This is it," Gabriel confirmed.

Charlie was asleep in her carrier strapped to his chest,

one fluffy white wing peeking out from the navy-blue fabric sling.

Raven's stomach rumbled, and her muscles trembled with exhaustion as she hobbled toward the gate. For the middle of the night, it was remarkably bright in the Garden District. The homes on either side of their Prytania Street address were adorned with twinkling lights. Across the street, a small herd of glowing reindeer nibbled on the lawn. The others seemed to notice that at the same time she did.

"Fucking hell," Avery said. "What day is it here?"

Raven frowned. "I have no idea." Her phone was at the bottom of the ocean, lost in the shipwreck before they'd reached Aeaea. "Let's get inside and find out."

"It looks like Christmas, but it couldn't be. We haven't been gone for that long," Clarissa said.

Gabriel groaned. "Time flows differently here than on Ouros. Raven's right, though. We should move inside. We're not safe here." He glanced furtively in both directions.

Nathaniel puffed on his pipe. "No worries. The time shift is a bit disorienting but nothing a few days of rest won't cure."

"Are you kidding?" Avery asked incredulously. "With it being the holidays, once my mother finds out we're in town, we won't rest for a minute."

"Shh!" Gabriel gestured toward the gate. "Raven, if you please. We can continue this conversation across the threshold and inside the wards."

She approached the gate, the granite slab under it inscribed with *to aíma tou aímatós mou*, roughly translated: blood of my blood.

Xavier stared at the dingy home beyond. There were no lights up in their yard, the front garden was poorly tended, and the window screens of the butter-colored house looked as if they'd started to rust. He grunted. "Have you no oread? The place looks abandoned."

"No. It looks exactly as it did the day we bought it," Raven said. "Nothing to see here. An old home in need of renovation but not dilapidated. The type of thing the eye simply skips over." Raven reached for the gate, its wrought iron showing the slightest bit of rust and wear.

Nathaniel took a puff off his ever-present pipe. "The dreadful appearance is intentional, then?"

Holding open the gate, Raven smiled. "Touch Gabriel or me as you step over the threshold."

Avery's hand landed on her shoulder. As she stepped across the granite, her expression morphed into one of pure wonder. Raven helped the others through and then followed them inside, closing the gate and the wards behind her.

The scene around her changed. The grass greened brighter than it should have for the time of year, and the house took on a fresh coat of butter-yellow paint. The shutters straightened themselves, and the windows lost a coat of grime, each one glowing from within with the light of a single candle. Lights twinkled from the rooftops like Christmas jewels.

"Holy shit." Clarissa sidled up to Raven on the lawn and elbowed her side. "You're some kind of magical genius. This spell held up even while you were gone?"

"It's complicated magic. Draws on the supernatural energy of the city. We're not the only thing that goes bump in the night here." Raven watched her mate stride to the front door. It opened before he reached it, and he stopped, spreading his arms. She pictured Juniper and Hazel clinging to him, feeding off his energy. She couldn't blame the two oreads for choosing to remain invisible. Not only were they in the presence of strangers, but they'd also been left alone without her mate's energy for months.

Finally, Gabriel lowered his arms and passed inside. She followed him, the others filtering in behind her.

"Welcome home, mistress," a silvery, disembodied voice said. "The rooms are prepared, and Juniper is serving supper in the dining room."

"Thank you, Hazel."

Inside, the house glowed. Bows of lighted evergreen hung around each doorframe and along the stair rail. The bright smell of pine and cinnamon filled her lungs. The feast that awaited them at the long ebony table of the dining room included hot chocolate and some sort of fluffy peppermint dessert that made her mouth water. Suddenly she was starving.

"Mama?" Charlie stirred in her carrier, and Gabriel lifted her out of the sling and put her on his hip. She spread her fluffy white wings and pointed at the leg of lamb at the center of the table.

"Out of the mouths of babes." Xavier selected a plate and handed one to Avery.

Stomach rumbling, Raven didn't hesitate to reach for a plate too but screamed when a blur of calico leaped toward her face. She dodged, and her cat, Artemis, landed on the floor near her feet.

Whoosh!

Charlie dove from Gabriel's arms in a flurry of white feathers and swooped to the floor. Artemis screeched, and when her daughter turned, Raven could see why. Charlie gripped Artemis in her teeth.

"Charlie, no!" Raven yelled, finger pointing at the girl's button nose.

Charlie's mouth dropped open. Artemis fell to her feet,

meowed angrily, and scrambled away in a tornado of claws and flying fur. Tears welled in her daughter's eyes, which had grown as wide as saucers.

Gabriel swept her up and patted her back as a wail broke the barrier of her shock. "She doesn't know any better, Raven. Try not to yell. You're scaring her."

"She tried to eat the cat!" Raven said tersely. "Something had to be done."

With another poof of white feathers, Charlie wiggled from Gabriel's grip and flew to the table, where she landed near the lamb and unceremoniously sank her teeth into it.

"I guess she's hungry," Clarissa said, hiding a laugh behind her upturned plate.

Raven shook a finger at her sister. "Don't encourage her. It's not funny." She tried her best not to laugh and only succeeded in pressing her lips tightly together as the sides of her mouth lifted.

Avery snickered.

"Charlie, come here. I'll fix you a plate." Raven reached for her daughter, but the little girl tore off a piece of meat and flew to the top of the china cabinet, where she ate from her hands while she surveyed them all from above.

For a second, Raven just stared at her daughter, thinking how feral she looked tearing into the meat with her teeth. Then panic planted a seed and grew a little garden in her mind. "She can fly." Raven gaped at Gabriel. "Our daughter can *fly!*"

"Yes, she can," Gabriel said proudly.

"What are we going to do? She looks like a wild animal. I can't have her flying across the room every time she sees something meaty! What about Mom? The last time she saw me, I was pregnant. I can't bring this with me into her world." She pointed a hand at her daughter.

Nathaniel tapped his pipe against his chin. "We could drug her if you're not averse."

Raven gave him an incredulous look. "Of course I'm averse! I'm not going to let you tranquilize my baby."

"Perhaps ye could make a changlin' baby from magic. Animate a doll or such," Xavier offered.

Clarissa tipped her head. "That is a tall order. Sarah and David are going to want to hold their grandchild. It would take one hell of a spell to make a fake Charlie seem human."

"Can we borrow a baby?" Nathaniel asked. "Surely you must have some American friend who can—"

"Lend me their newborn?" Raven fixed him with a pointed stare. "Sorry, no."

"Now that you say it, it does sound like a rather steep ask." Nathaniel tugged at the cuffs of his suit jacket. "Only trying to help."

Avery's face turned solemn. "Maybe we should tell her the truth."

"Now I'm sure you're crazy!" Raven blurted. "Maybe I could pretend to still be pregnant. Technically, I conceived in February, which would make a human due date of November, but we were married in June. Could I convince her the pregnancy happened after?"

Avery rolled her eyes. "She suspected you were pregnant on your wedding day. Plus, you must have mentioned a due date to her."

"No. I don't think I did." Raven tried to remember. "It's the simplest solution. We can leave Charlie here with the oreads, and I can pretend to be"—she did a quick calculation—"seven months pregnant with a March due date."

"And in March, then what?"

"We'll cross that bridge when we come to it."

Avery sighed and started loading her plate. "It's Christmas, Raven. We are going to show up at Mom's, and she's going to have a million questions about where we've been and what we've been doing. Do you know how hurtful it's probably been for her not to hear from us all this time? All she knows is that her three daughters have fallen off the face of the earth for months. How long can we keep this up without breaking her heart? What excuse could you possibly give for not calling her when the baby is born?"

Raven felt her face grow hot, and she tossed up her hands. "I don't know, Avery! I've been a little preoccupied with staying alive and finding the golden grimoire. Oh, and raising a flying, meat-eating baby. Cut me some slack here!"

"I'm just saying sometimes the truth is the best option." Avery used her fingers to pop a green bean between her teeth and then took a seat across the table.

Gabriel rubbed a hand over his face. "What *would* happen if we told her the truth?"

Raven gasped. "Not you too? She'll never believe it. She'll think we've all gone mad."

Avery pointed at Charlie, who'd finished her meat and was dangling her chubby feet over the side of the china cabinet. "How can you deny it with that in front of you?"

Raven scowled.

"I think you underestimate your mom," Clarissa chimed in. "She's run the Three Sisters for most of her life. She herself told me the restaurant is steeped in folklore. Maybe she'd take it in stride."

With a shrug, Nathaniel raised his pipe in her direction. "If it goes terribly wrong, I can always wipe her memory."

Raven looked to Gabriel for backup, but her mate wasn't any help. He had the look on his face of a man who desperately wanted someone else to solve this problem.

He growled deep in his throat and rumbled, "If she did know the truth, it might make it easier for us to find what we are looking for. She could be a huge asset."

Raven crossed her arms and stared up at Charlie. The babe pushed off the cabinet, her little wings catching the air, and soared down into Raven's arms. Her big blue eyes seemed to hold a question and an apology. Raven hugged her and kissed her cheek. "I love you, but no cat. Artemis isn't food."

Charlie giggled in response.

Raven sighed. "So we tell Mom the truth. What could possibly go wrong?"

"Why focus on the negative?" Clarissa said, cutting around Charlie's bite marks to serve herself a chunk of meat. "Think about all that could go right."

Avery lifted her glass of wine and tapped the glass to her chin. "Personally, I'll consider it a win if Mom doesn't die of a stroke." She gave a breathy chuckle.

Raven met Gabriel's gaze. Neither of them laughed.

CHAPTER FIVE

Aeaea Island

W*hat had she done?* Leena bolted to her tent, so distracted she almost ran into the wrong one. All she'd wanted to do was feel what it was like to be kissed. She'd never been kissed. She'd lived in the temple since she was nine years old. Who would she have kissed?

Oh, but she hadn't realized what a single kiss could do. It seemed so innocuous from the outside, a simple touch of lips. With Colin, it had been so much more. She pressed her fingers against her mouth as she remembered the heat of it, the way her stomach had dropped and her body had tingled deliciously in his arms. That kiss had kindled an ache in her she'd never experienced before.

His flesh had been sinfully hard against her chest, but his lips had been soft and welcoming. And the longer their mouths touched, the more a strange and wonderful pressure had built inside her. It lingered even now, her inner self fluttering like a leaf in the wind while an unexpected weight pooled between her legs. How could one both ache and feel light as a feather at the same time?

The way his tongue had danced with her own enchanted her. She might have explored that dance for hours had the rumble in his chest not alerted her to how the encounter was changing. His hands, his mouth, had grown more demanding, and when he'd asked her to be *his*, she knew she was playing with fire.

Of all the sensations the kiss had ignited in her, the warmth that had blossomed at the center of her chest at the sound of his trill had been the most surprising and alarming. At that point, she knew without a doubt that the kiss would never be just a kiss. It wasn't only an experiment. The feelings it stirred up were far more permanent, more dangerous. She shook her head.

"Leena?" His voice came from outside the door to her tent.

She tangled her fingers together in front of her stomach. If she remained quiet, would he assume she wasn't there and go away?

"Leena, I know you're in there. We need to talk about what just happened."

Drawing a deep breath, she released it slowly and steeled her spine. She was an adult and an elf scribe. She could handle this.

"Come in," she said in the lightest, most unflustered voice she could find, even though inside she was trembling.

He slipped through the tent flap and moved to stand in front of her. Dear goddess, his gray eyes sparked silver in the dim light, and the muscles in his arms bunched as he crossed them over his chest. Nothing short of stunning. That fluttering ache grew stronger still.

"You kissed me." He stared at her as if he was expecting an explanation.

"It was an accident."

His eyes narrowed to slits. "An accident?"

"Can we forget it ever happened?"

"No." He chuckled, low and gritty as if his throat were lined with cinders. "Your lips didn't fall from the sky and land on mine."

She focused on his right biceps, on the wavelike scar that ran its length. He was not a man who was easily distracted from his goals. He wouldn't be the type to let this go.

Turning from him, she rubbed her palms together in tiny circles and paced the length of the tent. How could she explain? "I just wanted to try it. This was my one and only chance. Once I go back to my old life, I won't be free to... indulge in any... experimenting."

"Mmm-hmm." He rubbed the side of his jaw. "Why did you choose to experiment with me?"

A chill ran through her. She swallowed down an unexpected urge to tell him she'd wanted to kiss him and him alone for a long time. What good could come from admitting something like that? Besides, she was starting to think she was simply confused, caught up in the moment. "You were there. We were alone. I've come to trust you."

He jerked back. "You trust me? Do you mean you understood that I was *safe* to experiment on?"

She shrugged apologetically. "You said you'd help me try anything I'd like before I return to the temple."

He gaped at her, gobsmacked. "I thought you meant tribiscal wine or cliff jumping. I didn't think it would involve your tongue down my throat for sport."

Uh-oh. The look of disgust on his face made it clear that

she'd offended him. "You're a man of honor. I shouldn't have kissed you the way I did without asking your permission first. I am sorry, Colin. It was wrong of me."

He nodded slowly. "Nice story."

"Hmm?" She shook her head.

"I think you're full of shit."

She gasped. "Colin, I said I was sorry. You don't have to be rude."

"You are. Full. Of. Shit." He moved nearer. Leather and cloves filled her senses. His scent. Close, warm, dragon male. She'd noticed it before on the beach, but here in the cramped quarters of the tent, it was unmistakable.

She rubbed her nose to distract herself from the intoxicating fragrance. "I don't know what you mean."

Her back bumped the wall of the tent, and she realized she'd been retreating from him, but now there was no place left to go. His superior height left her tipping her head back so she could see him clearly as he moved in even closer, until only a fraction of an inch separated her from his distinctly male smile.

"This is what I think, Leena. I think you're attracted to me. I think you kissed me because you were drawn to me just as I am drawn to you and have been for a long time."

She shook her head. "No. No, Colin. I can't. Scribes don't—"

He laughed. "Scribes don't experiment with kissing?" He reached out and lifted her braid between his fingers, stroking it with his thumb in a way that made her long to be that plait of hair, long to feel that touch on her skin.

"Scribes..." She didn't want to hurt him, but she needed him to know the truth. "Scribes can experiment, but we don't mate or marry. We swore an oath to our work. Our only permanent attachment can be to the goddess. Kissing you was an experiment. Just physical. But when I heard your trill, I knew it was more for you. I knew I had to stop."

He chucked her under the chin with his knuckle. "Here's what I think. When you kissed me, you were experimenting with far more than a little lip-lock. You were testing what it might be like to have a different life. You're questioning whether being a scribe is the future you want. When I asked you to be mine, you considered it and that scared you." His last words came out as a whisper, but she had no problem hearing them. He was so close now he said it directly into her ear.

Her body started to tremble, and her eyes burned with unshed tears. "Yes," she blurted. "Does that make you feel better? I thought about it. I considered it. I was tempted. Is that what you want to hear?"

"Yes!" His brows lifted with his smile. "Leena, you don't have to go back. Quit the temple and become my mate. You can choose."

"Can I?" She scoffed. "Give up everything I've ever known for the promise of something I don't? I should leave one lifetime commitment for another so easily?"

He grunted and tugged at one ear. "Okay, when you put it that way, I can see why you'd have reservations."

"I have more than simple reservations, Colin." Heat from his body was doing wicked things to her insides. She sidestepped and moved to the other side of the tent. "The Temple of the Sacred Pools isn't a tavern or an inn. I can't leave and return on a whim. If I give up my quill and my duties as a scribe, there's no going back. If I make a mistake, it can't be undone."

His brow furrowed. "There's no rejoining after you quit?"

She shook her head.

"When dragons mate, they mate for life," he rumbled. "I would never leave you."

"There is nothing more permanent in Rogos than the devotion of a scribe to their work for the goddess." Leena toyed with her braid. They were talking in circles. "You were right before."

"About what?" Hope flared in his eyes again, and her stomach dropped to know she was about to extinguish that hope for good.

"My actions weren't an accident. I kissed you, and I meant to kiss you."

"Leena..." He reached for her, and she dodged.

"This is a warning from the goddess. I've stayed too long outside the temple. I've allowed the wider world to influence my mind. And the temptations I'm feeling, they're just a symptom of my distraction."

He raised his palms to her. "No, Leena, I don't think that's it."

"I want you to take me back to the temple now... I mean, as soon as possible," she said firmly. The answer came to her like a light in the dark. She'd thought he was safe, but nothing could be further from the truth. Only distancing herself from him would break the attraction between them. She was too weak to withstand the temptation any other way.

"What?" All at once, a look of panic came over him, and he shook his head. "What about... what about the scroll? We're about to go to war, Leena. The Defenders of the Goddess don't have a prayer against Eleanor without *you*."

She did her best to hide the swell of pride it gave her to hear that he needed her, that the resistance needed her. It was too bad the feeling simply proved her hypothesis. She was becoming proud, lustful, and disconnected from her monastic life.

"You will have your scroll. You will escort me back to the Temple of the Sacred Pools, and I will request that my Quanling assign a replacement curator for the scroll. I will hand over my duties to him or her, and they will return with you here." She flourished her hand to drive home how simple the plan was. "You said it could take the three sisters and their mates a few weeks to find the tanglewood tree. Even with the difference in time flow between our worlds, you and my replacement could be back here before they are."

Colin became flustered, a muscle in his jaw twitching. "Don't do this, Leena," he said softly. "Stay here. Give this time. See where it might go."

The sheer need in his voice almost undid her. Right now, he reminded her of a mountain cat with a thorn in his paw. He wanted her to tend the wound, but doing so was a dangerous game that brought her far too close to his razor-sharp teeth. Worse, her entire being ached for his bite. She'd wanted more than just a kiss. If she weren't careful, she could lose herself in him. "I'm sorry, Colin. I wish to go. Today. If you will not do it, I will ask Sylas and Dianthe to escort me—"

"No!" The thought seemed to offend him, and he jerked as if the words burned. "I promised to guard you and the scroll if you would help us, and I will see that promise through to the end." His brows became two dark slashes over hard, ice-cold eyes. "Pack your bags. We leave in the morning."

CHAPTER SIX

Obsidian Palace
Paragon

G rigori sailed through the window and into Eleanor's ritual room looking worn, his gray feathers rumpled. Eleanor allowed the peregrine to land on her arm, its claws harmlessly digging into her skin. Hera herself had gifted her the falcon, transforming one of her prized peacocks into a replacement for Aborella after the fairy perished. Although the bird looked like the other messenger birds in her employ, this one was special. This one was a spy.

"You've come a long way, my friend. Your wings smell of the sea air. What do you have to show me?" She closed her eyes and allowed the peregrine's memories to fill her brain.

The three sisters sat on the beach, discussing where to find the golden grimoire. She watched the scene unfold, her heartbeat advancing to a gallop. So they had to go to Earth to obtain pieces of something called the *tanglewood* tree. Where had she heard of that before? Oh, she was aware it

41

was Raven's last name, but there was something else about the tree. Any recollection of the tanglewood tree slipped through her fingers as the vision ended with the sisters and their mates sailing toward Crete from Aeaea.

Eleanor blinked again and came back into her own head. She stroked the bird's feathers. "Well done, Grigori. You clever, clever bird. Let's find you a treat."

She rose and crossed the room to a glass tank where a narwit and her babies cowered in the corner away from her. She reached in and grabbed one of the tiny pink creatures, tossing it by the tail toward Grigori's beak. He snatched it out of the air and swallowed it whole.

"What to do with this information..." Eleanor sighed and reached for a second snack for the bird. "The sisters are certainly more vulnerable on Earth, but now is not the time for me to leave Paragon. Everfield has fallen, but the fairy kingdom is currently more of a burden than an advantage." She stroked the bird's feathers. "That annoyance, Chancellor Ciro, wants a legion of soldiers to help rebuild the Empyrean Wood. I may have promised him as much in exchange for his kingdom's submission to Paragon, and I fear if we don't deliver, the fairy kingdom will be hungry enough to align with the first ruler to offer them aid. Nochtbend has broken diplomatic contact, and each night, more dragons go missing under suspicious circumstances. The vampires have done everything but declare war. And Paragon's relationship with Rogos has gone similarly cold. My spies tell me the archers of Asfolk have started training again. The kingdom that has always remained neutral suddenly seems less interested in reminding me of that fact." She frowned at Grigori. "So, you see, I am needed here and cannot go myself to Earth, despite the temptation to kill that half-breed whelp on Raven's hip."

The bird squawked his understanding.

No, it would be counterproductive for her to leave this realm. If Grigori's vision was accurate, five heirs and their mates remained on Aeaea, including Sylas and Colin, the known leaders of the rebellion. She must remain in control.

But then, who could she trust to kill Raven's daughter? She couldn't send Ransom. She scoffed at the thought. The man wouldn't last a day against the sisters. She drummed her fingers on the edge of the narwits' tank, sending the creatures squealing into the corner again.

"What shall we do, my dear beastie?"

Grigori ruffled his feathers in response and snapped his beak. She frowned. There was only one thing to do—spy on the sisters in the earthly realm and find out more about what they sought there. Perhaps this tanglewood tree was a source of vulnerability. The plan came together in a flash.

"I want you to go to Earth," she said to Grigori. "Follow the sisters, but do not allow yourself to be seen. I want to know anything they do or say that might indicate a weakness. Perhaps this tanglewood tree is the answer to their undoing."

Grigori squawked his understanding and took to the air, shooting through the window like an arrow. Satisfied with the decision, she strode toward the door. She needed to contact the lord of the elves, Niall, again and put more pressure on Rogos to align with Paragon. Everything could be moved if one simply found the right lever. What was the elf's currency? There had to be a way to sway him.

She was interrupted when Ransom appeared in front of her, looking tentative. He had bad news. She could feel it. Tension coiled around him like an invisible snake, and he shifted back and forth on his feet with apprehension.

"What is it? Why do you look like you might be ill?"

She wished the man had spine enough to just spit it out. She could not take much more bad news, certainly not when it was prolonged in this dance of fear.

He cleared his throat. "I am sorry to report that this hour, just moments ago, the Dark Mountains closed at the border to Darnuith."

"What do you mean, the mountains *closed*?" Now her voice betrayed her true feelings, her tone becoming shrill.

He swallowed and took a step back. "It seems that the mountains have... moved and closed off the passage into Darnuith. We would now either have to traverse the mountain on horseback or fly over—"

"I know what it means," she snapped. "It means our only way to take Darnuith by force is now by air. A vulnerable position, to be sure, considering the constant storms in their territory. The snow will negate our invisibility. Effective air formations will be rendered impossible by the wind. They're preparing for war. The rebellion is rising."

"Would you like me to send an envoy to one of the Darnuith Highborn? Perhaps they could convince Queen Penelope to reopen the lines of dialogue."

Eleanor scoffed. "No. The time for dialogue is done. Station troops along the Sanguine River. Close all trade routes. Nothing goes in or out of Darnuith. Order your men to seize and confiscate anything they can get their hands on. Bring it to Paragon."

Ransom bowed. "Very well, Empress."

"One more thing. Send a falcon to Rogos and warn Lord Niall that if he aids Darnuith by allowing the flow of goods through Rogos, we will consider it an act of war."

Ransom bowed again, then strode from the room to do her bidding.

Eleanor turned on her heel and moved back into her

ritual room, going straight for the line of large gems on her shelf. Her hands landed on a massive diamond. The light inside flickered in her grip. Marius's heart. It held the most power, but that was why she couldn't use it. She'd need it later for something far more important than this. Instead, she grabbed Brynhoff's, the silver agate duller, just as her brother had been. Her nails clicked against the jewel.

Striding to the open space at the center of her ritual room, she surveyed the patterns there and chose her magical sigil for this spell. She'd perfected the shapes, already painted on the otherwise black floor. The base of her sigil was a spiral to symbolize creation. This was a place for manifesting her will. To the north, she'd painted a triangle capped with a U shape—a chalice to hold her ever-growing celestial magic. To the east, a wave symbolized her enduring and daunting power. To the west, two circles represented Ouros's suns—the bringers of light and life, and to the south, a serpent—the symbol of Hades and a link to the dark energy inherent in her blood magic.

She placed Brynhoff's heart in the center of the spiral. Pacing her row of dried plants and herbs, she selected a few branches of a cottony plant from the far reaches of Paragon and placed them on the wave. For the suns, she chose a ripe red tribiscal fruit, then smashed it under her heel. Over the chalice, a silver bowl filled with blue crystals to symbolize raindrops.

Eleanor herself stood on the snake. "With my blood, I send rain to Darnuith," she said, focusing her intention. She sliced a talon through her skin and watched her blood splash toward her toes. It never reached them. Wild and red, it spiraled into the center, wind whipping in a frenzy within the symbol. A thick gray cloud formed and cracked with lightning.

"Yes," she said. "More. More!"

She sliced herself again, and blood rained from the cloud onto the symbol. Every cell in her body contracted with the expulsion of magic directed at Darnuith. Soon, the kingdom of witches would find their land drowned in blood rain. Every citizen of every city in the Dark Mountains would watch their crops fail before their eyes. How sad for them that food from outside the realm would now be impossible to obtain. She'd made sure of that.

If Darnuith wouldn't bend, she'd make sure they'd break. She bared her teeth as the cloud rained on. Mountains closed. Ha! Queen Penelope had no idea who she was dealing with.

CHAPTER SEVEN

Aeaea Island

"We can't sail to Serenity Harbor now that Everfield has fallen. The port is crawling with Obsidian guards." Colin collected Leena's bags and stowed them on the boat, trying his best not to make eye contact with her. Every time he looked at her, he thought about the kiss, experienced again the deep ache of her rejection.

He flexed his wings and kept his mind focused on their goal. "We'll have to dock off the coast of Rogos. If we sail all the way to the shores of Niven, I can fly you directly to the temple. There's no port there, but all Indigo has to do is anchor offshore and I can take us the rest of the way." It pained Colin to have to borrow Sylas's Oread, but he didn't have one of his own for the same reason he didn't have a treasure room. He'd moved around too much to keep one.

Leena stared in the direction of Everfield before glancing toward Rogos. "I think that is our best plan. We can't return the way we came. We'll need to take care, though. The coastal area of Niven is rocky with rough waters. We can't get too close to shore."

"Then we don't land the boat. I'll fly you in from a distance. I have some business to attend to in Rogos anyway. Indigo can sail back tonight and meet me on the opposite coast tomorrow. I'll get there on foot." He needed to meet with the leader of the resistance in Rogos and bring her up to speed with recent developments. He could send a falcon, but this would be far more effective.

She smiled her approval of that plan but crossed to the rear of the boat, putting maximum distance between them. So that's how it would be. He growled and leaned his hands against the hull, staring at the horizon in the distance, at the dark brown line that was Ouros.

He was still there hours later, although he'd opted for a seat on the front bench. Better here than where he could see her, where her presence would taunt him.

After another half hour at sea, he blinked when a dark spot appeared in the sky beyond the boat, growing larger as it headed for him. Was that a falcon? He stood and held up one arm, and the peregrine landed in a flurry of flapping, digging in its talons.

"What brings you all the way out here, little buddy?" he asked the messenger bird. A small roll of parchment was bound to its leg. Colin untied it and read the tight script inside.

Rogos locked down—borders and coasts. Wards in place. Diplomatic ties to Paragon broken. All roads in and out of the kingdom, as well as the Sanguine River, are now occupied by Paragon. Nothing is getting through trade routes. DOG underground is compensating. Trying to meet demand best we can.—RZ1

Colin scribbled a message to Rook, the Rogos Red Zone

One leader of the Defenders of the Goddess. *Message received. Hold the course. Preparing next phase.* He strapped the scroll to the bird's leg and sent it back the way it had come. Then he strode across the deck to Leena.

"We've got a problem," he barked.

She started as if he'd woken her. *Didn't sleep well last night either, did you?*

"What's wrong?"

"Just received a falcon that Rogos has closed the borders and the coasts. They've cut diplomatic ties to Paragon."

"No..." Her face fell. "But that means sailing around to Niven will be impossible. If they've locked down the borders and the shoreline, Niven's beaches will be enchanted to keep out all foreign vessels. You won't be able to fly through. They're defending against Paragon. Every effort will be made to prohibit a dragon from getting in. If the wards don't stop you, the archers will."

Colin couldn't bring himself to feel bad about this turn of events. "We'll have to go back until I can arrange for safe passage."

Leena grew restless at this idea. "Wait... There's one place on Rogos's shores that I know will be safe for us to enter, a place used exclusively by scribes on the edge of the Mystic Wood. It's not easily accessible except by elves, but if Indigo can get us near, I can guide us in."

"Guide us in? That sounds ominous."

"In all the time you spent in Rogos, did you never learn about the Mystic Wood?" She raised a teasing eyebrow. At least she was looking at him again.

"I was there to earn the trust of the people. Aside from crossing through the wood on the main road to Asfolk, I didn't see the need for an in-depth study. I have heard that it's uninhabitable."

"That's an exaggeration. Not many elves live there, but it's not impossible. The wood is enchanted and fraught with peril. It's served a military purpose for Rogos for centuries. For example, had you tried to navigate off the main road on your journey, you might have found yourself stuck in one of the tar pools or attacked by one of the many venomous animals. Even the trees can be lethal if you eat the wrong berry or touch the wrong bark. It's designed to stop anyone who doesn't belong in Rogos from reaching its people undetected. Only an elf has any hope of navigating it, and even then, it is filled with deadly obstacles one must actively defend against."

He snorted. "It's a means of defense, then, similar to the winters in Darnuith. I never realized."

"We don't advertise it, and those that go in never come out to tell the tale. There is a reason we've been able to maintain neutrality all these centuries, Colin. Rogos's defenses are quiet but deadly."

"Hmm." *Like your beauty*, he thought, still feeling the sting from the night before.

"The scribe's pass is a small inlet on the southern shore. If Indigo can get us close, you can fly us to the dock."

"Why not keep going? I probably can't make it all the way to the temple, but I can fly us to the main road."

"I don't recommend it. You're a dragon, Colin. For the first time in centuries, Rogos has ended diplomatic relations with the dragon kingdom. It will be safer if we walk and you keep your wings tucked away until we reach the temple."

"Great. So now we're taking a stroll through the enchanted wood. This is a bad idea, Leena."

"Don't be concerned. I know a safe path... at least, in theory."

"In theory?" He raised an eyebrow.

"All scribes learn of the path, to use in case of trouble, but it isn't as though I've ever actually used it. What opportunity would I have had?" She gave a laugh that turned into a snort. "We left Rogos when we could take the main road through Everfield. I never thought we'd have to come back this way."

"Fantastic," he mumbled. "I'm all aglow with faith in this plan."

She shrugged. "Do you have a better idea?"

He faced her and circled one finger in the air. "Yes. We turn this ship around and return to Aeaea where we wait for the three sisters and then safely transport you home using magic, or else get special permission from High Lord Niall to drop you off somewhere."

Her eyes darted from his to the water rippling off the side of the boat. She seemed to consider it for a moment, then shook her head. "I know it's the safer thing to do, but I can't. I need to get back to the temple, Colin. I'm sorry."

"Why?" It was a fair question even though he suspected he knew the answer. They'd been over this. But he wanted her to admit it once again. He wanted to hear her say it.

"I don't trust myself around you," she blurted. She gripped the side of the boat but didn't turn her head to look at him.

"Then you admit you have feelings for me."

"If I didn't, we wouldn't be here. We wouldn't have had to leave Aeaea."

"We *didn't* have to."

This time, she did turn, and her expression held something close to torment. "We did. We do. We must."

It took the better part of the day to reach their destination. The Mystic Wood appeared on the leeward side of the boat in an explosion of deep green foliage and intensely colored blooms. Nothing in their world rivaled the beauty of this place. Roots tangled into the water off the bank, surrounded by an inviting silver mist. Teal vines coiled around the knotty tree trunks and grew in swags between the gnarled branches. A scent like pepper and tea blossom met his nose.

"There." Leena pointed to an inlet that was impossible to see if you weren't looking for it. "Beware of the vines. They're poisonous and plentiful here, where they survive on the salt of the sea."

Moments later, he heeded the warning as they neared the coast and he had to duck beneath vines that stretched from one bank to another. The boat slipped closer to shore, Indigo steering around a point of land that reached across the narrow way.

"Almost there," Leena said. "There's a safe place to disembark just down here."

Indigo nodded, his pearlescent face gleaming in the dappled sunlight. He dropped the sail and took up the oars.

Out of the corner of his eye, Colin saw a fuzzy brown creature the size of a small bear burrow into the ground offshore. "What was that?"

"Wood rat. Harmless unless provoked, but they carry a tick whose bite could kill you if you don't seek immediate treatment from a healer."

Colin grunted. "Any other deadly creatures I should be aware of?"

"*Dorinclees*. Uh, it translates roughly to silent cat. They're a type of cougar that lives in the trees. When their mouth is closed, it blends into the rest of their face, making it look like it doesn't exist. Thus, the name. Their claws likely won't break your dragon skin, but they could rip me apart."

"Good to know."

"Drop anchor here," Leena commanded.

The oread did as she requested. About a hundred yards ahead of him, Colin could make out a small wooden dock.

"It will be quieter if we fly to the end of the dock, but don't go any farther."

"And we need to be quiet why?" Colin slid on his pack and stretched his wings.

"The, uh... you'd call them razorwings."

"Razorwings." Colin didn't like the sound of that.

She tipped her head and spoke to him like a child. "Too much noise can attract a type of bat that slices its victim's skin with a barb on its wing and then drinks its blood."

"Fabulous. Just what I wanted to hear." He handed her the other pack.

"It's better to know what you're getting into."

"Mmmm." He swept her into his arms. "Ready?"

"Yes," she answered, but her voice sounded strained.

He understood why. He felt it too, how naturally their bodies fit together. Suddenly he was in no hurry to make it to shore. He'd hold her like this all day if he could.

"Indigo, remember to pass on that message I gave you to Sylas," Colin said, delaying their departure another moment. He'd given the oread the scroll the falcon had brought him from Rogos.

"I will not fail you, sir." Indigo's tinny voice came on a breeze.

Something large and dark moved in the water, perhaps awakened by their voices, and swam under the boat, sending waves lapping against the hull. Colin watched it circle behind them. With a sigh, he resolved that they needed to get a move on.

Colin flapped his wings and rose into the sky, soaring to

the small dock and landing gently on the wooden planks. But he took his time lowering her onto her own two feet.

Leena straightened her robes, brushing the natural fibers as if his touch had covered her in sparks. Well, the feeling was mutual. He smiled to himself and followed her as she walked briskly into the forest.

Not a word was spoken as they navigated a narrow trail through the trees. Even when he noticed a bright-blue snake swallowing a wood rat whole only a few meters from the trail, he held his tongue. This place was brightly beautiful but undeniably dangerous. *Not unlike Leena.* Gorgeous, exactly the type of woman he'd always dreamed of... and she'd crushed his heart into powder with one kiss. The thought balled into an icy knot in his gut.

They climbed a steep incline, and then the path widened into a suitable road, still surrounded by forest but with far more room on the trail.

She fell back to walk beside him instead of in front. "We've passed beyond razorwing territory. We can speak now."

He grunted his understanding but remained silent. She glanced back at him, noting his somber mood.

"You haven't forgiven me for the kiss, have you? I can't say I blame you. I should have been more cognizant of your feelings. Please accept my apology."

"You already apologized," he mumbled. "I'll tell you I forgive you if you want to hear it, although there's really nothing to forgive. I was a willing participant. You know I wanted to kiss you. I could have stopped you, and I didn't."

"Yes, but—" She grimaced.

"But what?" His tone passed exasperated and went straight into the territory of annoyed.

"It was a bit like offering you a bite of cake without offering you a whole slice."

Her tone was such he knew she didn't mean it to be insulting, but his dragon coiled tighter all the same. He stopped, his boots kicking up dust from the packed dirt road, and narrowed his eyes on her. "You're the one on the diet, Leena. I can have all the cake I want. I can eat it all day, every day. Breakfast, lunch, and dinner. If anyone is the cake in this scenario, it's me!"

Did he really just call himself cake? By the goddess...

"Uh, sorry. I didn't mean to suggest..."

"If you want to try another bite between here and the temple, you know where to find me," he added with more swagger than he actually felt.

For a fraction of a second, he thought he saw her eyes widen and her face pale, but then she turned from him and nodded as she walked quickly ahead. "It was a terrible analogy. I'm simply happy that you've forgiven me and we can put this all behind us."

"Good. I'm relieved we are both adults here and have moved beyond this whole situation, because the suns are setting and we're going to have to make camp soon. And there's only one tent."

He had to suppress a laugh when she turned to him, jaw dropping in horror. "Why is there only one tent?"

He snorted. "Because when we left Aeaea, I thought I'd be flying you into Niven. I only packed this thing for me because I was planning to visit our faction of rebels in Rogos before I returned to Aeaea."

"I can't stress what a bad idea it is for us to camp here." She shivered. "But it is getting dark... and cold."

"Can anything in these woods actually kill a dragon?"

She shrugged. "The tar pits, I suppose."

"Then let's find a place far away from those."

She rolled her eyes. "Honestly, right here on the road is probably our best option, but starting a fire would be a very bad idea. Light attracts wood rats."

He allowed his pack to slide off his shoulder. "All right, then. No fire and we camp on the road."

He got to work setting up the tent while she pulled her robes more tightly around her.

CHAPTER EIGHT

T his was a disaster. Leena helped Colin set up the tent, horrified at how the day had turned out. She'd insisted that he take her back to the temple in order to distance herself from him, and now she'd be forced to sleep in the same very small, very close tent with the dragon. Dear goddess help her. She couldn't decide if it was a night-mare scenario or a fantasy come true.

"There. Plenty of room for two," he said, putting the last two pieces together. "Unfortunately, without a fire, we'll have to settle for a cold dinner. I packed some bread and cheese for the journey back. We can share."

"Kind of you." She eyed the small tent in the darkness, then the big dragon standing at its door. Her mouth went dry. Maybe it was a test. If the goddess had put her in this position, perhaps she wanted Leena to prove to herself that the chemistry between her and Colin was a shooting star that simply needed time to burn itself out. It was a tent, not an altar meant for marriage. She held up her canteen and the small bag she used to hold her sundries. "I'll be right there. I just need a moment."

He nodded, then disappeared inside. It would take more than a moment to prepare herself for being so close to him again. The night wrapped around her like a shroud, creeping in intensity from a thin, gauzy twilight to an inky blackness that brought with it a chill that seemed to seep through her skin. She prepared herself for bed in the dark and then lingered on the road until a rustle of leaves deep in the woods sent a different kind of chill through her. Steeling her resolve, she slipped into the tent.

And had to force herself not to turn around and walk back out.

The interior glowed with the light of a small lantern, the dragon's naturally high body temperature warming the small space. He'd stripped down to a pair of shorts and was stretched out along one side of the tent, although his sheer enormity meant that he took up a bit more than half. She hugged the opposite wall before lowering herself to the wool spread he'd folded and placed on her side.

"You can have the blanket. I don't need it." He handed her a cloth wrap filled with a corner of a loaf of bread, a large hunk of cheese, and a handful of dried fruit.

"I suppose you don't get cold," she said, tearing herself off a bite.

"I feel the cold. It's just not uncomfortable to me. We dragons are highly resistant to extreme temperatures. I was born near the heart of a volcano."

She chewed, using the food as an excuse to think of a response that would take her mind off the smooth, taut skin that covered the swells and valleys of his chest and abs. "Elves are born at home," she squeaked, then coughed and took a sip of water to hide her nerves. "Usually, a midwife comes to the house."

"Were you born at home?"

Leena stared at the bread in her fingers and frowned. She hated talking about her childhood, but then, he couldn't know that. "Yes, I was."

He stretched back, nesting his fingers behind his head, and stared up at the roof of the tent. "I guess I was too, considering the Obsidian Palace is built into the mountain." He flashed her a grin. "No midwife required. We hatch from eggs, usually on our own."

As a scribe, Leena was vaguely aware of dragon reproduction, but she'd only read descriptions in scrolls. "Do you mean that your mother wasn't even there when you were born?"

He shook his head. "Dragon queens lay their eggs in a place we call the cradle. It's a cave, deep within the mountain—a holy place with a mural and an altar to the goddess. The queen lays her eggs in carved depressions in the stone, and they incubate there in the heat of the volcano under the watchful eye of Aitna. I don't remember much about the day I was born except seeing my twin, Sylas, for the first time. He was the same color as my paws and tail."

"You're born in your dragon form?"

He nodded. "I shifted for the first time a full season after I hatched. That's when our magic manifests our rings." He held up the garnet on his finger. "Mine matches Sylas's, although the setting is different."

"Fascinating." The tension in her shoulders relaxed, her natural curiosity trumping any discomfort that lingered at his nearness. "You weren't close to your mother, then."

"No." He snorted. "Hardly knew her."

Leena frowned. They had that in common. "What about your father?"

He sighed. "Killian was a decent dragon. He spent time with us... mostly in the training room, mind you. The pits.

59

He came from a wealthy merchant's family and was a champion in his own right. That's how he'd met our mother and become her consort."

"The pits are where you fight each other for sport?" She wondered what that was like. It sounded barbaric to her, but elf culture was so different.

"Yes, and for the royal family, status in the ranks was considered a badge of honor. It's all related to our military, the Obsidian Guard. We trained to be warriors and to fight side by side with the other soldiers if we ever went to war. All royal heirs are trained to be military leaders."

"Melee combat isn't practiced in Rogos."

"So I am told. The rebels I've met from Rogos say your army is made up almost exclusively of archers."

She nodded. "And engineers."

Colin's brow knit. "I hadn't heard that. What do engineers do in the army?"

Leena adjusted her legs under her. "Build things. The crypt key is just one of many feats of elf engineering. We're extremely gifted metalworkers. You fought in the pits as a youngster. We battle our mechanical creations in an arena where we animate them with magic. We call it the Animus Games."

"I never knew children here did that."

"That's not surprising. Elves are protective of their children. As far as I know, outsiders aren't invited to the Games."

"Did you participate?" he asked, brows raised in surprise.

"Once." She thought back to the time she was nine. "My creation's name was Monstrata, a two-legged beast with slashing blades for arms and a head with a snout of sharp, snapping teeth. My father helped me with the design." She fought back a wave of bitter nostalgia. "It was the first construction I'd ever animated. Anyway, my creature faced off against one built by an older boy named Newton who'd constructed his with a shelled back like a turtle. Mine was stronger and faster, but no matter how I tromped on his or sawed at the shell, it would not break. His was slower and less deadly, but his turtle chipped away at Monstrata until she was no longer functional." She sighed.

"Where is this Newton now? Do you want me to rough him up?" Colin winked.

She laughed lightly. "I have no idea, and thankfully I took the lesson he taught me in resilience and put it to good use. I didn't win that competition, but my creation was in the top ten for my age group, and that was enough for me."

He grinned at her. "Leena, the monster maker." He turned on his side and propped himself up on one elbow. "What other secret talents do you possess?"

She popped the last of the cheese into her mouth. "Nothing too exciting. But back to you. Do you think your military training is why you're so good at leading the Defenders of the Goddess?"

He shrugged. "*Good* is open to interpretation."

She carefully folded the now-empty cloth wrapper in her hands and placed it back in the pack. "You know you're good at this. If we succeed against Eleanor, it will be because of you. With your background, you'll know exactly where and how to strike."

His eyes darted to hers, his face growing somber. "It saddens me sometimes. I'll have to face the army I was born to help lead. Those soldiers in the Obsidian Guard... they're just kids. It's why I'm praying the three sisters find this tanglewood tree and then get their hands on that grimoire.

It's our only hope of taking Eleanor out with the least number of casualties."

Taking one last sip from her canteen, she stretched out beside him. "Maybe, when we get back to the temple, we can help things along."

"What do you mean?"

"We know approximately when the scroll was written. We might be able to cross-reference the date against the graves registered that year."

"Clever." Colin looked at her with something close to awe in his eyes. "Maybe there is hope of finding the grimoire even without the help of the tanglewood artifact."

Leena yawned and curled on her side. "Don't get too excited. Without translating the scroll, even if we can find the grave, we still won't have the code necessary to line up the cogs properly so that the key will work."

Eyelids heavy, she was relieved when Colin extinguished the lamp. "Hmm. This is one problem we're not going to solve tonight. Sleep well, Leena. There'll be time for us to figure it all out tomorrow."

To her surprise, she did.

CHAPTER NINE

As a dragon, Colin didn't need as much sleep as other species. Dragons were known to go days without a full night's rest with no ill effects. Perhaps that was why he woke first to dim light sifting through the canvas walls of the tent. With his first breath, Leena's sweet, wild scent filled his lungs. His inner dragon stretched and sniffed toward the bundle beside him.

She'd grown cold in her sleep and edged into the curve of his body, her head tucked under his chin and her back skimming down his front. His heart quickened at the exquisite torture. He longed to kiss her temple, glide his hand over the length of her spine, press the rock-hard erection that had formed the moment he smelled her into her backside.

He closed his eyes. No. He wouldn't give in to the temptation. It already ached to be taking her back to the temple, to know he'd likely never see her again afterward. Every kiss, every touch, would make it harder for him to part with her. His dragon already pined for her. Why make things harder than they needed to be?

She sighed in her sleep and rolled over, her hand and cheek replacing her back against his chest. She nestled in.

"Leena," he whispered. Maybe he should push her away. She'd made it clear to him what she wanted and didn't want. Maybe he should just get up and leave the tent, take care of his need for her outside, with his own hand.

He started to move, and her lids fluttered open. That purple gaze locked on to him, the color seizing him violently, freezing him into place. Her fingers traced an arc above his left nipple, and he clenched his fists to keep from touching her.

"Leena," he said again.

She swallowed, lifting her cheek off his chest. "I can hear your heart."

"You're making it pound."

Her hand hovered over his skin.

Colin's dragon coiled tighter inside him, and at that moment, the crafty beast came up with a truly diabolical plan, and Colin's lips began to move before he could censor himself.

"Would you like to experiment more, with my permission?" His voice sounded throaty and rough, as raw as he felt. "A kiss alone is hardly an education. If your goal was to sample the delights of the flesh before returning to the temple, you should expand your course of study."

Her long, tapered fingers traced the edge of his scar where it ended along the base of his neck, her lips parting on a shaky breath. "You're sure it wouldn't make things difficult for you? I thought you said before—"

"That was before." He forced his expression into something casual, almost impassive. "Before I understood what you wanted."

Her tongue stroked along her bottom lip. "Then may I... touch you?"

His lids heavy, the corner of his mouth twitched as he gave her a slow and certain yes. Her fingers traced light and soft across his collarbone, over the scarred mound of his shoulder, and down to his nipple. She pinched and rolled it between her fingers.

"Would you like to know what that feels like?"

A spark flared in her purple eyes.

He reached up to her neck, into her robes. Her lips parted as he traced her collarbone, then cupped her breast, rolling the nipple between his thumb and forefinger.

"Mmmm," she moaned, arching into his hand.

He caressed her breast again before pulling his hand away.

"Would you like me to show you something else?" he whispered.

He almost cheered when she met his gaze with wide eyes and nodded. Slowly, tentatively, he rolled her onto her back and stroked a hand down her front, not stopping until he reached the slit in her robes at her knee. He worked his hand under the material until his fingers met warm flesh. His erection twitched with need. Slowly, he swept his hand up her inner thigh, watching her gasp at his touch, arching, head back. He stroked again until the very tips of his fingers met the warm crease at the apex of her thighs. A growl rumbled in his chest at the wet heat he found there.

"Scribes don't wear anything under their robes?"

Pink tinged her cheeks. "Why would we?"

He licked his lips and traced the tips of his fingers back to her inner knee, then began the slow climb again, loving the way her body reacted to his touch.

"Colin, I feel..." She pressed a hand to her lower belly. "I need... more."

LEENA THOUGHT SHE MIGHT EXPLODE FROM THE pressure building inside her. Colin's fingers were teasing her in a way that sent sparks shooting through her like velvet lightning. A feeling was building low within her core. Exquisite pressure. If he'd just touch her in that spot again, where her nerves seemed to ache for him...

"You want more?" he asked her, his eyes dark as a thunderstorm.

She writhed beside him, too distracted by pure sensation to speak.

His fingers crept up again, and this time, they lingered, pressing and circling right where she needed it. A rush of heat traveled from his touch, through her torso, puckering her nipples and making her breasts feel fuller, heavier.

"Colin..." Everything on her had grown hypersensitive at his touch. She desperately wanted to strip out of her robes, to free her breasts from the constricting fabric. She wanted more from his fingers, and she worked her hips to increase the pressure.

"Oh, Leena, you're so damn wet," he whispered, and the sound of his voice was like velvet over her skin.

Two fingers dipped into her, spreading her. She parted her knees, pulling her robe up to give him access. The growl that rumbled through the tent sent another storm of lightning through her, to the tips of her fingers, her breasts, her lips. Every inch of her skin seemed to wake up.

His fingers moved faster, dove deeper, spread her wider. Her breath caught. She was so close, achingly close, to something—she didn't know what, but it was something she needed... Something...

With a gasp, she arched off the floor of the tent, pleasure ringing through her body like a bell and radiating out, out past the stars, into the beyond. Magic, enchantment, pure light! Slowly she came back together, back into herself.

She gazed up at him, panting. "That was..."

He smiled wickedly. "Better than a kiss?"

Yes, it was much better than a kiss, but she couldn't speak. Just nodded dumbly, shaken by the power of what he'd just done to her. He adjusted her robes around her. "Come on. We should get moving if we want to get you to the temple before nightfall."

❧

COLIN TOOK APART THE TENT IN RECORD TIME, anything to distract him from Leena and the absolute frenzy his dragon was in to mate with her. He'd made certain she experienced her release, but he hadn't taken his own. If that wasn't painful enough, he'd done it all while forcing back his mating trill. It took supernatural restraint not to come when he saw her arch off the floor, but he knew if he let himself go there, his dragon would bond with her and there'd be no going back. Now his inner beast was making his skin feel tight and his head throb.

"Is everything all right?" she asked him as he swept the pack onto his back, trying his best not to make eye contact.

"Perfect," he said. "I'm just anxious to get going. We've got a long trek ahead of us."

She nodded, but a look he couldn't quite read passed behind her eyes. Thankfully, whatever it was didn't linger. They fell into step, making their way at a quick pace toward the main road to Asfolk. At this rate, they'd make it to the city by late afternoon and from there could catch a carriage to Niven.

"Oh!" Leena hopped beside him. "Ow, ow, ow, ow!"

"What's wrong?"

She reached down and plucked something from the bottom of her leather slipper. She scowled at the two-inch-long creature with the barbed shell. "You're not supposed to be here."

"What is that thing?"

She flung it into the woods as far as she could throw it, then wobbled on her feet. "Mystic snail. They're not usually at this elevation. They like the swamps better. Fucker's shell broke my skin."

He cleared his throat, not used to hearing Leena swear. "Is that something to worry about?"

She looked at him and started giggling. "Perfectly harmless. Just makes you a little..." She waved one hand and staggered forward, a smile spreading across her face. As she came closer, he noticed her pupils were dilated.

"Are... are you high?" He laughed. "Are snails intoxicating?"

"That's the word!" She held up a finger between them, then pressed the side of it to her widening smile. "Shhh. I am intoxicating... *intoxicated* by snail venom."

She attempted to whirl around and continue down the path but tripped over her own feet. He lunged forward and caught her by the waist. Something crunched under his foot. Steadying her in one arm, he turned his boot to see another snail's remains smeared across the bottom. He could feel it now. The shell had poked through his boot but couldn't pierce his dragon skin. Still, now that he knew what the little bastards looked like, he saw them everywhere.

"Leena, the path is covered with mystic snails. You can't walk here. Let me carry you. They can't hurt me."

Before he could lift her into his arms, her chest slapped his as she leaped into him, standing on the tops of his feet, arms circling his waist. He let out an *oof* at the impact.

"They aren't ssssupposed to be here," she slurred. "They belong in the valley."

"Someone forgot to tell the snails that. I'm going to lift you into my arms and carry you until it's safe." He tried to do just that, but she grabbed his hands, wriggling against him. If his inner dragon had wanted her before, any effort at cooling his libido was undone by her exuberant closeness.

"Dance with me, Colin," she said, wrapping one arm around his neck. "I've never danced with anyone."

"Mountain help me." He tried to hold her so there was a bit of distance between their bodies without setting her feet on the snail-infested trail. "Just... just hold still, and I'll pick you up."

"No! I want to dance." She giggled like a child and squeezed his neck harder.

He cursed again and rolled his eyes heavenward. "Fine, but I swear you're going to regret this later." He positioned one hand at the small of her back and gripped her right hand in his left. "Hang on, darling, I'm taking you for a spin." He moved up the hill, snails crunching under his feet, in a way that couldn't be mistaken for dancing.

In his arms, Leena glowed. She tipped her head back and laughed, the sound ringing through the woods like silver bells. Damn it, but he loved that sound. Soon, despite himself, he broke into an actual dance, spinning and swaying to a song he remembered from Paragon. He hummed it to her as he picked up the pace.

"Oh goddess, it feels like flying." She arched her back in his arms. "Not as wonderful as before in the tent, but so freeing."

He slowed, his mouth suddenly dry. "So, you liked what happened before in the tent...?"

"Goddess, yes. It was like nothing I've ever felt before, like unraveling and then being knitted back together." She smiled up at him, and his chest swelled with satisfaction. But then her brow puckered with worry. "Only I don't think you liked it as much."

"I liked it very much," he admitted, searching her wild violet eyes and wondering how much of this she'd remember later. "Too much. I had to stop, or I wouldn't have been able to stop. Do you understand?"

A laugh bubbled out of her throat and between them. "No."

He found the genuine honesty in that answer endearing. She was completely innocent. And didn't that make him a lecherous asshole for putting his hands on her?

They'd covered a considerable distance, and he didn't feel the crunch under his boots as before. Once he confirmed the trail was safe, he stopped. Her cheeks were flushed, her lips full and velvety pink.

"Why are you stopping?"

"It's safe now," he said. "You can continue on your own."

Her eyes met his, their electric intensity driving straight through to his inner dragon. "But what if I'm not ready to be on my own? What if I want to hold on to you while I can?" Her lips parted, her head tilting to the side. She leaned closer.

Don't kiss her, you fool! But who was he kidding? Her hands were in his hair, and his inner dragon had already rolled over and was begging for a belly rub. Her lips met his, and this time, his trill filled the space around them. The kiss went deeper, and he showed her with his tongue exactly what he wanted to do to her.

"I'm going to need you to come with us," a male voice said.

Colin stopped kissing Leena, turning his head toward the voice... and got a close-up view of the sharp end of an elven arrow.

CHAPTER TEN

L eena spun off Colin's feet, drew one hand back, and released her invisible arrow into the nearest male. The curse landed in his gut. He staggered back, black veins spreading out through his arms and climbing his cheeks. He swore before toppling over.

"Was scribe magic necessary?" one of the other two elves said to her, his arrow still drawn. "We're just doing our job."

Leena turned toward him, arm cocked back, hand raised. "Lower your weapons, and I won't do it again."

The two uninjured male elves stood down, while the one on the ground groaned and writhed. Her poison would wear off in a moment—it wasn't designed to kill other elves.

"What was that?" Colin whispered, but she silenced him with a raised hand.

"What do you want with us?" she asked, and even she could hear how she slurred the end of that sentence. The world tilted and she steadied herself.

"We've been ordered to escort you to the palace," one

said. "We thought he was... bothering you." The guard gestured toward Colin.

"Not bothering me," she mumbled to them. "It was the shhhnails!" She pointed a finger at the trail behind them. *Shhhnails? Was her tongue swelling?* "But... why did you say you are here?"

The blond elf nearest her relaxed a bit. "We've come to collect you. Lord Niall requests an audience with you and the dragon immediately."

"What's this about?" Colin kept nudging one of her shoulders. Now that she thought about it, the world was tipping unevenly to her left, and each of those nudges seemed to right it temporarily. Damn it all, he was keeping her from falling over.

"What is wrong with her?" the first elf asked, climbing to his feet and shaking off the remainder of her magic.

Leena opened her mouth to try to explain again, but Colin did it for her. "She stepped on a mystic snail back there." He pointed toward the trail with his thumb. "I was trying to carry her."

The one who appeared to be their leader furrowed his brow and gave them both a disapproving look. "By the mouth?"

"Asshole," she mumbled, louder than she meant to.

"Please proceed, dragon. We can travel faster if you carry her, and Lord Niall will appreciate our haste."

"Name's Colin. I assume you're an archer of Asfolk?"

"Captain Haldir." The elf gave a shallow bow, his pale blue eyes never leaving Colin's face.

"I'm Leena," she blurted. "Nice to meet you, Haldir."

The elf frowned at her exuberance. Or maybe she was slurring her words again. "You as well, Leena." He gestured toward his partner to the right, an elf with bright red hair and eyes the color of maple syrup. "This is Garret, my second." And then to the blond on his left. "And Bartelon."

With a nod of acknowledgment to the three, Colin dropped his arm to the back of her knees, and she found herself draped in front of his chest. This wasn't nearly as fun as the dancing, but she didn't argue. She still couldn't walk herself.

"How did you find us?" She tipped her head back and stared at Haldir upside down. She had to close her eyes to keep from vomiting.

"I think it's best if we leave that explanation to Lord Niall."

Leena rested her head against Colin's shoulder and wondered at that. The scribes would be able to call up her location in the sacred pools, but only if they were specifically looking for her. And why would they be looking for her? It was very strange indeed for them to be escorted back to the palace to visit with the high lord. She'd never met the elf. He didn't often associate with the scribes except through his counselors when he needed to request a scroll for some political business. She had no idea what *this* might be about.

By the time they reached Asfolk Palace, her head was throbbing and every step Colin took set off a jab of pain between her temples. "Put me down," she protested. "Please... I'm feeling better."

Colin did as she asked, and she adjusted her robes, wincing at the light that bounced off the gleaming palace. Asfolk was a study in arched walls and circular patterns. Built from pink and white marble, the building's multiple turrets were capped in royal-blue slate, its doors and windows round. The outside reminded her of a snail's shell —shiny, smooth, and gracefully curved. Adorned in flowering ivy, Asfolk was considered the most beautiful palace in their world by many, although she had nothing to compare it to but Circe's temple on Aeaea. Certainly it was more formal than that.

She winced and shaded her eyes as another spike of pain stabbed through her head.

"You okay, dancing queen?" Colin whispered. "Do I need to sign you up for a ten-step de-snailing program?"

She giggled, then grabbed her head when the pain grew worse. "Don't make me laugh. It hurts my head."

"Apologies." He followed the word with a slanted grin.

She rubbed her temples as two attendants opened the doors to the palace for them. "I don't suppose you have any willow bark or a tonic in that bag of yours?"

He frowned. "Sorry. Dragons don't use them, but surely if you asked..."

"This is where I leave you." Captain Haldir gestured toward another set of doors. "You'll find Lord Niall inside."

Colin bowed to the elf before reaching for the door's golden handle. Head still throbbing, Leena followed him into a place she'd never thought she'd see—the throne room. She balked. She stood at the head of an aisle carpeted with a long purple runner. At the end of the aisle, sprawled across a wooden throne atop a raised dais, was an elf with jet-black hair and an aristocratic nose. Lord Niall. Were they supposed to walk the length of the room to speak to him or address him from back here?

Colin didn't seem to share her reservations. He passed her and strode forward with his arms spread wide. "Lord Niall! Such a pleasure to be in your presence again."

Before Leena could pick up her chin off the floor, the ruler of Rogos leaped off his seat and embraced Colin like they were old chums.

"Colin of Paragon! I had a feeling you'd return to Rogos sooner than anticipated. You've fallen in love with our kingdom." He wagged a finger at the dragon. "It will always be home to you now."

Colin grinned and glanced back at Leena. She didn't like the way Niall followed that glance, as if he could read something into it. Like his piercing green eyes could trace an invisible string between Colin and her.

"I'm actually returning Leena to the temple."

"Then you've translated the scroll?"

Colin scratched the back of his neck. "Not yet, but—"

"I needed to discuss something with my Quanling." Leena strode forward until she was in the company of the two men. She'd had no idea that Niall had known about their quest or her part in it. "Colin was kind enough to escort me."

Niall clapped his hands together. "What luck. Quanling Marjory will be attending my banquet tonight. You can talk with her then."

Leena's hand pressed into the base of her throat. It was very unusual for the Quanling to leave the temple and unheard of for any scribe to be invited to the high lord's banquet. "But surely I... I mean, I assume..." What could she say that wouldn't be insulting? While her mind reached for some hint of what to do, Lord Niall put her presumptions to rest.

"You, of course, are invited as well. Someone must be there to record the event for posterity. After all, what I will announce tonight involves all of Rogos, even the scribes."

Lifting his eyebrows, Colin scratched his chin. "Sounds serious. Is that why you summoned us here?"

Colin's question was quite forward, and Leena wondered if it would anger the high lord, but Niall only smiled wider. "You are here because my fiancée predicted your arrival and because you and the Defenders of the Goddess are an integral component in ensuring the future of Rogos."

Leena couldn't stifle a gasp. "Fiancée?"

Colin patted the high lord's shoulder. "Congratulations. I hadn't heard."

Niall turned toward the dais.

"Darling?" A woman appeared beside his throne. One second, it was just the three of them, and then there she was, leaning against the side of the chair as if she'd been standing there the entire time. Had she been invisible or somehow manifested?

However she'd arrived, Leena was baffled by her appearance. She wasn't an elf. Her blue eyes barely gleamed. They were almost human-looking, as were her ears, which were rounded at their tops. Her skin, the color of freshly poured cream, was enhanced with a blush at her cheeks and full red lips. Platinum hair twisted along the back of her head and was managed into intricate curls at her crown. And her gown—Leena had never seen anything like it—was shiny, silver blue, and draped to the floor. Together with a tiara, four diamond-covered spikes that peeked out from her curls, the outfit made her look like an ice queen.

Beside her, Colin lowered himself to one knee and bowed at the waist. "Queen Penelope, it's an honor."

Queen Penelope? Leena curtsied low and bowed her head. Penelope was the witch queen of Darnuith! Now that she knew who she was, she recognized her from drawings in the scrolls. No wonder she'd seemed to appear out of nowhere. The woman had the magic to do so and then some. Her outfit now seemed fitting. Darnuith was a kingdom of ice. But could it be true? Could the high lord be uniting with the queen in marriage? If so, what did that mean for Rogos?

"My heartfelt congratulations on your betrothal," Colin said, rising from his knee. "Is this the news you'll be sharing at the banquet tonight?"

Queen Penelope moved to Niall's side as gracefully as a dancer.

"Yes, and more," Niall said. "But there will be plenty of time to talk politics. For now, I'm sure you'll want to rest and freshen up before the banquet. Grindel and Sylvia will show you to your rooms." A pair of elves appeared at his summons.

As Sylvia led her from the throne room and in the opposite direction of Colin, Leena wondered briefly if Queen Penelope had somehow enchanted the high lord into proposing marriage. But the more she analyzed that theory, the more she found the very notion to be absurd. Elves were resistant to elemental magic, and Queen Penelope would have had to, at least initially, be magically restrained to get within ten feet of him. Plus, he looked at the witch as if he honestly loved her.

She would have liked to talk to Colin about the turn of events but wasn't surprised they weren't given rooms in the same part of the palace. He was an exiled heir of the kingdom of Paragon, and she was a scribe. He'd be treated like a royal, and she... Well, she wasn't sure how she'd be treated. She'd never been here before.

"Please make yourself comfortable." Sylvia gestured inside the door to a small bedroom. "There's a dress in the closet appropriate for the banquet tonight. Please be ready by sunfall."

"I won't need the dress." Leena held her hand out to the woman. "It is against the rules of my order to wear anything but my sacred robes."

The older woman folded her hands and lowered her gaze. "It is against palace law to attend a royal banquet in anything but fine attire. I believe, in this case, royal law supersedes temple law." Sylvia gave a shallow bow, then left her alone.

Leena flopped onto the bed and stared up at the ceiling. Her headache had faded and left a lingering malaise in its place. All she'd wanted to do was return to the temple and go back to the way things were. But that end seemed to be barreling toward her both too quickly and not quickly enough. It was all so confusing.

This morning, she'd experienced the pleasures of the flesh. Some pleasures, at least. She understood there were others. Deeper temptations.

Unbidden, her thoughts turned to Colin, to the tent. Now that she thought back, she realized there must be more. Something was supposed to happen next. She sensed she was supposed to do something... something Colin avoided when he'd ducked out of the tent so quickly. She never thought she'd miss having a traditional mother until now. A true mother would have taught her about men, about sex.

What was she saying? This was exactly why she had to return to the temple as soon as possible. Oh, how he'd branded her soul. Was the inner heat he commanded in her a product of his being a dragon, or were all intimacies with the opposite sex kindling for that fire? She'd never know. He was and always would be her only one.

At least she'd learned one positive thing—her Quanling was coming to Asfolk. With any luck, the leader of her order would agree to escort her back to the temple herself, assign Colin a replacement scribe to help him with his research, and she could leave him, and all the temptation he brought with him, behind for good.

CHAPTER ELEVEN

New Orleans
December 24th, 2018

"What do you buy a woman who's about to learn her granddaughter is a witch/dragon hybrid?" Raven asked Gabriel. They'd stopped by Blakemore's Antiques to pick out a Christmas gift to bring with them to her mother's the following morning. She was relieved that Avery and Xavier had offered to babysit Charlie while they shopped. The thought of keeping the child contained in a store full of priceless valuables made her itch, especially now that they'd learned she could fly.

Gabriel slanted a grin in her direction. "There is that bronze dragon figurine from the Qing dynasty."

"Oh for the love of the goddess, can you imagine? Not only would we stop her heart with the news, but she could also relive the experience repeatedly every time she saw it."

Agnes came out of the office and rushed to embrace both of them in a firm hug. "I thought I heard your voices!" Her sleek silver bob was as sophisticated as ever, and the wide-legged pants she wore looked sharp with a cropped, textured sweater. She kissed Raven on both cheeks. "It's been an age!"

"Too long," Gabriel agreed.

"Where's Richard?" Raven asked.

"Off for the holiday. It's Christmas Eve, after all, and unlike me, he has family. Now tell me what brings you here today. I'm sensing it isn't to check up on the store."

"Never. I trust you implicitly. There's something we need to find, and something we need to do to find it."

"Do tell."

Raven glanced around the store and lowered her voice. "No customers in today? Not even on the second floor?"

She shook her head. "Midmorning lull."

Raven moved to the door and locked it, flipping the sign to CLOSED. "Do you want to tell her or should I?"

As it turned out, Gabriel volunteered to fill Agnes in on everything that had happened since they'd left Blakemore's. They joined her in what used to be Gabriel's office, where Raven conjured them a pot of tea and added details her mate forgot. It took the better part of an hour to explain where they'd been these past months and everything that had unfolded. When Agnes heard about Charlie, she almost came out of her skin, insisting she must meet the baby before they left to return to Aeaea.

"So, you're here to find the remains of the tanglewood tree. My god, Gabriel, I thought the mess you were in with Crimson Vanderholt was the worst that could happen. How do the two of you get yourselves into these situations?"

Gabriel growled and reflexively glanced at his ring, no doubt remembering the curse that had brought them together. "Don't talk about Crimson. I still have nightmares."

"One good thing came of Crimson Vanderholt," Raven said through a smile. "It was because of her spell that I was able to get pregnant with Charlie."

The room grew eerily quiet. Gabriel sipped his tea. Agnes rubbed under her eye.

"Well, it's true. Thank goodness she's dead, but her spell, as dark and evil as her intentions were, brought Charlie into this world." Raven poured herself another cup.

Gabriel cleared his throat. "I'd rather not think of it."

Agnes stood. "Then let's do something productive, like finding you a gift to bring to Raven's mother, shall we? I think I have just the thing. How do you think she would feel about a stained-glass panel for one of her windows?" Agnes pointed at the small window in the brick above her head. "It was reclaimed and refurbished from an old church that was torn down years ago."

Raven squinted at the colorful leaded glass. There was a large bird outside the window, and its silhouette blocked the sun, obstructing her view of the pattern. She stood and crossed the room to view the simple geometric art at a better angle. Easter lilies. Her mother did have a front window in her apartment above the Three Sisters that let in the morning sun, and the bright colors matched her decor.

"I think she'd love that."

THERE WERE TWO WAYS INTO THE APARTMENT ABOVE the Three Sisters. One was to enter through the bar itself and use a narrow staircase that ascended between the back office and the kitchen. The other way was to employ a staircase that rose along the outside of the building and doubled as a fire escape. Since it was Christmas morning, the bar was closed, the front door locked. They'd have to use the outside stairs.

"Gabriel, you are going to have to carry Charlie," Raven said. "I'm not strong enough to keep her wings tucked into the blanket. She keeps squirming out of my grasp." She rewrapped her daughter in the red plaid they'd bought for the occasion and tried her best to make her look human even though there was no way her size was anything close to natural. Once she was a veritable burrito, Raven handed her off to Gabriel.

"Even if you hide the wings, it's going to take Mom all of five seconds to realize something is wrong. Let's just hope Charlie doesn't try to eat her like she did the cat," Avery said.

Raven glared at her sister. "Since we're all being so honest with Mom, I'm not sure why you and Clarissa left your mates at the Prytania house? Shouldn't we rip off the Band-Aid and introduce them to her at the same time?"

"Hey, technically, she's already met Nathaniel," Clarissa said, an easy laugh warming the air around her.

"I just thought it would be easier on Mom if there were fewer... distractions." Avery adjusted the stack of gifts she was carrying. "Besides, Xavier is... hard to explain on many levels."

Raven understood what her sister meant. Xavier had spent centuries in a pocket of magic, living cut off from the modern world. It wasn't just that he was a Scot and a dragon—he was practically from another time. But she also knew that Avery's deepest fear wasn't about any of that. "You're afraid to tell Mom you got married without her there."

"Maybe," Avery admitted.

Raven crossed her arms. "Don't give me a hard time

about Charlie. Whatever happens in there, I'm doing my best. I need you to have my back on this."

They all stared at the door to the apartment above the Three Sisters. No one moved.

"Avery, give me the gifts. They'll hide my flat stomach until I can break the news gently."

"Oh hell." Clarissa released a heavy sigh. "Let's do this."

None of them even had to knock. As if by some sixth sense, Mom opened the door the moment they reached it and squealed with unbridled joy. "Merry Christmas! Oh, I'm so happy you're finally here! Come in! Come in!"

Gabriel glanced at Raven and tucked Charlie into his chest like a football.

"Merry Christmas!" Raven accepted a one-armed hug from her mom around the gifts. She'd missed her mother, and as Avery and Clarissa took their turns hugging her, she couldn't help but feel a wave of nostalgia for the cramped, brightly colored kitchen that used to be the heart of their home. Less than a year ago, she'd lived here, swaddled in the unconditional love of her mother and Avery. It hadn't all been roses, but it was what she'd needed to get her life back after her illness. The apartment seemed smaller now, but also cozy and safe. Maybe this would be okay.

"Mom, there's something I have to tell you," Raven said.

Her mom raised a finger. "Actually, there's something I have to tell you—all of you—and I'm afraid it can't wait." Her honey-brown curls bounced over one shoulder as her perfectly shaped red lips spread into a wide smile. Come to think of it, her mother's makeup was exceptionally on point, and she was dressed in an emerald-green jumpsuit Raven had never seen before.

"Mom, you look great, but you didn't have to get all

dressed up for us," Avery said. "We thought this was casual." She gestured to her own jeans and lightweight Christmas sweater.

Clarissa smiled politely and zeroed in on Sarah's left hand. "That ring is gorgeous. Is that new?"

Everyone stopped. Raven stared at the diamond on her mother's finger. "No..."

"Yes!" Sarah squealed. "David, come in here."

Raven's mouth dropped open as her father stepped into the door of the kitchen, wearing a suit and tie. She didn't miss the fact that his hair was gelled.

David smiled nervously at everyone. "I guess the cat's out of the bag."

Avery made a sound like a cough. "What cat? What bag? Why is Dad here? You didn't say anything about Dad coming to Christmas. I didn't even know you were speaking to each other."

Sarah shrugged. "We got back together. He lives here now."

"You what?" Raven couldn't believe her ears.

"Maybe we should go into the living room and have a drink," Sarah suggested.

"Congratulations!" Clarissa looked positively uncomfortable, and Raven and Avery pinned her with a barbed stare. Up until a few months ago, she hadn't known Sarah was her biological mother and, as the newest member of the family, still didn't fully appreciate the family dynamic. Raven's father had abandoned and divorced her mother when Raven was on her deathbed and had proved himself a selfish ass time and time again.

"No." Avery shook her head at their sister, her voice low.

Sarah folded her arms. "Avery Lynn Tanglewood, did you just tell Clarissa not to wish us congratulations? I'd say congratulations are perfectly in order. We're getting remarried."

Avery tossed up her hands. "What? Mom, how could this happen?"

Raven glanced at Gabriel, who stood positively still, Charlie sleeping in his arms. "Maybe Mom's right. Maybe we should go into the living room and have a drink. I need a drink. I think we all need a drink."

"It's really not that surprising," her mom continued. "You three were gone. David and I spent more and more time together. The pressure was off. One thing led to another."

Avery scowled. "Eww."

"Eww?" David said, wagging his finger at her. "Eww? That eww once led to all of you!"

Clarissa tucked her hair behind her ears. "Speaking of... um, nice to meet you, by the way."

Sarah froze. "Oh my god, that's right! You two have never actually met, I mean, as adults. Oh my god. We've gone about this all out of order."

Clarissa and David stared at each other, each jerking forward as if they were trying to decide if it was appropriate for them to hug. David smoothed his tie. "It's such a privilege to finally meet you."

The two laughed awkwardly and hugged each other.

"Did someone mention a drink?" Avery grumbled.

Raven sighed. "These gifts weigh a ton." She set the stack down on the table.

Sarah did a double take. "Why aren't you pregnant anymore?"

The room grew quiet. Sarah's eyes darted from Raven to

Avery to Clarissa and then finally to Gabriel and the bundle in his arms.

"Wait, is that...?" Sarah pointed at the red plaid burrito.

"That can't be our grandchild," David said.

Gabriel loosened his grip and gently rolled Charlie to expose her sleeping face.

Sarah approached tentatively, her features betraying her confusion. "But..."

Raven could practically hear her mother's mental calculator working. Sarah reached out and brushed a finger across Charlie's cheek.

"Mom—" Raven raised both hands as Charlie's eyes popped open and she took one look at her grandmother, burst from her blanket, and flew around the room, through the grasping hands of Avery, Clarissa, and Gabriel, before landing in a squat on top of the refrigerator. Her red velvet Christmas dress bunched over her bare toes.

Sarah looked at David and then back at Charlie. She pointed, then pressed the finger to her lips.

"Charlie, stay there!" Raven held out a hand to her daughter. "Mom, I can explain."

"Oh shit, she's going over!" David rushed forward and caught Sarah before she could hit the floor.

CHAPTER TWELVE

Asfolk Palace
Rogos

Colin's room in Asfolk Palace faced west, giving him a fabulous view of the setting suns as twilight enveloped Rogos. He smoothed the lapels of the suit he'd been given to wear, a black-and-white affair that was more formal than he was used to and a little tight in the shoulders. Tonight, he'd wear a burlap sack if Niall asked him to.

He needed Rogos to align with the Defenders of the Goddess against Paragon, and he hoped this recent engagement meant an end to Rogos's neutrality. Darnuith, after all, had never been neutral; their tentative peace with Paragon had been fraught with tension and political positioning. That said, Queen Penelope had avoided an alliance with the Defenders of the Goddess with as much passion as she'd evaded a close relationship with Eleanor. It was well known she didn't trust dragons. It didn't matter which side they were on.

The match between Niall and Penelope made him

uneasy. Was it a political marriage, or was romance involved? Only a fool would underestimate the power and influence of the witch queen of Darnuith. As much as he appreciated that Rogos might benefit from an alliance between the two kingdoms, it had to be a bit like grabbing a tiger by the tail.

A knock came on the door. "High Lord Niall requests your presence in the ballroom," a male's voice announced.

Colin slid his feet into his shoes and opened the door. The elf on the other side was elderly and small—his head only reached Colin's bottom rib, and his pointed ears bent at the tips.

"Hello again, Grindel."

The little elf bowed. "If you'll please follow me."

Colin allowed Grindel to escort him to the ballroom and then to what appeared to be a staging area near the front of the immense hall. But when he passed through the door Grindel indicated, Colin pulled up short. It wasn't Niall waiting for him inside but Queen Penelope, and she was alone.

"Apologies," Colin murmured, backing toward the door. "The elf who brought me here said I was to meet Niall. He must have put me in the wrong room." He reached for the door handle, but with the sweep of one hand, he heard the door lock before he could open it.

"He told you what I asked him to tell you." The queen's voice was warm and melodious. Instantly, he wanted to gather her in his arms and give her a friendly hug as if she were a long-lost acquaintance. He was resistant to her magic but not immune to it and felt himself relaxing under her influence.

"Why did you want to see me?" He leaned his back against

the door, keeping as much space as possible between them. Relaxed as her magic might make him, there was no mistaking he was in a dangerous situation. Simply being alone with her in this room could cause a diplomatic mess with Niall, and he'd be a fool to trust her after the way she'd lured him there.

Her icy blue eyes locked on to his, and her wide mouth spread into a smile. "I heard something interesting recently from a mutual friend of ours, and I thought you'd be the best one to confirm the rumor."

The scent of honey filled the room. Colin had the distinct impression that the air was wrapping around him like a cozy blanket. She was just so nice. He hadn't remembered what a kind and welcoming person the queen was. He shook his head to clear it. "Which friend? Which rumor?"

"Zander Wraithwing says that you have the three sisters and they may have one of Darnuith's most precious but missing historical artifacts, the golden grimoire."

"There is a golden grimoire, but it isn't Darnuith's. It was left to the three sisters by their ancestor Medea." Colin shook his head again, fighting the fog that kept clogging up his thoughts. He had to concentrate to think.

Penelope's smile grew wider. "Exactly. I knew you'd understand. An honorable dragon like you was sure to see the truth of it. Medea was our queen, and the three sisters are witches and her descendants. Therefore, by law, citizens of Darnuith. When Medea left the grimoire to them, she was leaving it to us."

"I don't think... I, uh, I'll have to talk to Raven. Truth is, we haven't even found it yet." The room grew hot. He tugged at the collar of his shirt.

She giggled and shrugged in the most charming way. It

made him smile. "A clever man like you must have some idea where it is."

He blinked rapidly against a shimmer that surrounded her like an aura. "It's here," he said. "Somewhere, locked in a grave in Rogos. We have a crypt key, but we need the three sisters to translate the sacred scroll to know which tomb it fits."

"The scribe was helping you, wasn't she?"

"Leena helped me find the scroll and was curating it while the three sisters attempted to break the enchantment over it."

"So why are you back here?" Her voice rang like a bell, and her warm smile never faltered.

"Leena wanted to go home. She was... afraid of how the greater world was changing her. I was escorting her back to the temple."

"Hmm. But you need her?"

"In more ways than one," he said softly.

Penelope rubbed her fingers lightly over her left collarbone, above the neckline of her dress. "You will find the grimoire, Colin. I just know you will. And when you do, you'll bring it to me."

"I, uh..." He couldn't make any promises, but he couldn't think of the words to tell her so.

"There then, it's all settled." She patted his arm, and he wondered when she'd crossed the room. "I'm so glad we had this talk."

She stood on her tiptoes and placed a kiss on his cheek. His eyebrows shot up, and he smiled after her as she opened the door and floated from the room.

Only after she was gone did a fresh waft of air come through the door and clear his head. He frowned. Had he just promised her the grimoire? No. No, he hadn't. But she'd wanted him to. She'd used her magic, hoping the influence would hold, consciously or unconsciously.

Even though it hadn't completely worked, he hated how much he wanted to give her the grimoire right then. He could just imagine how it would make her smile. He stepped out of the staging room, shaking off the last remnants of the interaction and knowing one thing for certain—there was more than one reason Queen Penelope was interested in the Defenders of the Goddess, and all of them needed to be very careful around her.

He accepted a bubbly yellow drink in a tall glass from a passing server and watched the ballroom fill fast with people from all over Rogos, everyone dressed in their finest. Colin recognized Quanling Marjory, dressed in a yellow gown that made her skin look sallow. He wondered if that was a purposeful compromise. The scribe leader couldn't wear her robes at the function, but she could wear a dress that made her look just as pious.

Colin scanned the crowd for Niall. If he could speak to the high lord again, if only for a few minutes, he could ask about Darnuith and how he'd met Queen Penelope. Working with the two kingdoms would require a gentle hand, but they'd all have to be in lockstep if they were to overcome Paragon's dragons.

If Niall was among the crowd, though, Colin didn't notice because before he could find the high lord of the elves, his gaze locked on to a vision in midnight blue floating into the room. *Leena.* Her dark copper hair had been freed from its usual braid and lay in soft curls that rested on bare shoulders, fire against ice. Her dress was strapless and hugged her figure, skimming her legs to her ankles and parting over her left knee when she walked. From her fingers, a matching satchel dangled, large enough to hold the scrolls she swore she never left behind. It made him smile to think of her dedication even while the sight of her silky, pale skin made his dragon coil and chuff within him. He scratched his arms through his suit to distract from the prickle of his heated blood.

Leena's violet eyes met his, her inner light making them violently purple, as bright as the lamps burning on the walls. Only, as soon as she saw him, her smile faded. He tried not to take it personally. Had he spent less time with her, he might have thought she hated him. But that wasn't hate he saw in her expression—it was fear. She wanted to hate him. It would make things far easier for her. Bastard that he was, he wouldn't let that happen.

He started for her, cutting through the crowd of faceless guests, unable to see anyone but her. Her gaze darted around the room, looking for a lifeline, anything to avoid facing him again. One more night. Tomorrow, she'd leave with her Quanling, her replacement would be assigned, and he likely wouldn't ever see her again.

One more night to feel the temptation she'd made it clear to him she wanted to avoid.

One more night to change her mind and win her over.

Turned out his dragon was okay with being a bastard.

"You look stunning," he said when he finally reached her.

Her eyes flicked down to her toes. "I'd rather be in my robes, and I can't walk in these shoes, but I'm told this is expected of me."

He frowned. He hated the idea that her upbringing had made it so she couldn't even enjoy one night of glitz and glamour. She'd always feel like she should be wrapped in burlap even when she was clearly a queen. "Well, we all have to do what is expected of us. I guess the dress is just one more worldly experience you can leave behind when you're back at the temple."

She smoothed a hand over the already smooth material at her waist. "Yes. It shouldn't be long now. Actually, I should try to find my Quanling. I'm sure Marjory will be happy to escort me home and name my replacement."

The thought burrowed into his heart, where it condensed into a heavy weight that threatened to make the floor cave in. "Are you sure you're ready? Have you... sampled enough of life to quell your curiosity?"

Her cheeks turned a delightful shade of pink, and her gaze swept toward her shoes. "There is one thing I'm curious about."

"Oh?"

She looked both ways, cheeks blazing.

"This way." He gestured to a door that led outside to the balcony. They stepped into the cool night air, and he tugged her out of view of the ballroom, behind a marble pillar and against the outer wall of the palace. "There's no one out here."

"Because it's freezing!" She shivered and hugged herself.

He stepped closer, extending his wings and wrapping them around her. "Better?"

Close now, within his shelter, those violet eyes turned stormy. "Better."

"So, what is it you're curious about?"

Her eyes flicked away from his. "What you did to me in the tent, it seemed... one-sided... Like there should be more."

Heat rose with other more interesting parts of his body as he remembered that morning. "You're right. There is more. Much more."

"Tell me." And just like that, the bashful scribe was gone, and the twinkling eyes and impish grin of the woman he'd first kissed on the beach were back.

"Well…" How to say this without scaring her away? "What I did to you, usually a woman would… reciprocate."

Her lips parted. "I was supposed to do the same to you?"

"No. You don't have to. There's no obligation between lovers." Now it was his turn to look away, his inner dragon chuffing for her touch.

"But you left the tent so quickly."

"I didn't want to show you more than you were ready for. I wasn't sure how much you wanted to… sample."

She sighed. "With you, Colin, I find every bite I take just leads me to want another."

"Maybe that means you need a steady diet." He leaned forward. Her mouth was so close her chin tipped up within the shelter of his wings. He stopped when she shook her head, a tear forming in the corner of her eye.

"That's exactly why I have to go." She backed up, breaking from his wings and heading for the door, her skin forming goose bumps in the cold.

"Leena…"

She patted the bag at her hip. "I've got to get inside. It's my job to record this big announcement for posterity."

"You're a good scribe."

She nodded.

"What about your idea to search for the grave using the year the scroll was created?"

"It will be the first thing I suggest to my replacement to pursue."

"I'd prefer you. You're familiar with the history."

"It will not be me." She smiled and sighed. "If you'll excuse me—"

"Was it my dancing?" He flashed her a crooked grin.

For a moment, she blinked at him. "I am sorry about that. The snail venom has an inebriating effect."

He shrugged. "I loved every minute of it. I've never seen such joy on your face."

She dropped her chin and stared down at her tangled fingers, her cheeks blazing again. "Yes, you have, just this morning." She pivoted away from him, leaving him dumb struck, and stepped through the doors into the crowd.

CHAPTER THIRTEEN

Leena's heart thumped in her chest as she strode aimlessly away from Colin and the balcony. She had to get back to the temple. He was too much of a temptation, becoming too precious to her. Already, she wondered how she would find the strength within herself to let him go.

And it was sinful what she was doing. Using him. Experimenting on him. How embarrassing to learn that she'd been so overwhelmed by the experience he'd given her in the tent that she hadn't thought to find out how he liked to be touched. She wondered now what that thick hardness he'd pressed against her belly would feel like in her hand. Why had she never thought to research male anatomy in the temple library? Why hadn't she read about sex?

But she knew the answer to both those questions. She'd never even been tempted to because what a coupling represented to her was a place of pain and suffering. She'd always felt lucky to avoid the trappings of coupledom. Until Colin. Until the strange feelings he ignited in her.

The most shameful part—the part she didn't want to admit, even to herself—was that there was more to her experimenting than simple lust. If her attraction to Colin was purely physical, it would be far easier to deny herself. No, there were definitely deeper feelings here. Layers of friendship and mutual admiration. He made her laugh. Made her feel totally accepted, just as she was.

Alone among the throng of people gathered for the ball, she smoothed her dress, hoping no one could see the turmoil raging inside her. Surprisingly, her dress showed none of it. On the outside, she was as calm and collected as when she left her room. Small favors.

She was relieved when Quanling Marjory came into view, her austere yellow dress far more appropriate than the one the palace had loaned her. She wondered if the woman kept it for such events.

"Goddess, it is good to see you, Mother," Leena said, using the term of endearment that scribes used for the head of their order. Although they were not physically related, Marjory was as much a mother to her as the woman who had delivered her into this world.

"Leena, my daughter, how lovely you look," the older woman said in a low voice.

"I know it's disgraceful, but I was told my robes were inappropriate."

"Oh, they are, dear. You really had no choice. But your appearance is quite pleasing for the circumstances and is, in fact, appropriate. Try not to feel out of place. The goddess loves adaptability."

She pressed a hand to her chest. "I'm relieved you think so. I miss the simplicity of temple life."

"Don't we all," Marjory said, but there was a hint of humor in her voice. She followed it up with a sip from a bubbly yellow beverage. Was that wine? The Quanling did drink alcohol during certain ceremonies at the temple, but for some reason, this seemed different. That sip was entirely for pleasure. She'd never seen Marjory do anything entirely for pleasure before.

Leena sighed. Pleasure was exactly why she needed to speak with the woman. "I wonder if I might have a moment with you?"

"Of course, but quickly. People are starting to take their seats. I believe both the food and the big announcement are coming soon."

Leena didn't let on that she knew what part of that announcement would be. It wasn't her news to tell, and disclosing the betrothal now could undermine the event. "I was wondering if you might escort me back to the temple when you return tomorrow. As the leader of the resistance, Colin has much to do. I hate to distract him from his responsibilities."

"Of course you can travel with me. Frankly, I'm surprised you're returning so soon. Have the rebels learned all they can from the scroll?"

"All that *I* can help them with. I'd like you to name a replacement for me."

That earned her a sideways glance. Marjory opened her mouth to respond, but they were interrupted when a servant near the head table rang a loud and persistent bell with a sweeping motion that required the use of his entire body.

"We'll discuss this later," Marjory said.

Leena followed her to their assigned table. Soon, the room was flooded with servers bringing out a parade of dishes that Leena had never tasted before. There was roast elderbeast and razorwing pie, a noodle dish she didn't know the name of, and she was served a glass of the bubbling yellow wine.

She glanced at Marjory, who gave her a reassuring smile. "Enjoy yourself, daughter. You have my permission to indulge fully in the banquet. After all, we serve the goddess, and the high lord is her named ruler of Rogos. Rejecting his banquet would be an affront to her name."

Leena reached for the glass and took a tentative sip. The liquid was herbal, definitely alcoholic, but crisp and refreshing. The slightly sweet flavor left the taste of apple and citrus in her throat. "Mmm. What is this?"

Marjory grinned. "Dornapple wine. Incredible, isn't it? The fruit is inedible before fermentation. Most people consider the tree a weed. But for the elf who is willing to invest the time, the rewards are theirs to reap." She raised her glass, the lines in her cheeks growing deeper with her smile.

Leena had to agree. The drink was delightful, and it helped to relax her as they progressed with the meal.

"Does anyone know what this might be about?" the man seated across from her asked.

"It has to be about the trade routes," an elderly woman beside her stated. She clutched the oversized, polished jade necklace she wore around her birdlike neck. "Paragon has never gone so far as to cut Rogos off entirely. It's dastardly. That awful Eleanor has gone too far. Everfield has already fallen. How long until her dragons are at our gates?"

Marjory chewed her food carefully before speaking. "Eleanor will realize soon enough that her actions won't achieve the desired effect. Rogos prides itself on being self-sufficient. We produce enough within our boundaries to feed and clothe every citizen. I wouldn't worry."

The heavyset elf beside her gave a hearty guffaw that made his jowls shake. "Spoken as a true scribe. With all due respect to your ministry, the rest of us have grown accustomed to choice and luxury, not to mention reaping the profits of selling our goods to the other kingdoms. We need those routes to preserve our way of life."

"Thank the goddess for the resistance," the lanky elf beside Leena chimed in. He sipped his wine before adding, "Almost everything is still available via the black market, although the prices will rise, I'm sure. Worth it, though, considering the risk they take now that Everfield has fallen. Word is the Obsidian Guard is permanently stationed along the east side of the Sanguine River."

"I don't think it's a coincidence that the queen of Darnuith is sitting in a place of honor at the head table," the man beside her added. "They likely called us here to tell us what they plan to do about the blockade."

"I don't trust her," the woman with the jade necklace added. "You can't trust witches any more than dragons. If there's anything our history teaches us, it is that both are only interested in more. More power. More things to collect. More magic."

Leena couldn't hold her tongue. "Excuse me, but didn't this gentleman just mention that the resistance and its black market are keeping Rogos afloat during this difficult time?"

The woman's prominent upper lip curved like a duck's bill as she tucked in her chin to stare down her nose at Leena. "Yes, girl. What has that got to do with anything?"

"Well, it's only that the Defenders of the Goddess are led and run by dragons, the former heirs to the kingdom of Paragon. And there are witches helping them too. I've met them myself."

"What's your point?" the heavy elf said.

"Only that it's probably not fair to judge an entire species based on the actions of a few. I'm sure to dragons and witches, elves seem stubbornly hands-off during times like these. Neutral and independent we may be, but we are more than ready to enjoy the benefits of those who are not when it suits us."

The lean elf grunted and drank the rest of his wine. "The young always have such idealistic views."

Leena leaned back in her chair, regretting that she'd said anything.

"You were right, daughter," Marjory whispered. "Don't be discouraged to speak your mind. These elves always want to have it both ways."

"I'm just looking forward to returning home to Niven," Leena said softly. "All of this unsettles me."

Marjory frowned. "It should unsettle you, dear. The world is changing. Nowhere is immune to it, not even the temple."

Before Leena could say another word, the servant rang his bell again and the crowd went silent. "If I can have your attention, please," the tiny man announced. "High Lord Niall has an announcement."

Leena reached for her bag and pulled out her quill and a blank scroll.

⁓

Asfolk Palace
Rogos
Year of the Goddess: ,βιθ, Capricorn 3rd

I, LEENA OF NIVEN, SCRIBE OF THE ORDER OF THE SACRED Pools, am honored to be a guest of Asfolk Palace, charged with recording the historic event unfolding this night. High Lord Niall has called in representatives from every district in Rogos for an exclusive banquet and special announcement.

Speculation is high about what this announcement might be given the recent closure of trade routes and the occupation of the Sanguine River by the empress of Paragon. With the traditional meal concluded, the attendees wait patiently for our high ruler to speak.

Murmurs slowly fade and then stop altogether as Niall stands and accepts from one of the servants an enchanted crystal meant to amplify his voice. At the head table behind him, the witch queen of Darnuith, wearing a silver-blue gown that makes her appear as if she's brought the icy power of her kingdom with her on her person, looks on with nothing but admiration in her expression. Beside her, the ambassador to Darnuith, Claxon, watches stoically from his place of honor.

A weighty silence spreads across the room as the high lord prepares to speak. "It pleases me that so many of you could join us on such short notice for this celebration and announcement." *His sleek ebony hair frames his face as he looks out over the tables.* "The kingdom of Rogos has a long tradition of maintaining neutrality. For the four hundred years I have ruled, our isolationist policies have served us well. We have flourished and become self-sufficient."

The crowd gives a short round of applause.

Niall frowns. "But times have changed. The empress of Paragon has recently closed off all trade routes between the five kingdoms. Everfield has fallen under her heel, giving her control of the entire Sanguine River and what remains of the Empyrean Wood. She claims to want to unite the kingdoms, but what we've seen in Everfield is the manifestation of her true desire, to destroy them and enslave their people. Enslave our *people!*" *Niall's voice rises, passion bleeding through his words.*

A quorum of boos rings out. Elves dart glances at one

another and thump their tables with their fists to communicate their displeasure at the thought.

"You may have noticed that Queen Penelope has joined me tonight," Niall continues. "You may have wondered why. The day before yesterday, it rained blood in Darnuith, a dark spell cast by the empress, meant to poison their crops and force that kingdom into her hand. Thankfully, their queen, our powerful ally, thwarted the curse. Darnuith has closed their border with Paragon and cut off all diplomatic relations with the empress."

A cheer rings through the ballroom. The crowd applauds the queen for her courage standing up to Paragon.

"But the threat is still there to both our kingdoms. Daily, I receive a falcon from the empress of Paragon asking for me to bend the knee. What she tried in Darnuith, she will try here in time."

Now the room grows so quiet this scribe can hear the bubbles in the wineglasses fizz. No one needs to speak for everyone to understand. While Queen Penelope has the type of magic that could shelter Darnuith's crops from blood rain, Rogos does not. Elfin magic is strong but, unlike Darnuith's, their crops and industry are spread across the kingdom. A protective spell of impossible size would be needed to protect it all, an effort far beyond elf magic.

"I am convinced that neutrality is no longer an option for Rogos," Niall says.

Murmurs rise like a wave in the crowd. Tension in the room ratchets up.

"Never fear—your high lord will keep you safe." He licks his lips. "I am pleased to announce that just this morning, Queen Penelope of Darnuith accepted my proposal of marriage, and we were united in matrimony only hours ago."

The murmurs grow louder. A desert dweller pops from

his chair and moves to storm from the room, but another at his table grabs his arm and escorts him back to his seat. No one looks happy. The expressions in the room range from alarm to disgust.

Niall lowers his head, his voice growing serious. "With our marriage comes an alliance between our kingdoms. Darnuith has promised protection to Rogos, and Rogos has agreed." He scans the crowd as all levity melts from his face. "Come sunrise, Rogos, together with Darnuith, will prepare our troops, we will align with the Defenders of the Goddess, and together, two kingdoms united, we will declare war on Paragon."

LEENA DROPPED HER QUILL AS THE BALLROOM exploded into shouts and confused murmurs. The woman in the jade necklace whimpered and appeared to faint in her chair. The heavyset elf jumped to his feet, shaking his fist and yelling his displeasure at this turn of events. Guests headed toward the doors, anxious to find other guests and to speak about the announcement.

"By the goddess," Marjory said, her face paling. She grabbed Leena's arm. "War? A political marriage? Now? Do you know what this means?"

Leena wasn't sure she did. After spending time with Colin, she'd come to realize that war was inevitable, but the other citizens of Rogos in the room seemed to come out of their skin at the thought. Admittedly, she'd never expected it to happen this fast. What did this mean for the temple? She blinked back a flood of anxiety, then realized that her role was the same as always.

"I need to get this down." She tapped her quill to her

scroll. "Everything that I see and hear. When we get back to the temple—"

Marjory's gaze snapped to hers, and the look in her eyes bordered on panic. Leena recoiled.

"Our high lord has just declared war, my daughter," she whispered. "I believe it is still to be learned what the future of the temple will be."

"What do you mean?"

"Rogos will prepare its army, and we have a number of able-bodied men and women in our ranks, all of them trained to defend themselves."

"We're trained to defend the scrolls," Leena said. That was why she'd learned to shoot poison arrows with her bare hands.

Marjory gave her a pitying look, tipped her head to the side, and pursed her lips. "We need to prepare ourselves. Everything will change." Marjory laid a hand on her arm. "The ambassador to Niven is heading this way."

A lithe but elderly elf that Leena had met once years ago came to stand before them, extending his hand. "Quanling Marjory, it's a pleasure to see you again."

"And you as well, Ambassador Rajesh." Marjory gave a small bow. "You remember my scribe Leena?"

"Of course. Actually, she is part of the reason I've sought you out tonight."

Oh no. A dark, sinking feeling welled in Leena's gut.

"First, I must inform you that troops will be descending on Niven in the near future to harvest the goddess's tears for use in weapons against Paragon."

Marjory bowed her head. "I expected as much. We have preserved the knowledge of these weapons from long ago, and our scribes will aid our soldiers in any way needed."

"Excellent."

Leena's stomach clenched. Soldiers at the temple?

"Which brings me to Leena," Rajesh added. "It seems her help is an integral part of the war effort. Something about finding a crypt and a weapon. I can't say I understood it all. But High Lord Niall has insisted that her role is key and she must not be removed from the task."

Panic rose like bile in Leena's throat. "No," she blurted. That was louder than she'd intended. She cleared her throat. "Excuse me. I'm sure what he meant was that a scribe's involvement is key. The Defenders of the Goddess need a scribe to research graves to find a potential weapon hidden there. Any scribe could do it. It doesn't have to be me."

The ambassador shook his head. "He made it very clear. Only you."

Leena turned toward Marjory. "May I speak with you privately for a moment?"

Her Quanling pursed her lips until tight vertical lines appeared beneath her nose. "Excuse us, Rajesh." The older woman gripped her arm and pulled her to the side. "What is wrong with you? When the high lord asks for your service, it is your duty to comply."

"I... I can't." She pressed a hand to her stomach and lowered her voice. "The reason Colin escorted me back here now was so that you can assign an alternate scribe to the task, Mother. Our... relationship... has become inappropriate." Heat crept up her neck to her ears.

She knew her Quanling noticed the blush because her eyes narrowed on her cheeks. "What do you mean, inappropriate?"

"He has expressed feelings for me," she whispered.

"You, of course, have done nothing to invite these feelings."

Leena's gaze shifted to the floor. "Not intentionally."

Marjory made a sound deep in her throat. "And you have explained to him your oath and obligations?"

"Yes, Mother." She was a horrible scribe for acting on her impulses. She must go back to the temple. Must put distance between Colin and herself.

"Then I fail to see the problem. I am sure he will respect the boundaries of your oath." Leena's gaze snapped up to her Quanling's and found the woman's eyes cold and hard.

"But I think it would be best—"

"The temple is not a place to hide, daughter, especially now, not with a world at war. You and Colin will come with me back to the temple where you, and no one else, will help him find what he is looking for. Am I understood?"

Leena swallowed. "Yes, Mother."

"Very good." She ushered her back to the ambassador. "Apologies for the delay. Leena misunderstood her assignment. She will help in any way she can to protect and advance the kingdom of Rogos."

"Splendid," Raj said. "The high lord will be pleased."

And so, Leena thought with a scowl, would Colin.

CHAPTER FOURTEEN

New Orleans
December 25th, 2018

Raven chewed her lip while her mother and father stared at Charlie with a look of total surrender on their faces. They'd been like that for the better part of an hour, just trying to let everything sink in. She thought it was not unlike the stages of grief. They'd journeyed through denial and then anger, when her father had chastised them all for keeping this a secret for so long, and now she suspected they were entering depression.

They sat shoulder to shoulder on the floral sofa in the living room, both looking a little light-headed, and leaned into each other as if they were holding each other up.

"You're a witch," Sarah said absently. "All three of you are witches."

They'd gone over this a hundred times. "Yes. Just like the family legends always said." Raven nodded. "It was all true. It runs in our blood."

Sarah glanced at David as if he were to blame, but, in

fact, it was the Tanglewood bloodline, Sarah's bloodline, that gave them their magic. "I guess it skipped a generation."

"And you're a dragon?" David squinted at Gabriel and ran a hand down his face when her mate nodded slowly. "Our grandchild can fly."

"Yes," Raven said in her most soothing voice... again.

"It's really not that big of a deal." Avery flipped one hand in the air, garnering looks of horror from her parents. "Once you get used to the idea, it will seem perfectly normal."

Charlie chose that moment to soar across the room and land in Raven's lap. David's mouth dropped open in a frown so exaggerated it was almost comical. Gabriel rubbed Raven's shoulder and pulled Charlie into his arms.

"I never had a family like this," Gabriel said in a voice like scorched embers. "My childhood was filled with weighty expectations and clenched teeth. My uncle assassinated my father and my eldest brother."

Sarah inhaled sharply, and David wrapped a comforting arm around her.

"My father was more concerned with how well we fought in the pits than showing us any sort of affection. Still, I missed him after he was gone. Our uncle, as it turns out, was acting under my mother's influence. She tricked my siblings and me into thinking we must stay apart, and so for three hundred years, we didn't even have one another."

A gagging sound came from Sarah's direction. "Did you say three hundred years?"

Gabriel glanced toward Raven, a resigned look on his face. "I am approximately five hundred years old, give or take a few due to the differences in the time flow between our worlds. I am a dragon. I am immortal. As are your daughter and your granddaughter."

Now Sarah pressed both hands into her mouth.

"I keep waiting for you all to tell us the punch line," David said. "But we're the punch line. The human grandparents." He gestured toward Charlie, shaking his head. "Is this real?"

Gabriel spread his wings. Her mother looked as if she might faint again. Raven snapped her fingers, and a spark of magic spelled out MERRY CHRISTMAS in the air between them. Sarah and David looked like they'd stopped breathing.

"It's real. And you're not a punch line, Dad. Neither of you is. We thought about keeping this from you, but we think you can handle it."

Clarissa laughed nervously. "Hey, but it's not nearly as exciting as you two lovebirds getting back together, am I right?"

Everyone turned and stared at her.

"Just trying to lighten the mood." She grabbed the sides of her chair and stretched her legs out in front of her.

Charlie started gnawing on Gabriel's arm.

"Mom, I know you're still processing all this, but Charlie is hungry. The meal smells delicious. Can I feed her?"

Her mother shook herself like she was waking up. "Hungry? But surely she..."

"She eats everything we eat, although she prefers meat... rare." Raven felt her smile falter. That was one of the odder things about Charlie that she hadn't quite gotten used to herself.

Sarah sat up straighter. "I have just the thing." She pointed over her shoulder. "I made prime rib. She can have the center piece." She popped off the couch and headed for the kitchen.

"You know your mother," David said. "Nothing trumps her instinct to feed people."

Her father must have been right, because in a matter of minutes, Raven found herself at the dining room table, passing bowls of whipped potatoes and fried okra. Her mother had produced a high chair that must have been from the restaurant and succeeded in getting Charlie into it, wings and all.

"Now, you stay right there," she said, pointing a finger at Charlie's nose. "And I will get you some nummy beef."

Raven couldn't believe it. Charlie stayed absolutely still, watching with widened eyes as her grandma cubed up the red portion of the center cut of prime rib and put it on her tray. She started eating without a fuss.

"That's incredible," Raven said. "How did you get her to mind you?"

Sarah waved a hand dismissively and spread her napkin on her lap. "It's all in the voice. You have to tell them what to do. You don't ask a toddler, you tell them. She knows I'm serious."

For the next glorious hour, Raven enjoyed a relatively normal family meal. She kept exchanging glances with Avery. Her sister had been right. Mom and Dad could handle this. Everything was going to be so much easier now that they knew.

And then David asked a question. "Now that you're back, are you going to live above Blakemore's? Or in that Garden District place you bought before the wedding? I've got to tell you, I think that place needs work. If Charlie is going to be growing up there, we need to fix up the yard. Maybe buy a swing set."

Sarah held up a finger. "Oh, Bob from church is selling

their swing set. Beautiful castle-like thing with a slide. It would be perfect for Charlie."

Raven swallowed what was in her mouth. "We, uh, can't stay."

Forks rattled against plates as her mother and father stopped eating.

Avery came to her rescue. "You heard Gabriel talk about the horrible things his mother did, but he hasn't told you about the horrible things she's doing right now. We came here because we think that the three women who started the Three Sisters hid something here for us to find, something that could help us conquer her."

"Conquer her?" David chuckled. "You make it sound like you're going to war."

"We are," Gabriel said gravely. "Now that Marius is gone, I am the heir to the throne of Paragon, and with the help of your daughters' magic, we plan to right the wrong my mother has inflicted and take back the kingdom."

Sarah's eyebrows rose. "You plan to be king?" she squeaked. Her fingers tugged nervously at her ear.

Gabriel nodded darkly. It took all Raven's self-control not to elbow him in the side. He was brooding, and his eyes were doing that fiery devil thing they did when he was thinking about something serious. He was going to scare her parents out of their skin.

"More potatoes?" Raven asked lightly, taking a heap for herself, then attempting to pass the dish. Nobody took her up on it.

"Which means you will be queen," David said, staring at her, slack-jawed.

Clarissa stopped chewing, her gaze ping-ponging around the table. "Mmmm, potatoes. Pass those over here."

Raven handed her the bowl, then turned back to her father. "Yes. I will be queen. If we can conquer Eleanor."

"Can we... visit?" Sarah asked.

Gabriel smiled. "Once it is safe, we would love to have you as our guests."

Sarah nodded and absently stroked back Charlie's platinum curls, then took a deep breath and blew it out slowly. "Well then, we need to find whatever it is the original three Tanglewood sisters left for you."

The entire table seemed to release a collective breath, even David, as if he was happy as long as Sarah was happy.

"Do you know what it looks like?" Sarah asked.

Raven nodded. "A tree. Or part of a tree."

Sarah snorted. "Not the tanglewood tree?"

All three sisters leaned forward.

"Yes, Mom," Avery said. "We need a piece of the tanglewood tree."

"You know the legend is that our ancestor was burned at the stake over its pieces." She rubbed her chin.

"I'd heard," Raven said. "But we think there might be pieces of it left."

Sarah nodded. "Well, yes. There are three."

"What?" Raven, Avery, and Clarissa yelled in unison.

"Sure. Well, you two know." She wagged a finger between Raven and Avery incredulously. "It hangs above the bar. The wands. The magic wands!"

When Raven stared at her blankly, her mother clarified. "Right above the beer taps. On the wall. Oh, for Christ's sake, let's go down there. I'll show you." She pulled the napkin from her lap and tossed it onto the table.

They all followed Sarah through the back door and down into the closed restaurant. She walked behind the bar and pointed up. A dropped section of ceiling ran the length of the bar in the same shape as the counter. And there, hanging so that only the workers would likely see it, was a shadowbox with a framed piece of wood.

"I can't believe I never noticed that before," Avery said.

Sarah grabbed a stepladder and climbed up to pull it off the wall. "I'm surprised we can still see it through all the dust." She blew along the top, and a cloud settled down around them. She handed it to Raven.

"How do you know this is part of the tanglewood tree?" Gabriel asked.

"It says so, right on the back. That's why I left it up there all these years. Grandma said it was lucky because it came from our family tree."

"Literally," Clarissa said.

Gabriel, Charlie in his arms, tapped the back of the box, and Avery and Clarissa leaned in as Raven turned it over. Etched into the wood on the back was TANGLEWOOD 1625 with a triquetra beside it.

"It's three, you know." Sarah pointed a manicured finger at the box, and Raven turned it back over and stared at the blur of brown behind the glass. "Grandma told me it's actually their three magic wands, wrapped so tightly together that it looks like one solid branch. She said it was a symbol for the three sisters' undying affection for one another."

Clarissa reached for the box. "Let's get this baby open and see for ourselves."

Raven tried to open the back, but it was nailed shut. "Mom, do you care about the frame?"

Sarah shook her head. "Not a bit."

"Clarissa?" Raven held it up and turned her face away. Without another word, Clarissa sang a high note and the glass shattered. Avery caught the brown hunk of wood as it fell from its mount.

"I see it now," Avery said. "Mom was right. There're three separate branches." Avery grasped the stub of one. "It tingles." Raven reached for another, and Clarissa looked between them before grasping the third. The wood vibrated, then stopped.

"This isn't mine," Clarissa said slowly.

Raven looked at her. "I thought it was just me."

They switched sides. Instantly, a flood of heat flowed through Raven's body.

"Ugh," Raven said. "My mouth tastes like basil, and my veins feel like they're sprouting leaves!"

"Mine feels cold, like dark ice." Clarissa smiled.

Avery looked between them excitedly. "Mine feels hot and bubbly."

"I think... Try to pull. I think mine is slipping! Maybe we can pull them apart!" Avery said.

"Careful. They're so old. We don't want them to snap," Clarissa added.

But Raven could see a faint light growing between the coiled branches. "It won't snap. Slow and steady. One... Two... Three..."

Raven pulled evenly on her wand. The light grew brighter, and then the wood untangled, one from another. She grasped her piece tighter as wind rushed up between them. Hers was six inches in length, polished smooth, and twisted naturally from its base to a slightly upturned tip. Through a column of light, she stared at her sisters, their hair blowing back from their faces. Clarissa held up a sleek and dark wand slightly longer than Raven's with an elongated knot in the wood of one side. Avery's was crooked and held a hint of bark.

For a second, Raven smelled something sweet, like blossoming fruit trees. And then a flood of power surged between them. It knocked the air from her lungs before crashing to the ground and flowing across her toes. Once she could draw breath again, she locked eyes with her sisters. She could hear their hearts beating. Without a shadow of a doubt, something important had just happened. They were even closer now than before. Bound. Before by blood, now by an even stronger magic.

"Oh my god," David said incredulously. "It's all true. Your crazy family. This damn bar. All true."

The wind and the light faded away, and Raven drew in a deep, cleansing breath. "It's true. You have no idea how much you've helped us, Mom." Tears filled her eyes as she stared at her beautiful mother, her father's hands supporting her shoulders. "This... this means everything to me."

Sarah placed a hand over David's on her shoulder. "That's all we ever wanted for you. For each of you." She met Raven's eyes, then Avery's, and finally Clarissa's. "Every choice we ever made was meant to give you everything. Everything you needed."

Raven leaned forward and kissed her mother on the cheek, and then, because the feeling gripped her, she kissed her father too. She'd carried so much anger toward him for so long. He'd skipped out on her and her mother at the darkest point of her illness. But somehow, if her mother could forgive him, so could she. Tonight, she'd challenged both of them in ways they'd never been challenged before. And here they both were, looking as though either of them would cut off their own pinkies to help.

Behind her, Charlie started to fuss in Gabriel's arms. There was a loud pop, and Nathaniel and Xavier appeared behind them.

"Clarissa, I felt a charge down the bond," Nathaniel said.

Raven noticed her parents' faces turn ashen. "Mom, Dad, this is Clarissa's... Well, Mom, you've met Nathaniel, and this is Avery's husband, Xavier."

"Yes, we've met," Sarah said absently, gaping at Nathaniel. Then her face morphed from surprise to anger as she took in Xavier. "Wait... Avery, you got married? *Without telling me?*"

David's eyes raked down Xavier to his kilt. A muscle in his jaw worked wildly until he blurted, "I need a beer."

"'Tis a fine idea," Xavier said. "And a pleasure to meet ye both!"

Gabriel raised his chin. "May I suggest we continue introductions upstairs? Charlie needs to finish dinner... and there are gifts."

Thankfully, after drinks were poured, everyone agreed, and Raven thought perhaps the truth really had set them free.

CHAPTER FIFTEEN

Obsidian Palace
Paragon

Eleanor closed her eyes and opened them again, coming back into her own head. She'd been in and out of Grigori's mind for days, following her children and their mates in the earthly realm, listening through windows and air vents. And still, she wasn't certain any of it would be of use to her. She dug her nails into the arms of her throne, her teeth gnashing. What she needed was a plan.

Ransom charged into the room, looking as if he might be sick. "My empress."

"What is it now, Ransom? I'm in the middle of something."

"I'm sorry to disturb you. It's Rogos. I have word from our spies that Lord Niall announced tonight his intention to declare war on Paragon."

The arm of her throne cracked beneath Eleanor's grip, the wood splintering angrily up to her elbow. She tossed it aside. "Are you certain of this?" she asked through her teeth.

"Our informant has always been accurate in the past." Ransom inched backward, his gaze darting away from her. "There's more."

"Well? Out with it!"

"Niall has wed Queen Penelope of Darnuith. Their kingdoms are aligned."

This time, she popped out of her throne and paced, her rage causing her skin to bubble from within, her need to shift raising the temperature in the room. With a slap to her own cheek that made Ransom jolt, she tamed her inner dragon. This was not the time to lose control. This was the time for cunning, and that was something Eleanor always had in spades.

"This is a complication," she said softly. "But it will be nothing once we have the book. All I need is for the three sisters to find it and remove it from the wards that now protect it from me. Then I will take it."

To his credit, Ransom didn't say a word.

She wrung her hands, remembering all she'd seen through Grigori's eyes. "Does the name Crimson Vanderholt mean anything to you?"

He shook his head. "Only the witches of Darnuith have such names."

"Or those from Earth." She drummed her fingers on her bicep. "I've recently learned that one by that name is the reason Gabriel and Raven's child exists. She must have been a witch of great power to perform such a feat."

"Would you like me to try to find her? If she's in Darnuith—"

"Oh, I am quite sure she is dead." Eleanor frowned. "But death is not the end, and to one such as I, one who is destined to be a goddess, death is no barrier to knowledge."

"What do you plan to do?" Ransom shivered.

She rolled her eyes. The man was truly a coward. "All you need to worry about is locking down all trade routes between the kingdoms. Let nothing through. I'll take care of the rest."

"Yes, Empress." He bowed low and started for the door.

"Bring me a child."

Ransom stopped, waiting for a beat before turning to face her. "A child? I wouldn't know where to find one."

"Figure it out. I need a child's blood. Find one. Look among the peasants or in the pits. Do it, Ransom, or I will use your blood in its place, and believe me, the spell will require much more of it to compensate for your age."

"Yes, Empress." He all but ran from the room.

Eleanor strode to the library and passed behind the tapestry into her ritual room. She'd never raised the dead before, but it was possible—she could see the spell in her head. It was dark magic, blood magic. Nothing she wasn't familiar with, in theory.

She flipped through her grimoire but didn't find exactly what she was looking for. This would take creative magic. She was up to the task. Grabbing a piece of chalk, she carefully constructed a pentagram on the floor, correcting any imperfections until the shape was as perfect as she could make it. Now for a power source. Her gaze landed on her collection of hearts. Brynhoff's had dimmed from her earlier spell. Too weak. She'd never waste Marius's diamond on this. Her eyes fell on a navy-blue sapphire. Killian's. She snatched it from the shelf, placing it at the apex of the pentagram.

On the top westward point, she positioned a bunch of dried wolfsbane, the queen of all poisons. Any sorceress that would manipulate another woman's fertility would share a connection with the plant. Across from it, on the top, eastward point, she situated a black candle. With a snap of her fingers, the wick ignited. Below the candle, she offered a loaf of freshly baked bread she conjured from the kitchen. Surely any soul she called up from Hades would be hungry, and she wasn't above bribing information from the witch. On the last point, she rested a silver chalice.

A sound came from the entrance. She drew a symbol in the air to open the ward, and Ransom entered with a young boy at his side. He couldn't have been more than seven and was dressed in the black uniform used for training in the pits. He trembled under her gaze although his chin stayed high.

"You're a brave little dragon," she said.

"Yes, Empress."

"Ransom, you may leave us."

The man hesitated but turned on his heel and left when her eyes met his.

She held out her hand to the boy. "You have no reason to be afraid. From you, I'll only need a few drops."

"Drops of what?"

She reached out and grabbed the boy's arm, dragging him toward the symbol on the floor. His face went ashen as she sprouted her talons. "Push up your sleeve, brave boy."

He did as she requested, although he could not hide the terror that painted across his young face. She speared the boy's skin and allowed his blood to drizzle into the chalice. She had to hand it to the child; he didn't even scream, just wept silently.

"There." She shoved him away, and the boy grabbed his arm, although it was already healing. "Speak nothing of this. Go find Captain Ransom and tell him that I have found you braver than him and I said you could take the entire day off training to feast on whatever you choose."

That turned the corners of his mouth up. She waited until he'd left the room to return to the ritual.

"Crimson Vanderholt, I call you from Hades. Come forth and answer me." She repeated the mantra in the language of her ancestors, concentrating on the symbol.

The inside edges of the pentagram bubbled with black oil. It bled like ink to the center of the symbol, pooled, then spiraled into itself.

"Come forth!" she commanded again, and the oil rose, broke apart, became smoky. Legs formed, then a torso. When the smoke faded, a worn woman with wavy blond hair stood before her, wearing a bustier, a tattered skirt, and leather boots. Every part of her was black or a shade of gray, including her somewhat translucent skin. The bags under her eyes loomed the same color black as her lips. Not resurrected, then. A ghost. Good enough for now.

"Who the fuck are you?" the ghost asked.

"I am the one who has called you forth. My spell will force you to respond to my questions. It will be easier for you if you don't fight giving me the answers I seek." Eleanor paced around the outer band of the pentagram, assessing the woman. She certainly didn't look powerful. She had the presence of a half-drowned rat.

"Why would I fight it? No matter what they tell you about Hades, it isn't the party you expect." She glanced down at the wolfsbane. "You should have used cannabis," Crimson said, placing her black-nailed hands on her hips. "I would have come faster."

Eleanor didn't know what cannabis was, but she didn't appreciate her spell being critiqued. "Tell me what role you played in making the offspring of Raven and Gabriel."

Crimson's eyes narrowed, and then she laughed. "So my spell worked." She rubbed her thumb across her chin.

"Simple fertility spell with a trap door. I wove Raven's magic into it so that she couldn't absorb it and undo it. Tied his life to the sexual act. Forced them to couple within the symbol. Child's play."

"Why did you do it?" Eleanor asked through her teeth. "You must have known the offspring of a witch and a dragon would be a monster capable of limitless power."

Crimson shrugged. "Sort of the point. If you must know, I planned to eat the kid's heart to achieve immortality."

Eleanor studied the woman, respect blossoming despite her haggard appearance. Crimson must have been a powerful sorceress, indeed. But something didn't make sense.

"Are you human?"

"I was."

"What made you so sure you'd ever see the whelp again?"

Crimson smiled, displaying a mouthful of black-lined teeth. "Raven agreed to it. Witch to witch. A magical covenant. If I broke the spell over her beloved Gabriel, she would owe me her firstborn child."

"You are owed the child?" Eleanor's heart began to pound with excitement.

"Unfortunately, a witch's death causes any magical agreements they entered into to become null and void. I am, shall we say, corporeally challenged? I couldn't enforce our agreement even if I wanted to."

Eleanor toyed with the citrine ring on her left hand. "What if you were resurrected?"

Crimson's dark mouth gaped, the tip of her tongue sliding across her teeth. "I don't know who you are, lady, but I like the way you think."

CHAPTER SIXTEEN

Asfolk Palace
Rogos

After a long, sleepless night dreaming about Leena, Colin was relieved to learn they'd been given the use of a carriage to travel to Niven and the Temple of the Sacred Pools. He'd been approached by Ambassador Raj last night, after the big announcement, and told that finding the crypt that held the golden grimoire was now the top priority of the lord and new lady of Rogos. Therefore, both Quanling Marjory and Leena would escort him to the temple, where Leena would remain assigned to the mission. After all, no time could be wasted bringing another scribe up to speed.

This was good news to Colin, who considered it a stroke of luck to get a few more days with Leena. It also meant he could meet directly with the commanding general of the archers of Asfolk as they made their plan of attack. He'd already sent a falcon to Sylas, informing him of the turn of events, and met briefly with Rook, the leader of the DOGs in Rogos, at the ball last night. The underground was alive and well, circumventing the Obsidian Guard through a series of tunnels and private homes. With any luck, the move by Rogos and Darnuith would spur Nochtbend to join their cause. The vampires were already heavily invested in the underground.

Only, as he climbed into the carriage, Leena might as well have been a block of ice sitting across from him. She barely looked in his direction. Quanling Marjory boarded behind him, and the carriage jerked into motion. Leena's mouth seemed bent into a permanent frown, her eyes affixed to a spot outside her window.

"Did you enjoy the banquet last night?" he asked them both to break the tension.

Marjory lit up. "Very much. You must suspect I do not indulge in that sort of eating and drinking very often as Quanling. Our sacred texts encourage a simple lifestyle. It is pleasing to the goddess." The wrinkles around her lips grew more pronounced. "I suppose it is true that a scroll written by an intoxicated elf would be rather useless to the future of our race, but I must say that an occasional dalliance with such luxuries feels good for the soul. That cake! Glorious."

He glanced toward Leena, but she did not turn from the window. "I agree it was delicious. I couldn't quite place the flavor."

"That is because it was thornfruit. Very rare. As you might guess by the name, it isn't any fun to harvest and so is only used for extremely special occasions. I'm not surprised you've never tried it, even with the time you've spent here. I've only had it twice in all my years."

"That explains it. We don't have thornfruit in Paragon."

"I doubt it would grow in the volcanic soil." She

smoothed her robes. "Here, it flourishes in the marshes of the Mystic Wood."

"I've heard there are snails that live in those marshes that can be intoxicating to elves." Colin watched Leena carefully for a reaction. A muscle in her jaw twitched like she was grinding her teeth, but she didn't turn her head.

Marjory gave a heady laugh. "Now you're making me revisit my adolescent years. Oh, I remember doing snails. Harmless good fun, although a huge waste of time. I'm afraid they won't work on dragons, though."

"Pity. I'll have to stick with elven ale."

"No one brews it better!" She gave him an authentic smile. "All this talk of banquets and ale... Are you sure you're up to returning to the simple meals and hard beds of the temple, Colin?"

He grinned. "I've spent most of my life on a military cot. It doesn't bother me at all. Anything to find the information we need. I do wonder, though, if Leena is sad to leave the palace. She hasn't said a word since we departed."

Now she turned her head, her purple eyes narrowing to slits. If looks could kill, he'd surely be dead.

"Oh, you'll have to forgive Leena," Marjory said. "I believe this was her first banquet and her first time out of robes since she was a child."

Leena glanced at her and nodded once.

Colin furrowed his brow. "Surely you must have attended one before you entered the order."

The smile faded from Marjory's lips, and she glanced at Leena as if to say *shall you tell him or shall I?*

"No." Leena's eyebrows bobbed with her words, her expression softened by a hint of what he interpreted as embarrassment. Her cheeks tinged pink. "Never. Actually, I entered the temple at nine years old. I'd never experienced

131

anything like that. Well, not as far as I can remember anyway."

There was something about her tone that made his dragon grow cold. Nine was the age she'd told him she'd competed in the Animus Games with her father by her side. What had happened that year to make her a ward of the temple?

"Is it common for a child to take the oath to become a scribe?"

Leena looked away and licked her lips. This time, her Quanling did answer for her. "No, it's not common, and she didn't become a scribe as a child. Leena was orphaned that year. The temple took her in."

"I didn't become a scribe until I was an adolescent," Leena added, glancing at him again. "Sixteen."

Colin's stomach filled with lead. This wasn't right. How could anyone make a decision that required giving up a normal life when they'd never had one? No wonder she'd kissed him. She'd never had the opportunity to kiss anyone before. She'd never had the opportunity to experience any of the world as an adult.

"Colin, are you unwell? You look as though you might be sick," Marjory said.

He cleared his throat. "Fine." He straightened and focused on his own window.

"Oh," Marjory said softly. "I have been thoughtless. After what happened with your mother, of course talk of being orphaned must disturb you."

He gave her a slight nod, only to appease her.

"At any rate, we should be arriving soon. We've left the wood." She gestured to the window and the stretch of desert beyond it.

An orphan. Colin tried his best not to stare at Leena, but his eyes were drawn to her side of the carriage again and again. He kept picturing her, small and vulnerable, dressed in robes before she even understood what they meant.

But he couldn't think about that now. They'd arrived and were pulling up to the stone building that was the Temple of the Sacred Pools. He followed Marjory and Leena out of the carriage.

Sand blew across his toes, and the sun baked him with a concentrated and brutal intensity that would be uncomfortable for most creatures. As a dragon, he wasn't bothered by the heat of Niven's desert, but the dust and sand instantly turned his throat dry as a stone.

The closest sacred pool shimmered a half mile in the distance. He'd always wondered who was the first to discover that it wasn't water reflecting the burning sun but an acid so strong it could burn a dragon. Absently, he ran his fingers over the scar on his right arm. When Leena helped him find the orb of Rogos, they soon discovered that any tool they tried to use to retrieve it would dissolve before they could get the orb to shore. In an act of desperation, he'd shifted his arm and reached in for it.

Although his dragon scales had survived the ordeal, he'd suffered permanent burns that were present on both his *soma* form and his dragon. He didn't regret it. That orb and the cog it'd concealed were part of the answer to winning this war.

"The room you stayed in before in the west wing is still available," Marjory said. "Shall I ask the Fratern to show you the way?"

"No, I remember." He adjusted his pack on his shoulders.

"Very well. Leena will meet you in the library to begin work as soon as you've settled in."

Leena's eyes widened. "Wouldn't you like to rest from the journey? We could start after the evening meal."

Colin frowned. "No, I'd like to get started right away."

Her face fell, but she bowed and retreated toward the east wing without a word of protest. As he turned to go to his own room, Marjory caught him by the elbow.

"Did something happen between you and Leena?" Marjory asked. "She seems quite preoccupied with avoiding you."

He gave her a reassuring smile. "She stepped on a snail in the Mystic Wood. She made me dance with her. Said she'd never danced before and wanted to try it. Perfectly innocent but embarrassing for her, I'm sure. I admit my earlier snail comment was to tease her about it. She's right to be angry with me."

Marjory studied him. "I always worried Leena had taken her oath too soon. What you say does not surprise me. I think I should like to dance again if I had the excuse." She grinned then. "I'm relieved it's nothing serious. I'm sure she'll be over her embarrassment soon enough to help you. Meanwhile, I suspect she'll be highly motivated to find that crypt."

⛬

As soon as Colin dropped off his pack, he made his way to the sacred library. Stone and darkly stained wood shelves extended in rows from the massive wooden entry to the outer boundary of the room, each laden with leather tomes and stacks of tightly rolled scrolls. At the center of the library, the ceiling was open to the floors above. He counted six balconies above him. There were more, he was sure, hidden beyond a silver mist that hung like a storm cloud at the base of the seventh. He knew the floors extended below ground as well; just how many was anyone's guess. The temple library was physically massive, but Colin understood that elven magic was at play here as well. Just as a scribe's quill never ran out of ink and their scrolls never ran out of room to write, the sacred library never ran out of shelf space.

The scribes had recorded history since the founding of the kingdom of Rogos. At the center of it all was an altar of white marble. He found Leena flipping through a massive dusty tome at one of the many library tables scattered between the shelves.

She looked up and gave him a questioning look. "Do you know what year Medea hid the book?"

"It had to be right after Tavyss died and she was resurrected."

Leena narrowed her eyes. "Where is Tavyss buried? Is it possible this is as simple as finding his grave?"

Colin raised his eyebrows. "That would be unlikely. When dragons are killed, their body disintegrates. The only thing left behind is their heart... Um, a gem about this big—" He formed a circle with his hands in front of his chest. "It matches our rings. Usually, whoever kills us takes it as a trophy or leaves it for the earth to swallow with time. We don't have cemeteries because, well, we don't die of natural causes."

Leena scowled. "So Eleanor might still have Tavyss's heart?"

Colin shrugged. "It's possible. She's not beyond keeping

it. It wouldn't even be the worst thing she's ever done."

With a grunt, Leena closed the book in front of her and placed it on the white stone altar at the center of the library. She scribbled a few symbols, and the book disappeared back to the stacks.

"I have the year the scroll was created. I'm calling up all references to Tavyss. We should be able to find a record of the exact date of his death. Then we can cross-reference all graves sealed around that time." Leena wrote the request on the scroll, and magic swirled across the white table. "This will take some time. The magic needs to sift through scrolls and reference books dating back centuries."

"There is the chance Medea hid the grimoire before Tavyss died." Colin scratched the stubble on the side of his jaw.

"Wouldn't Medea need it to attack Brynhoff and Eleanor?"

"Maybe. But it seems likely that Medea and Tavyss were double-crossed. If they thought they were going to Paragon to make peace, she might have left it behind. Or maybe she knew there was a risk of it falling into the wrong hands, so she preemptively locked it away."

Leena groaned. "So we must consider all graves from just before the war to just after Tavyss died." She scribbled again on the scroll, and Colin watched the magic absorb her request. "You know, we can narrow this down, but even if we identify the grave, without the three sisters translating that enchanted scroll, I don't know how we'll be able to use the key. It requires a code word in order to position the gears properly. I pray they find what they went looking for."

"I've learned not to underestimate the three sisters. They'll find it."

With a nod, she turned from the altar and started

shelving a few reference books left in a cart nearby.

"While we're waiting for the scrolls, there's something I want to ask you." He lowered his voice. "Why didn't you tell me you were orphaned? You told me your dad helped you animate your creation when you were nine. Marjory said you were orphaned that year. What happened?"

Her gaze shifted away from his, and she dusted her hands over the leather spine of one of the books. "It wasn't pertinent to our mission. Why *would* I tell you?"

"The kissing and other things weren't pertinent to our mission either, but you seemed to have time for that."

Leena's eyes narrowed, and she looked over both shoulders. "Shhh. Please. Colin, please don't tell anyone what we've done."

She looked as if she might cry, and he knew she meant more than the kissing. And didn't that make him feel like a total ass? "I'm not going to tell anyone, okay? I just... I thought we were friends. We talked about things other than the scroll and the orbs. We've spent weeks together."

Her face fell. She finished with the books and braced herself on the table. "It's not something I like to talk about."

Colin couldn't stand the pain he saw in her eyes despite being curious about the cause. "I understand. I'm sorry. You don't have to tell me. If I had the option of keeping the actions of my murderous mother a secret, believe me, I would."

She frowned, seeming to roll that over in her mind. "It's not a secret. In fact, the year it happened, everyone knew. But I don't want to talk about it. It isn't a happy topic of conversation." Leena glared at him, her hands landing on her hips. "I'd like to talk about something else. What did you say to the high lord to make him demand I remain on this mission?"

CHAPTER SEVENTEEN

L eena's head felt hot. She wanted answers. Every
instinct told her Ambassador Rajesh's insistence she
remain on this assignment was somehow because of Colin.
The way he'd looked at her in front of the high lord... Had
he said something to him? Asked for a favor? Colin wanted
her. He'd made that perfectly clear. The problem was, she
wanted him too. That was precisely why she needed
distance.

"Admit it. You are the reason my Quanling won't name
a replacement." Leena focused all the anger she'd felt since
the ball into the point of her stare.

Colin gaped. "Of course not!"

"No? You said nothing about needing me specifically?
Because our ambassador said the high lord and lady thought
I was *indispensable*. What exactly would give them that
idea?"

A low growl emanated from Colin's throat. "You *are*
important to this mission."

"You admit it! Knowing full well I desired to be released

from this assignment, you intentionally made it so that I couldn't go. You did this on purpose, Colin."

He smiled, or was he baring his teeth? "Why would I do a thing like that?"

She scoffed. "You know why."

Colin approached until the scent of leather and spice permeated the shelves around her. She backed up a step, but he kept coming, and she kept retreating until her backside bumped against one of the library's tables at the end of the row. He stopped so close to her she could feel his radiant heat.

"Colin..." She shook her head.

He leaned in and said, "I never asked the high lord or lady to keep you on this mission. I wanted to. I've made no effort to hide that I want you to be mine. My inner dragon reminds me of it constantly."

His lips were close, and she could feel his breath against her cheek. Heat coursed through her body, her torso, circulating out each of her limbs and settling heavily in her core. Why did he affect her like this? She should move away. She swallowed but couldn't make her legs work. "You know I can't."

"See, you keep saying that, but the truth is that your body is communicating something else. You were the one who kissed me—"

"That was a mistake—"

"It didn't feel like a mistake in the tent."

"I wanted to try it. Nothing more. You said you understood."

"I do understand. And if that's all you want, it's okay with me, dancing queen. It's just I'm not convinced you really believe that. When you forced me to dance with you, you said—"

"I was high on snail venom!"

"High or not, you stared at my lips just as you're doing now. Are you wondering if I'll kiss you this time?"

Damn it all, she *was* staring at his lips. She snapped her gaze back up to his eyes and gripped the table behind her until her knuckles hurt. "Where else am I supposed to stare? You're right in front of me."

He sighed. Only the slightest space remained between them. She could feel the heat coming off him. Any closer and he might brush against the hardened tips of her breasts. His lips might touch hers.

"So then, you don't want me to kiss you?"

"If you did, I couldn't stop you."

His eyes narrowed to slits, and the heat she felt earlier turned icy as he moved away from her. "I'd never force myself on you. Don't insult me. And I did *not* ask anyone to keep you on this mission against your will."

"I... Of course you wouldn't. I just don't understand why you keep... tempting me."

"Then you *are* tempted."

"I am. I've told you as much." She looked away, her brow furrowing as she attempted to intellectualize what she was feeling. "I think all scribes are tempted at one time or another. But with the help of the goddess, we don't have to give in to our temptations."

"No, we don't."

The scrolls she'd ordered manifested on the altar. She moved to get them, but Colin held up a hand. "Make yourself comfortable. You're the only one who can read these things. The least I can do is carry them over to the table."

Nothing about this situation was comfortable for Leena, but she took a seat at one of the large library tables. Colin gathered the scrolls carefully in his arms and brought them to her. She chose one and scanned the contents but struggled to concentrate on the words.

What was she looking for again? Graves. Which graves were constructed within the years relevant to their search? She shuffled the scrolls in front of her and found the one she was looking for, unrolling it on the desk.

"I have the list of graves. Unfortunately, the notes say there was a plague that year. Firesickness. Curable now, but it killed hundreds then. The library found over five hundred crypts registered within the years we've time-boxed."

"Goddess, this is hopeless." He scrubbed a hand through his hair.

She'd always known it was a long shot. "I'll keep rereading the history. I might find a clue in the other writings about Medea and Tavyss. There are several perspectives here. Maybe with context, we can narrow it down. Otherwise, we wait for the three sisters."

"And hope they return before the first shots are fired."

"Anyway, you should go. I can do this alone. You can't read Elvish, so..."

He didn't go anywhere. She stared at him. He stared back.

"Do you think the reason you wanted to experiment with me was because you were orphaned as a child and never had an adulthood outside the temple?"

She tipped her head back and groaned. "Not this again."

"I'm curious." Colin pulled up a chair across the desk from her and sat down. "And considering I'm the one you experimented with, I think you owe me an explanation."

Maybe he was right about that. She had used him. Even if he was willing, she'd taken what she needed and given him little back. Only, her family history was a secret she would have liked to keep buried forever. She still didn't understand why her Quanling had shared that she'd been orphaned. She must have realized that Colin would be curious, that she'd feel pressured to tell the rest of the story.

She didn't want to talk about this. She never wanted to think about it. But it crossed her mind that this might be a lifeline from the goddess herself. If she told Colin the truth about her past, he might understand why she wasn't a suitable mate. If she could push him away, he'd be so much easier to resist. Telling the truth might make it simpler for both of them.

Leena frowned. "Marjory told you I was orphaned at nine and that's why I came to the temple. That is only partially true. Strictly speaking, I'm not an orphan at all. My mother is still alive."

"Then why were you left here?"

"The year I was nine, my mother was pregnant with my little brother." Leena shifted, hating this story. It was best to get it out. Get it over with. "The animus competition I told you about was the last significant time I spent with my father. The day after, my mother went into labor. The midwife was called, but there was something wrong. Something was wrong with the baby."

Leena swallowed, the library melting away, replaced by a memory of hiding in the room that used to be hers and listening to her mother scream. Her heart thudded in her ears. "My brother died in the womb, and the midwife had to use magic to help my mother expel his body. But the pain and anguish, it drove my mother mad. There's a rare condition among my kind, a mental break that occurs in some women who experience this. Her body and her mind could not handle my brother's loss."

It was so quiet in the library she could hear her breath

flow from her lungs. Colin held deathly still on the other side of the desk, his face impassive.

"My father and the midwife tried to comfort her, tried to give her herbs to help her recover, but the midwife had made a fatal mistake. She'd left one of her tools, a special blade she'd used to help extract the infant, and my mother took hold of it."

"I wasn't in the room. I didn't see what happened next. All I knew was that the midwife ran into my room, her clothes soaked in blood, and swept me from the house. I tried to protest, but when archers were called, I knew whatever had happened was serious. Later I learned that my mother had stabbed and killed my father and then turned the knife on herself."

She watched Colin carefully, waiting for any reaction. She expected shock. She didn't want his pity. Any normal person would want to distance themselves from her and her awful past. But his face remained expressionless and attentive. Damn it. She'd have to tell him the rest.

"The midwife kept me at her house for a few days, and then the authorities brought me here. I was led to believe both my parents had died. From that day on, I grew up here in the temple. I've been happy here. I feel loved."

"Marjory is a true mother to you, then." He studied her, nothing but kindness and empathy in his expression.

"She is. But when I was sixteen, she told me that before I took my oath to become a scribe, it was important I know all the facts. She wanted me to be sure. I couldn't devote myself fully to the goddess until I knew the entire truth about who I was and how I'd come to be here. Because even though I thought the temple was my only choice, it wasn't. I could have left if I wanted to."

"Where could you have gone?" Colin asked. There was a note of disbelief in his voice.

"There's a place just outside Asfolk that we call the Borough. It spans a city block and is constructed of simple dwellings financed by the high lord to support elves who can't support themselves. I am told that the people who end up there are often elderly, ill, or are physically or mentally unfit." Elves lived a few hundred years, short lives compared to dragons. Leena wondered how much she should explain. "I suppose dragons do not have such a place, being immortal as you are."

Colin scratched the side of his jaw. "But we do. Immortal we may be, and physical deficiencies are extremely rare among our kind, but we are not immune to mental problems. Dragons tend to be obsessive about things, some to the point of becoming destructive. We have homes and caregivers that specialize in the condition. A few witches who live permanently in Paragon have had success healing their minds."

She nodded. "Then you do understand that the people in the Borough have terrible personal problems, some that they were born with, some that they bring upon themselves. As it turns out, my mother did not die from her injuries as my father did."

Confusion muddled Colin's expression. "What happened to her?"

She stared down at the scroll in front of her. "My mother stood trial for the murder of my father. She was found to be insane and institutionalized in the Borough. She was unfit to care for me, which is why I was brought here."

She hazarded a glance at Colin. There it was. That was what she was waiting for. Horror darkened his gray eyes. Now was the time to drive the stake home.

"Marjory took me to the Borough to visit my mother. We found her living in a filthy block of concrete with a straw bed. She's cared for there, but there isn't an ounce of luxury. It's a hard life. Harder than here in the temple, even with our oath to live simply.

"I don't know what I expected. In retrospect, she hadn't seen me since I was nine. But we looked so much alike I couldn't help but recognize her. We visited for a time under the guise of scribes interested in the happenings there. And then, at my Quanling's prodding, I introduced myself."

Leena locked eyes with Colin. "My mother admitted she'd recognized me the moment I'd walked into the room, but all she saw was my father in me. She said she should have killed me too when she had the chance."

"Goddess, Leena, that's awful. I—"

"It is where I come from. The only reason I am alive, well cared for, at peace, is because of this temple and the goddess. The people here are my family now. I took my oath soon after that, willingly. I wanted to be part of this. I wanted to remain here always, sheltered from that terrible life I saw in her eyes."

"It scarred you. You were young. Seeing her must have been traumatic."

"Here, I have love, I have acceptance, I have safety. I belong here."

Colin stood and paced across the library, the scar on his arm looking especially red in the lamplight. "But you don't have freedom."

"What? Why would you say that? I am free."

He turned back to her, his gray eyes glowing deep red with intensity. Those were the eyes of his dragon, she realized. And when he spoke, his voice was lower, grittier than before. "If you were completely happy here, completely free, you wouldn't have kissed me, or invited my touch, or wanted to dance as you did. You wouldn't look at me the way you do."

She shrugged and shook her head. "Curiosity. That is all. Nothing more."

"That's not true. You meant it. There was more behind our interactions than just testing the waters."

Leena brought her fist down on the table. "Don't you understand? Before Aeaea when I met your siblings, I'd never witnessed couples showing love to one another as an adult—never with a mind for understanding it. When you come across something for the first time, you want to experience it. Think about it. The first time you were here, didn't you want to gaze into a sacred pool or call up a scroll from the stacks?"

Colin's mouth turned into a cynical slash. "True. I was curious. But I didn't grab you and force you to show me those things. I didn't lose myself to the experience of being a scribe."

"I didn't—"

He slashed a hand through the air. "I can't say what you felt or what you thought, but I do know one thing—you chose me. You didn't experiment with another elf, or a nymph, or ask one of my brothers to help you."

"They have mates. I would never—"

"You may not have experience with the opposite sex, Leena, but I do. And what happened between us was a culmination of something more, something that has been growing since I first set foot in this temple. You know it and I know it."

She took a deep breath. She did know it, or maybe she suspected it. Whenever she was near him, she felt a tug deep within her, drawing her to him. And if she was being honest, it was more than physical. She preferred his company to all others. It was why she needed distance. She swallowed the lump that had formed in her throat, remembering their weeks together. "No. I'm sorry. It wasn't that for me."

He stared at her and shook his head.

"You should go to bed. I'll skim through these scrolls and let you know what I find."

He knew she was lying. She could tell by the way his head tipped to one side and his eyes narrowed at the corners. Colin leaned toward her, the tension between them growing to epic levels. Her senses were overwhelmed with his leather-and-spice scent.

"You know what I think?" The hint of his dragon she'd noticed in his eyes earlier gave way to a softer gray as he seemed to regain his cool composure. "I think you told me about your parents because you thought it would push me away. You thought it would make you an undesirable mate."

Her gaze drifted away from his, her chest heavy with how close he'd come to the truth. How did he know? How could he tell?

"But I am a man whose mother murdered his father. My parents all but ignored me, forced me to fight in the pits of Paragon, forced my siblings and me into hiding. And it is my psychopathic mother we are going to war against."

Leena leaned back, suddenly feeling cold.

"Knowing you've had to overcome your roots only proves why we would be perfect for each other." He raised an eyebrow. "Sorry to disappoint you, but it doesn't make me think any less of you."

Just a table length. All she'd have to do was lean forward, give in to this pull between them and the heat singing in her blood, and she could feel his lips again. Her face moved a half inch toward him before she realized it. She stopped, pulled back. Her eyes locked on to his. A dizzying feeling caused her to inhale deeply and her stomach to drop. The temperature in the room climbed a degree. She remembered his touch, how it had felt for his hands to coast over the hardened tips of her breasts, to do what he did before between her legs. Another quarter inch evaporated between them. The goddess could forgive one more kiss.

He straightened, backing away from her. "But you know what you want, right?" His eyes narrowed on her. "If you change your mind or decide you'd like another taste, you know where to find me. You're free, right? It's your choice."

He gave her a little bow and then left the room, leaving her breathless and with a deep, hungry need she had no idea what to do with.

CHAPTER EIGHTEEN

Another restless night. Colin didn't stop in the dining hall for breakfast the following day, instead taking advantage of the cool desert morning to perform his training exercises. He moved through his routine, trying to concentrate on the kicks, blocks, and punches he'd mastered over a lifetime of practice, but Leena's face kept breaking through his concentration.

It didn't help that he could see the scribes in the distance, the special red robes they wore for morning ceremonies flowing in the wind around one of the sacred pools. Between the motion and the light reflecting off the goddess's tears, it made them appear like part of the desert, a flower blooming from the sand. Their chants carried across the arid grounds. He didn't understand the language, but the melody was beautiful, and he pictured her among the other scribes, singing her heart out in devotion to the goddess.

Leena had meant to push him away last night, but her story only made him more certain they belonged together.

She'd taken her oath too early. She hadn't known what she was getting into, let alone what she'd be missing.

By the time the scribes marched in formation back toward the temple, he'd finished his hand-to-hand combat exercises. Legs trembling, he picked up the sword he'd borrowed from the temple arsenal and started practicing his weapons routine, testing his balance as he attacked invisible opponents around him.

He couldn't force Leena to want him. Nothing would change unless she decided she wanted more for herself, wanted the love that he knew hovered just beyond their reach. While he was ready and open to it, she wasn't. And until she altered her way of thinking, there was nothing he could do.

It had to be her choice. His arms throbbed with the effort of wielding the weapon. Sweat dripped down his face. He'd been at this for hours. Exhausted, he dropped to his knees in the sand. No amount of self-flagellation was going to solve this problem. Only one thing would. He had to let her go.

Thankfully, his dragon had not yet bonded with the woman, not in the permanent way of his kind. The desire was there. The offer had been extended. But he was still free. Leena said she wanted to remain a scribe. He had to believe her and honor her wishes, no matter how wrong he thought she was. It was the right thing to do. The only avenue that wouldn't end in his destruction.

He closed his eyes and said a quick prayer of thanks to the goddess for her help in his preparations for battle, then climbed to his feet to return to the temple. A bird's cry came from above, and he whirled. Searching the clear blue sky, he was surprised to spot a falcon heading toward him.

Sheathing the blade, he raised his arm for the bird,

which landed on the proffered perch with a flourish of wings. A message was attached to its leg.

Master Demidicus is pleased to inform you that Nocht-bend has officially broken ties with Paragon and offers its full support to the Defenders of the Goddess. All representatives have stepped down from the Highborn Council. We await your word on next steps.

Colin's heart leaped. They had Nochtbend! He dug in the pouch on his belt for a charcoal pencil and a piece of parchment and scrawled a response. *The Defenders of the Goddess gratefully accept alliance with Nochtbend and vow to aid in its defense against the kingdom of Paragon. Preparations are being made. An envoy will be sent with more information.*

He bound the scroll to the falcon's leg. "To Master Demidicus," he told the bird and with a lift of his arm sent it flying for Nochtbend. He strode toward the temple, in need of another falcon to send to Aeaea. He had to get word to Sylas. Then he had to find Leena. Time was running out. They needed to find the book, with or without the three sisters.

❧

NORMALLY, THE MORNING RITUALS WERE SOOTHING TO Leena. The routine was meditative. She woke early, donned the red robes that represented the volcanic home of the goddess, and gathered around Premia, one of the seven major sacred pools, with the rest of the scribes. After the Quanling and Fratern read from the Book of Creation, they'd sing the songs of the morning, the songs of beginnings, the song that told the story of a goddess scorned whose existence created their world and whose tears filled the pool between them.

She'd longed to come back here, longed to lose herself again to this, but no matter how she tried, her eyes kept wandering to the patch of desert in front of the temple, where Colin trained in the same way he had on the beach their last days on Aeaea. It was all she could do to remember the words to the songs she'd sung every day since she was nine.

Now, as the group strode back to the temple for breakfast, she avoided glancing toward him, kept her head lowered inside her hood, tried to look straight ahead. And failed miserably. Something inside her kept turning toward the place where she'd last seen him; some internal compass kept urging her to seek him out. Only when she did give in and look toward where he'd been practicing, he was no longer there. He wasn't in the dining hall either as she picked at the porridge all scribes enjoyed every morning, but that didn't stop her eyes from darting around the room in search of him.

"Are you all right?" Marjory said.

Leena snapped out of her reverie, a daydream that included golden skin patterned in waves and the flash of gray eyes. Standing on the other side of the table, her Quanling inspected her and her full bowl, looking concerned.

"Fine," she said, flustered. "Just considering how best to interrogate the scrolls to find the right tomb."

"I have every confidence that you can do this, Leena. You've always shown exceptional talent at research. I'd go as far as to say that if you are successful at this task, you will solidify your nomination as my replacement when I retire. Certainly you will earn the favor of the high lord himself."

Leena took a deep breath and let it out slowly. This was

her future. This was what she'd always wanted. All she had to do was focus on her goal. "I won't fail you."

Marjory reached down and squeezed Leena's hand. "You won't fail *us*. What you do, you do for all of Rogos, my dear girl. Now finish your breakfast. You're excused from the rest of the day's rituals. Your work is far more important."

"Yes, Mother."

An hour later, Leena sat at one of the large tables in the most secluded corner of the library, surrounded by scrolls. She'd started reading about Tavyss's upbringing in Paragon under the reign of Villania the Fire Queen but found her mind drawn to another scroll she'd called up on a whim, one with red edges. She looked both ways and unrolled it furtively.

The symbols at the top in ancient Elvish translated loosely to *coupling*. Leena's eyebrows lifted as she perused the many ways a male could be with a female. Him behind her. Her on top of him. Both on their sides, legs intertwined. She brought her face closer to the scroll and touched her bottom lip as she studied a sketch of how one could use their mouth to pleasure another.

"Any breakthroughs?"

She dropped the scroll as if it were hot, and it rolled itself up on the table with a rustle and zip. She brushed the scroll into the bottom of the pile with one hand and reached for another of the ones she knew were about Tavyss. "Colin!" she squeaked. "You startled me!"

"Clearly." His gaze narrowed on her face, and the corner of his mouth twitched.

Damn it, she was blushing. Her cheeks blazed. "I was... in another world." She giggled awkwardly. "I've been

155

reading about Tavyss's childhood. Did you know he was pit champion four years in a row?"

Colin snorted. "I'm sure that was every year he competed. The eldest heir always wins."

"Always?"

"Anyone who beats him in a match gets pummeled outside the ring. Xavier beat Marius once, and I think our father snapped his wing. We heal quickly, but it still hurts."

"That isn't in the scrolls."

"I guess there's only so much you can see from the outside."

Leena couldn't help but flash back to the scroll she'd been studying. What would all those positions feel like to a participant? Had the scribe responsible for the scroll tried them all? What would it feel like with Colin? He'd be gentle and considerate. He had such a kind heart for someone raised a warrior, someone who'd been hurt the way he had by his parents. How could something so good come from someone so evil?

"Leena? Are you sure you're okay?"

She jolted. "Yes. Sorry, just distracted. I was thinking what a miracle it was that someone so good... Tavyss... came from the same parents as Eleanor."

Colin rubbed the back of his neck. "It's something I think about sometimes, how my siblings and I could come from that and all have turned out okay. I mean, none of us are megalomaniacs like her. I think it has to do with the lot of us learning how to lose. We all experienced what it was like to be bullied into submission against our brother Marius. Then seeing Brynhoff murder him. And afterward, what she did... She took everything from us, even one another. None of us would do that to someone else."

His expression turned vacant, and Leena studied him,

the absolute perfection of this man who had no goal but to do the right thing. If the Defenders of the Goddess won this war, he would not be king. He'd have no position at all. Yet he wanted nothing more than to fight his way out of a job.

"Why are you here?" Leena asked, suddenly realizing that they weren't supposed to meet again until she found something.

"We have Nochtbend. I received a message this morning that the vampire kingdom has joined the resistance. I also had the pleasure of bumping into General Lore of the archers of Asfolk while I was in the falcon mews borrowing a bird to notify Sylas. The general and I have both been sending falcons all morning. He's here to oversee the mining of the goddess's tears for weapons."

"He is?" Leena knew it was possible. There were scrolls on building bombs filled with tears, but she'd never witnessed the process. They'd never needed to use them in her lifetime.

"Yes. All able-bodied males in Rogos have been called up, Leena. Even the male scribes. They aren't going to wait for the three sisters. That's why I'm here. We have to find that crypt and a way to get that book, or we'll be going to war without it."

She sighed and looked at the massive pile of scrolls beside her. "I'll do my best. But honestly, perhaps the best thing both of us can do is pray to the goddess. We need the three sisters. If there's one thing I've learned today from studying these scrolls, it is that Eleanor is exceptionally evil. I'm convinced the only way to defeat her is with exceptional magic."

Colin frowned but nodded. "Then we pray."

CHAPTER NINETEEN

R aven popped through Nathaniel's portal, clinging to
the hands of her sisters as they stumbled onto the
steps of the Temple of the Sacred Pools. Sand crunched on
the stone beneath her feet, the grit blowing across her toes
and seeming to hang in the air around them. The dual suns
of Ouros had set hours ago, and the desert was surprisingly
cold. She crossed to Gabriel, who gathered her next to
Charlie in his arms without a word. Her daughter reached
out from her carrier and patted her cheek.

"Nathaniel, you've outdone yourself with this portal,"
Raven said. "I felt the drag between here and Aeaea. I'm not
sure I could have moved this many people."

Nathaniel tamped out his pipe, his face glistening with
sweat in the moonlight. "I don't think I can do it twice, and
I'd rather not try. Let's hope the Quanling and Fratern are
welcoming."

Xavier made a deep grunt. "Welcoming to the sons of
the enemy? We'll be lucky if these scribes donna land our
arses in a sacred pool." He pointed toward the nearest glint
of water in the sand beyond the temple.

Raven had seen what that water could do to a dragon when she'd met Colin. She hoped none of them would come in contact with it anytime soon.

"I just want a bed," Avery said. "I still don't know why this couldn't wait until morning."

"According to Sylas, the morning might be too late," Gabriel said. "We need access to the enchanted scroll before Eleanor or her troops attack. There's too much at stake to wait."

Clarissa took a deep breath. "No time like the present, then." She stepped forward and delivered three firm raps using the substantial metal knocker fastened to the front door.

A second later, a small door slid aside, and the partial face of a young male scribe appeared in the viewer. "The temple is closed to outsiders."

"We're looking for a scribe named Leena and the dragon who accompanies her, Colin. We have news from the Defenders of the Goddess." Clarissa met Raven's eyes. With one note, she could unlock the door with her voice, but both of them knew it was better to do this diplomatically.

The little door slid shut, and a quorum of voices, three male and one female, argued behind it. Raven couldn't make out everything, but it sounded as if there was some disagreement about if they should be let in or not. Finally, there was a click, and the door swung open to reveal a lanky and stony-faced woman who pursed her lips in their direction.

"I am Marjory, Quanling of this temple. I was *not* informed of your arrival."

"I imagine Sylas's message will arrive tomorrow," Gabriel said.

Marjory's eyes fell on his emerald ring. "My word. You're the heir." Her gaze scanned the others. "The Treasure of Paragon and, dare I guess, the three sisters?"

"Yes," they said in unison.

"It's very important that we see Leena right away, ma'am," Raven said.

The older elf made a face like she'd tasted something sour. "Please call me either Marjory or Quanling."

Raven bowed her head. "Marjory. My apologies."

"This way. Colin and Leena are in the library."

Raven followed the Quanling into the strange building. The walls reminded her of the pyramids, at least what she imagined they'd look like on the inside. Great slabs of unadorned limestone surrounded them. Their footsteps echoed as they walked, made louder by high ceilings and lack of carpeting. Long shadows stretched between patches of light cast by sconces on the walls. Although the temperature in the temple was comfortable, she walked closer to Gabriel to try to stave off the cold and impersonal feel of the rooms.

Marjory stopped before a set of large doors just as they flew open of their own accord, and the group came face-to-face with a very surprised Colin.

"You're back!" he said, then started pulling his brothers into swift hugs.

Raven noticed that Leena sat at a wide table behind him, looking more than a little flustered. "Have we interrupted something?"

"No." Colin rubbed the back of his neck. "Leena's been sifting through every scroll we could find that referred to Medea or Tavyss. We've been at it all day. I was going to take a break, but now that you're here..."

Leena rose from her seat. "Thank the goddess. Did you find the tanglewood tree?"

Clarissa crossed to her, drawing her wand. The tip glowed a bright, icy blue, and she held it high for the scribe to see. "The only parts that matter."

"I have the enchanted scroll here." She patted the satchel at her hip. "I keep it with me at all times. Should we try again to translate it?"

Everyone grumbled a tired yes, and Raven followed the others to the table.

"Let me just clear a space." Leena quickly shifted armfuls of scrolls, putting them on a white marble platform where they were promptly swallowed by swirling purple magic. She pulled out the palimpsest and unrolled it on the table.

Raven perused again the strange scroll. Although she couldn't read ancient Elvish, Leena had told her what it said. The grimoire was brought to Ouros at the beginning of Eleanor and Brynhoff's reign by Medea, who became the witch queen of Darnuith. Her mate, Tavyss, was the older brother of Brynhoff and challenged him for the throne for reasons unknown. In the fourth century, when Eleanor and Brynhoff did not comply, Medea attacked Paragon. She and her dragon mate were killed during the uprising, despite having the grimoire. Medea was pregnant at the time with their young. The scribe had noted a common belief at the time that Eleanor or Brynhoff somehow tricked Medea and Tavyss into letting their guard down and took advantage of their lapse.

Medea, Tavyss, and the baby were killed, but Medea was resurrected by her sisters. The sisters hid the golden grimoire somewhere and split the key into five pieces, enclosing them in magical orbs and hiding one in each of the five kingdoms. Colin had found the first orb here in Rogos; then Sylas and his mate Dianthe had succeeded in retrieving the other four. With the help of Charlie, they'd opened the orbs and reconstructed the key. The scroll included sketches of the orbs but not how or where to use the key.

But it was what was under the writing that they were after now. Symbols glowed and moved beneath the ink, appearing and then disappearing. Scrambling themselves. The document was a palimpsest, and the true message of how to obtain the golden grimoire and use it against Eleanor was hidden underneath, encrypted, waiting for them to unlock it. A message from the past meant for them and them alone.

"We have to do this together. I sense it in my bones," Raven said to Clarissa and Avery. She drew her wand and watched the tip glow to life as if its magic had come alive in the presence of the scroll. "Are you ready?"

Avery backed up a step. "Whoa! I don't even know how to use mine." She drew her wand but held it awkwardly in front of her, as if it were a bomb that might go off at any moment.

Raven took her hand supportively. "All it does is amplify your magic. I can feel it. The tanglewood tree was born with our ancestors. Its magic fed them for decades. It's all here." She stared at the wand in wonder. "All we have to do is ask it to work for us."

"It's a branch, Raven, not the neighbor boy. I don't think asking is going to be enough." Avery frowned.

"Think of it like your sword," Clarissa said. "It's a tool. With the right intention, you can make it work."

Avery adjusted the wand in her hand, her knuckles turning white from her grip. "Okay. I'm ready to give it a try. I hope you know what you're doing."

Raven glanced down at the scroll. "I do. I can see it now, like a bow that just needs to be untied. As we did before. Avery, drain the encryption spell. Clarissa, strengthen Avery. I'll take the magic apart and then translate what's underneath."

Clarissa grinned. "I can't wait to see what's on the other side of that spell."

"On the count of three. One... Two... Three."

Avery grabbed the corner of the scroll. The strange moving text disappeared, replaced by ancient Elvish. Clarissa's voice rang out, supporting Avery. And Raven uttered a spell that came to her straight from the wand, as if the tree itself were whispering in her ear. With another incantation, Raven watched the symbols jumble and then right themselves in her language. She crossed her arms and made the motion of tying a knot.

It worked! The letters glowed brighter and then settled into the scroll, the locking spell successfully holding the words in place.

Avery let go.

Clarissa stopped singing. "Fucking hell, it worked! Finally." She tried to bend her neck to get a better view, but Raven was in the best position at the table. "Read it to us, Raven."

"With the help of Daluk of Niven, I, Medea Tanglewood, witch queen of Darnuith, bequeath my golden grimoire to the three foretold to free Ouros from the tyrannical rule of Eleanor of Paragon. I don't know your names or from where you will come, but my sisters and I have seen you in our visions. Now, as we prepare to leave this world, we put our faith in you.

"My dearest love, Tavyss, is dead, as is our son, Phineas. We know now that we must leave this place. A traitor lurks within the court of Darnuith, and now that Tavyss is dead, I am mortal and Eleanor is not. We have seen the future, and you are Ouros's only hope.

"Daluk has helped me seal the grimoire inside my heart's tomb. It had to be done. Only its inherent magic could keep my protective spell active past my death. The tomb is hidden, but it will be easy for you to find as its shape is in the form of my beloved and it guards the gate of a garden that reminds me of the one where we first met. I've placed it in Rogos where Eleanor's prying hand cannot reach.

"Now my vengeance is in your hands. Our visions have shown us the way, and I pray you will be brave enough to follow it. We've seen a child, a descendant. The beginning and the end. Only this child holds the magic to both make and undo what is to come.

"Eleanor grows stronger by the minute. Beware, her supporters hide like vipers, waiting and watching from the tall grass. You must call upon the goddess of the mountain and ask her to intercede on your behalf. Everything you need resides within the grimoire. Use it.

"Know that my sisters and I cannot guarantee your success. The future we see is constantly shifting. We know not in what year you will come or the circumstances of your arrival. All we can promise you is that wherever it is we go after we pass from this existence, we will be watching, waiting to aid you in any way we can. The only word I leave you with is goodbye. Goddess be with you."

Raven looked up from the parchment. From her carrier

strapped to Gabriel's chest, Charlie clapped her hands, grinning.

"She likes to hear you read," Gabriel mumbled.

Nathaniel rubbed Clarissa's shoulders. "Did that make sense to anyone? A tomb in the shape of her beloved... Is that Tavyss? In what form? Or the baby?"

Xavier raised a finger. "'Tis in front of a garden, it said. Can only be so many of them, eh?"

Leena shook her head. "Rogos has many gardens, and if there is a tomb shaped like a dragon or a man or a child, I have never heard of it. It's not traditional."

"Not just a garden," Colin added. "Fruit trees. Our family crest is a dragon wrapped around a golden fruit tree. Sylas learned it represented Tavyss in the Garden of the Hesperides. That's where he met Medea."

Nathaniel took a fortifying drag on his pipe. "What type of trees do you have in Rogos that bear hanging fruit?"

Leena walked to the altar and scribbled something on a piece of parchment. A scroll manifested before her. "A map of Rogos. Let's take a look." She unrolled it on the table. "There's a Ramblefig orchard here. That's an oblong purple fruit we use in pastries. It's on the border of Darnuith. She might have put it there."

Xavier shook his head. "I'd not hide something so important so close to the road as it is."

Colin nodded. "I'd have to agree with my brother. Not only is it close to a border and the road, she mentions a traitor from Darnuith. Wouldn't she want to have it farther inland?"

"What about that one?" Gabriel pointed at an orchard on the edge of the Mystic Wood. Charlie reached toward the map, her chubby hand opening and closing.

"That's sandberry fruit—the Dune Orchard. That could

very well be what we're looking for. It borders the desert and is owned by the desert dwellers. It will be hard for me to gain access. Even harder for a non-elf. The desert dwellers do not like company."

Colin scanned the map again. "The only other ones appear to be around Asfolk Palace."

"Asfolk is the capital and a hub of commerce. Having a variety of fruit grow there benefits the palace, and it's also centrally located to ship across Rogos."

"An odd place for a crypt," Nathaniel said.

Raven wished Medea had been more specific about the location of the tomb, but everything the witch had done thus far was to keep the grimoire out of the hands of Eleanor. She couldn't make it too easy. And the hardest place to reach on this map was the Dune Orchard. "Let's search there." She pointed to it on the map. "We have to start somewhere. We can leave in the morning."

Leena shook her head. "Why not look now?" Everyone flashed her a confused look. "We don't actually have to go there to know if it's the place. I can look from here." She strode behind the white marble platform and through a door at the back of the library.

Raven followed into a room with a sanded wood floor and a line of hollowed-out stone bowls filled with liquid. Each was next to a desk with shelves of blank scrolls and a quill.

"Stand back—the tears will burn you." Leena positioned herself at one of the desks.

The scribe sat down and passed her hand over the pool beside her. Raven gasped as the tears started to swirl with color and light, images flashing within the bowl's depths. This wasn't familiar magic. This was something else, a type of power unique to the scribes.

"Show me Dune Orchard," Leena commanded.

The waters settled. Raven made out a garden but couldn't see more from her angle. Leena's eyes actively scanned the surface.

Clarissa cracked her neck. "Google Earth in a bowl."

Gabriel, Nathaniel, and Avery chuckled. Colin and Xavier stared at her blankly.

"I don't see a gate or a tomb," Leena said. "I don't think this is it. There's no place that fits the description."

Everyone groaned.

"Try the one next to Darnuith," Gabriel suggested.

She circled her hand again. "There is a cemetery next to this one and there is a gate, but I'm not seeing a dragon. Also, these graves aren't old enough to be what we're looking for. The style is consistent with the past fifty years."

"Sylas found the golden orb in the floor of the Obsidian Palace," Colin said, placing a scarred hand on Leena's shoulder. "I think Medea was a clever woman who would enjoy hiding something in plain sight."

Leena stared ahead, eyes unfocused, memories passing through her expression like ghosts. She glanced back at Colin and then circled her hand over the pool once more. This time, she said something in her native tongue, and when the picture formed in the bowl, she gasped.

"What is it?" Raven asked.

"Asfolk Orchard. It's a few miles outside the city. I only remembered it because of the dragon statue... I read some-where it was a gift from Paragon."

Raven tried to look in the pool, but she couldn't see what Leena saw.

"There are no graves near this orchard, but the fruit is gold and round. And the dragon sculpture is right outside the gate." Leena lifted her chin and stared at Raven. "It's not a grave, but it has to be it. It's exactly what she described."

Raven exchanged glances with Colin. The dragon nodded and said, "We go first thing tomorrow. I'll send a falcon to Asfolk. With any luck, Rogos and Darnuith will see reason and wait until we have the book to attack."

CHAPTER TWENTY

Colin closed himself into his chambers in the west wing, looking forward to a good night's sleep. Spending time with Leena that day had been exhausting. When he'd first found her in the library, his dragon had locked on to her mating scent, the same one she'd put off in the tent. He'd hunted her down like a predator and found her at a table in the back of the library. But if the hot blush that had stained her cheeks was any indication that she'd been thinking about him, she'd made it very clear she did not intend to act on those feelings.

After their initial interaction, she'd been all business for the rest of the day. She was attracted to him. He knew she was. It didn't matter, though. She'd made up her mind, chosen the life of a scribe, nothing more.

He couldn't blame her. What did he have to offer her, actually? The youngest son of a murderous tyrant. He had no crown, no income. He could not promise her safety or comfort. Hell, he was the leader of a rebellion, a bringer of war, a warrior without a home, who was fighting for someone else to take the throne. Even in the best of circumstances, he had nothing but death and destruction in his near future, followed by a life of... What exactly? He had no idea what role, if any, he'd play in the future of Paragon if they succeeded.

Although he had no trouble seeing in the dark, he lit the thick white candle on the lone dresser. He wanted the fire, the flicker of life to cast out the shadows forming in his heart. He used the pitcher and basin to wash himself, then flopped down on the small bed. A rendering of the goddess of the mountain hung on the wall. A woman on fire—not burning but thriving. He glanced down at the red waves and divots that permanently marred his skin. He couldn't feel sorry for himself. Dragons were created to endure.

He closed his eyes. All he saw was Leena's face. He turned on his side. She'd feel warm tucked in against him. He flipped on his stomach. The tent. Oh goddess, he remembered how she'd felt in radiant detail. He groaned. Thank the Mountain dragons didn't need much sleep. He doubted he'd be getting any tonight.

A faint knock came on his door. He raised his head. It was late. None of the scribes would be up at this hour. The knock came again. Barely a brush of knuckles on wood. He climbed out of bed and pulled on his breeches, leaving them unbuttoned at the top. Whoever it was, he planned to deal with them quickly.

He cracked the door. *Leena?*

She pressed one finger to her lips. Silently, he opened the door wider to let her in, then looked both ways to make sure the hall was clear before closing it behind her.

"What are you doing here?" he whispered.

"I... I couldn't sleep." Her face flushed, her eyes drifting to his breeches and the open fly.

He didn't move to fasten it. He was in his own room, and it was the middle of the night.

Colin sighed, his hands landing on his hips. "Don't you elves have a tea for that? If not, I'm sure Raven could help."

"We never finished our conversation."

"I think we did."

She licked her lips, and Colin's cock twitched at the sight of the tip of her pink tongue. What was she doing here? Was this some way of torturing him for embarrassing her earlier?

"We're going to open the tomb tomorrow. The scroll is translated. You won't need my help after that."

"You must be relieved." He frowned.

"Not as I should be." She dropped her gaze to the space between their feet. "You said that if I wanted another taste, with your permission..."

Colin froze. Had he misheard her? If the severe blush staining her cheeks was any clue, he hadn't. But this was dangerous. His dragon wanted her as his mate. He'd better know exactly what his boundaries were, or this would end badly for them both.

"A taste. What does it mean to you? Tell me exactly. I can't color within the lines if I don't know where the lines are."

She released a held breath. "You're going to make me say it? I thought men took what they wanted until a woman said no."

"Not this man. Not this dragon."

Her throat bobbed. "I want one night," she whispered, her gaze flicking up to meet his. "Just between us. No one can ever know. Just one night to..." She gestured in front of her chest, as if there was something physically there. Something large and unwieldy. "...appease this hunger."

"Hunger?" He knew exactly what she meant, but he wanted to hear her say it.

"I ache for you," she said, her violet eyes misting as if she might cry. She tugged at her dark copper braid, and her voice cracked as she continued. "My every fiber yearns for more of what we did before. It burns inside me. I can't sleep or eat. It is a beast that must be fed or I might die."

At once, Colin's mouth went dry as a bone. He was far more experienced with the opposite sex than she was. What she was describing was lust, plain and simple. He could help her with that, but it would mean more to him. He had far more than physical pleasure at stake.

Although, his intentions weren't completely charitable. He refused to tell her that feeding that beast might make it hungrier in the long run. He was too much of a bastard to give her any excuse to back out now.

"One night." Colin hooked his knuckle under her chin and lifted it until she looked him in the eye. "Kissing, touching, or... everything?"

That pink tongue emerged again, and he could see her pulse fluttering. "Everything," she said breathlessly. "I want to touch you. I want to..."

He narrowed his eyes. "What does everything mean to you?"

Her eyes drifted, and that blush was back. Goddess, he loved that blush.

"I'm not sure."

"Then I'll teach you."

His dragon coiled inside him, his skin heating with urgency to take her. But he only had one chance at this. All he had to give her was his body. Himself. As he saw it, he had to make tonight so good, such a mind-blowing experience for her, that she'd leave the temple for him. That was the only way he'd have what he wanted. The only way he'd have *her*.

He walked around her, noticing her slight shiver under his gaze. She was nervous. He'd try his best to alleviate that. He took her braid between his fingers and untied the leather cord binding it. "A dragon has a highly developed sense of smell." He unbraided the plait, running his fingers through the dark copper strands. "Do you know what you smell like to me, Leena?"

She shook her head.

"Blackcurrants and wild primrose. Dark floral ambrosia." His touch reached the back of her skull, and he scraped his nails along the skin there before dragging his fingers through her hair. He buried his nose in it and inhaled. "I wonder what you'll taste like."

She released a shaky breath and tried to turn toward him.

"Stay where you are." He traced his fingers behind her ear, pleased when she did as he commanded. She tipped her head to expose her neck to him—the long, graceful neck of a dancer with pale skin as perfect and smooth as spun vilt. He brought his lips to where he'd just touched and brushed them featherlight across her skin.

At the collar of her robes, he traced along her neckline, tugged the fabric down between her breasts. The inside of the arm he had wrapped around her brushed over her nipple, and he found the tip hard. Good. He'd explore her breasts soon.

He stroked over her abdomen and dug his fingers into her belt. "I'm topless. Only fair that you join me," he whispered in her ear.

Her throat twitched with her swallow. He pressed a kiss to her pulse as he untied the knot at her waist. The folds of her robe fell open, and he stepped back to pull it off her shoulders.

Her back was lithe, lean perfection. He tossed the garment on the chair, using the excuse to walk around her once more. Naked before him, her form held a willowy grace, from the tips of her pointed ears to the stretch of her waist to her elegant limbs, proportionally longer than a dragon's. In the moonlight, her skin shone like carved marble, perfectly smooth and white.

Behind her again, he wrapped her hair around one hand, tugging until she gasped softly, then placed a kiss on her top vertebrae, just under her hairline. She released a deep, shaky breath, and he stemmed a self-satisfied grin. If she'd liked what he'd done to her in the tent, she'd love what he had in mind for her now. He cascaded kisses like a waterfall along her spine, releasing her hair and dropping to his knees to reach her tailbone, palms cupping the twin mounds of her ass.

"Now you can turn."

She did. In his current position, her navel was level with his lips. He slipped his hands around her waist, and he placed a kiss there, worshiping it with his tongue and nibbling lower. She dug her fingers into his hair.

He would have liked to taste her right then. But she wasn't ready for that. In fact, she was trembling so hard he was afraid she'd lose her balance. He needed to move her to the bed.

Rising, he met her gaze, then dropped his lips to hers. He skimmed his hands up her waist and cradled her breasts, flicking his thumbs across their taut peaks. Her fingers in his hair became more demanding, and he plucked and rolled her nipples in response. Heart pounding against his chest in time with his, she drove her tongue deeper into his mouth.

"We're uneven again," she said against his lips.

"Hmm?"

She glanced down at her nakedness and then pointedly at the breeches that still hung around his hips. Her fingers trailed down his stomach. To his surprise, her hand didn't dawdle with removing them but drifted inside, wrapping around his rock-hard shaft and stroking him from base to tip.

"Leena," he whispered. "You keep doing that and this is going to go faster than you deserve."

"I want to see you."

He backed up a step and removed his breeches. Her lips parted as she studied him by candlelight.

"Do I frighten you?" he asked.

"No. It's just different from what I expected. Different from scrolls and sketches. You're... huge."

A wicked grin spread across his face. "Kind of you to say so." He traced the backs of his nails along the outer curve of her body. "I think you're walking poetry."

That brought color to her cheeks. Her violet eyes seemed to give off their own light in the darkness. She scoffed and looked away. "I'm plain by elf standards. Flat."

He closed the gap between them. "Perfect." He guided her to sit on the bed and spread her knees so he could kneel between them. Once again, his lips found hers. He trailed featherlight kisses down her throat to her breast, his fingers drifting between her legs and stroking along her center. She was wet, ready.

She pressed her hands into his shoulders. "What are you going to do?"

He looked up at her from under hooded lids. "I'm going to give you an experience to remember."

"Trust me."

Leena had to have lost her mind to have come to Colin's room. By the goddess, she was wicked. Only, she couldn't bring herself to regret her actions with his fingers doing decadent things between her legs.

Something was building inside her, that same strange, dropping ache she'd felt in the tent. It centered around his touch, and she thought he'd continue the same as before. She leaned back on her elbows, noticing the exquisite sensation of the night air across the tips of her breasts.

"Colin..."

His lips landed on the curve of her stomach, and his tongue traced a wet trail lower. He couldn't possibly mean to—

Leena's head tipped back, and she inhaled sharply as Colin's tongue replaced his fingers. The world narrowed to the steady rhythm of his flicking tongue against her flesh. She bit her lip to keep from crying out. Closer. Closer. Her skin tingled. Her breath caught in her throat.

Her soul exploded through her skin, even stronger than the first time in the tent. He had transformed her into pure light, and the pleasure that resulted filled the room. Spinning. Unraveling. Weightless, she came apart and then back together.

And still, she wanted him. Wanted more. His mating trill buzzed like a purr between her legs. He turned her on the bed and climbed on top of her. This was happening. He loved her. She knew he did. And that trill was important, his dragon coming to the surface, claiming her.

She should stop this. It would be harder for him after

this. All she could give him was one night, and she knew he wanted more. Had always known.

But when her hands landed on his shoulders to push him away, her body betrayed her and pulled him closer. Her legs wrapped around his hips. She was so wet from his mouth and her need that it was all too easy for him to slide partially inside her. She sucked in her breath at the size, at the way he stretched her to the limit.

"Am I hurting you?" he whispered. His muscles coiled above her as if stopping his movement was causing him pain.

"Not at all." She pressed a kiss to the underside of his jaw. "Why would it hurt?"

"Sometimes the first time hurts for females."

"Not for me. Not for elves."

"Thank the goddess." All at once, he thrust into her. He hadn't given her everything before, not even close. And although it didn't hurt, it made her gasp. The fullness, the depth. He was everywhere, and her flesh reveled in it.

He began to move over her, in her, until she felt that now-familiar building again.

"Please," she whispered. She hadn't meant to say the word. Hadn't meant to beg. But the feeling was so intense, so intimate, it spilled from her lips like a prayer.

And he was there for her, hooking her knee over his shoulder and driving in deeper. When the light filled her this time, it seemed to come from a deeper place. She had to bite her wrist to keep from screaming. And when he tensed over her and she realized he was experiencing his own magic, the sight of his face in the throes of ecstasy fed her own.

It was a long time before it seemed she could breathe

again. Longer still until he rolled off her and dragged her against his chest, covering them both with the thin blanket.

"Another taste," he whispered in her ear. "Was it what you expected?"

She shook her head. How could she explain what she was feeling? "I didn't know you could get to heaven by joining bodies."

His voice was serious when he responded. "Neither did I."

"But you have done this before."

"I've had sex before. I've never done this before."

For some reason, that made her heart glow. "I wish things were different."

He stiffened behind her. "Different how?"

Tears filled her eyes. "If I were a different person. If we'd met at a different time. If I hadn't yet taken my—" She stopped. She'd been about to say if she hadn't yet taken her oath and become a scribe. But did she mean it? If she'd met Colin before she'd devoted herself to the order, would she have chosen him over being a scribe?

A lump formed in her throat. There was no sense thinking about such things. "I should return to my room. I can barely keep my eyes open. I have to get back while everyone's still asleep."

He pulled her tighter against his chest and kissed her temple. "You said you wanted a taste, that you wanted everything."

She laughed softly. "I think you gave me a full meal."

"Not even close. The after-sex cuddling is an important part of the experience." His breath was warm against her ear. "Sleep, Leena. I'll wake you before dawn. Plenty of time to make it back to your room."

She yawned and snuggled deeper into his embrace. She

should go. It would be wiser if she returned to her chambers now and didn't prolong the inevitable. Every minute she lived in this fantasy made it harder for her to return to the real world.

But in the end, she wasn't strong enough. She wanted more of this, wanted to drink the night dry of its indulgences. She closed her eyes and drifted off in the protection of his embrace.

CHAPTER TWENTY-ONE

For all intents and purposes, last night was a disaster for Colin. His dragon had fallen scales over talons for Leena. He'd given her everything and bound himself to her, and she'd made no such vow with him. She'd be the only woman for him now, ever. He'd condemned himself to a long and lonely life.

Still, he wouldn't change a thing. A single night with her was worth any cost, including a lifetime alone. He watched her sleep as the hours passed. It never occurred to him to close his eyes and rest himself. Why would he? And willfully miss a second of this?

But alas, the hour came when he could wait no longer without putting her at risk. He'd promised her a taste and then to return her to her own life. It was time. She had to go, and he had to complete a mission. He had a war to lead.

"Leena," he whispered in her ear.

She took a deep breath and smiled in her sleep.

"It's time to wake up."

Her eyes fluttered open, and then her smile faded. "It's time for me to go, isn't it?"

He nodded.

Slowly she climbed out of bed, out of his arms, and pulled on her clothes. Only when she was fully dressed did she turn back to him. "Thank you for this."

He inclined his head. She reached for the door.

"Leena." Why was he doing this? He was only going to make it worse.

"Yes?"

"No matter what happens now, I want you to know something." He watched her throat bob, saw the way she hugged herself against the well of emotions that made her eyes glint with tears. "Last night was everything to me. No matter how long you live or what the future brings, I want you to know that I love you and have loved you, above all others. This was a taste for you. A first taste. For me, it was the last. And I don't regret a single moment of it."

"Oh, Colin..." She gave him a pitying look he could not abide. It was no secret that once a dragon bonded, they could not find pleasure in another. Whether she realized that he'd bonded with her unilaterally last night or simply thought his words were romantic pillow talk, he didn't want her sympathy. He wouldn't have changed a damn thing. Every second of last night was sacred.

He gestured toward the door. "Go. You don't want to get caught."

She gave him a slight bow and left without another word.

Cold shards of ice stabbed through his heart in the empty room. Some invisible creature had dug its claws into his chest and torn and shredded until there was nothing left but wispy twists of his soul blowing in a dark wind. Everything that mattered was over.

But a soldier, a warrior, was trained to fight through the

pain. He'd keep moving and leave everything on the battlefield.

Colin washed and dressed, forcing himself to move the shattered pieces of his heart. The suns hadn't yet risen outside his window, but he took up his sword. Time to lose himself in his practice routine. Whatever this war would bring, he was ready, because after tonight, he had nothing left to lose. And if there was one thing universally acknowledged in Ouros, it was the hazard of a dragon with nothing to lose.

❦

It was all Leena could do to keep her eyes open as they rode toward the orchard on the edge of Asfolk. Unlike the palace, the temple did not have access to a carriage large enough to transport four dragons, three witches, and one exhausted scribe, and unlike the night before, it was decided that Nathaniel's magical reserves could not be wasted on transporting them by portal.

What the temple did have was plenty of horses. The dapple-gray steeds carried scribes to the distant pools in Niven to make sacrifices to the goddess. They'd saddled up that morning after breakfast and set out for Asfolk, Leena carefully distancing herself from Colin to avoid suspicion. Every time she came near him, she thought that her skin must be glowing, branded with light everywhere he'd touched her.

How was it possible that no one seemed to notice she was different? The idea boggled her mind. How could they not notice that she'd been completely turned inside out and put back together? Her night with Colin had shaken her to her core. She'd never be the same. Never.

She adjusted herself in the saddle, her muscles deliciously sore from their lovemaking. Despite her best efforts, her mind went back there, back to the sight of him moving over her, in her. Sweat on his forehead. The muscles of his arms bunching with the effort, caging her in, making her his willing prisoner.

They reached a crossroad and got a firsthand view of exactly what was happening in Rogos. A battalion of archers rode by in front of them, dressed in their purple uniforms. The captain bowed his head in her direction. She bowed back, watching absently as the unit continued on. When they resumed their journey, she allowed the dragons to go ahead of her toward their destination. She was too tired for the responsibility of leading the way.

"Earth to Leena." Clarissa popped up beside her. When had she found her way to the back of the group?

"Why would Earth be calling me?"

Clarissa laughed. "It's an expression. We say it to each other on Earth when someone spaces out."

"What a strange expression."

"What's with the matching luggage?" Clarissa motioned under her eyes. "Looks like you haven't slept in days."

She glanced away nervously. "I haven't been able to sleep lately."

"Clandestine affair?"

Leena's head snapped around, her eyes widening. "Why would you think that?"

Clarissa laughed, buckling over the neck of her horse. "It was a joke. Obviously. I mean, you're a scribe, right?"

"Oh, right." Leena forced a giggle.

Clarissa's smile faded, and she leaned back in the saddle. "Seriously, what is it? Why can't you sleep?"

She lifted her eyebrows, thinking fast. "Isn't everyone

missing sleep these days? Our world is on the brink of war. Even now, the high lord has likely lined up troops at the border."

It wasn't a lie, but Clarissa's face fell as if it wasn't quite what she'd expected her to say. "Hmm. Well, if we get our hands on that book today, my sisters and I are going to end this war before it begins. Take heart—you'll be sleeping well soon."

How she wished that was true.

It was late morning when they reached Asfolk Orchard and found the metal sculpture of the dragon guarding the gate. There was no one here. No need to guard it. Not only was the thornfruit dangerous to pick and inedible to anyone who didn't know how to prepare it properly, it wasn't even in season.

Leena hopped down off her horse and inspected the dragon. She brushed years of dust and debris off the metal sculpture. Dead leaves had gathered along the side in the dip between its tail and its body. This wasn't a crypt. There was no inscription anywhere on it, no marker. It wasn't even big enough to contain an adult body. More relevant to their cause, there was no place to put the crypt key.

"I don't understand," Raven said. Charlie reached for the shiny dragon from the carrier on her chest and Raven redirected her hand away from the sculpture. "This is exactly what Medea described in her message, but this *can't* be it, can it?"

Leena traced the metal with her fingers. "Elves are geniuses at metalwork. Let me just..." There was a ridge under the dragon's jaw. A latch. She squeezed it.

A metal-on-metal groan preceded the rattle of a chain somewhere inside. The clockwork dragon vibrated, the copper mouth yawning open to expose a network of bronze and platinum gears around an indentation. The crypt lock.

Clarissa gasped. "Holy shit, that is badass!" She ran her fingers over the gears.

"Let's try the key." Raven dug in her saddlebag for the collection of gears they'd retrieved from the orbs.

"Gives me the creeps." Avery shivered. "Be careful, Raven. Anyone talented enough to make this thing is smart enough to booby-trap it."

"Aye. Seems an odd contraption to me as well," Xavier said. "Are ye sure it's safe? Perhaps one of us should do it." He looked worriedly at Avery, and a pang of jealousy cut through Leena at what passed between them. Her eyes slipped to Colin, who was scanning the surrounding area for threats, his eyes everywhere but on her.

Raven shook her head. "Medea left this to us. We have to do it." She navigated Charlie's grabby fingers to fit the key into the dragon's mouth. "Leena, I need your help. What's the key word? The symbols are all in high fae."

"I don't remember one. Did Medea even leave us a key word?" Leena pulled the scroll from her satchel and unrolled it for the witch. She stood beside it as they both read it again. "It could be the baby's name, Phineas..."

"The only word I can leave you with is goodbye," Raven read. "How do you spell goodbye in high fae?"

Leena reached into the dragon's mouth and turned the gears, matching the symbols to spell out the valediction. Then she backed away with the others as the clockwork dragon started to tick and grind.

CHAPTER TWENTY-TWO

The dragon, Raven noted, wasn't a sculpture but a machine. As soon as they turned the key in the lock, it started to tick. Inner gears turned, and the mouth grew bigger and bigger until it was possible to walk into the gaping maw.

"This is dangerous, Colin," Gabriel said. "A few of us need to guard the perimeter, especially the main road into the gardens. I don't need to tell you what will happen if anyone sees this, and I do mean *anyone*."

The men exchanged worried glances.

Colin gestured to Xavier and Nathaniel. "Station yourselves to the north and east. Gabriel and I will take south and west. Make yourselves invisible, but don't be afraid to use force if you have to."

Gabriel kissed Raven lightly on the lips. "Are you going to be okay?" His eyes flicked to the dark entrance to the crypt.

"I'm with my sisters. Medea left this for us. I think I'm in more danger from something out there"—she gestured toward the road—"than in here."

189

Gabriel nodded. "Leave out there to me." He kissed Charlie's head, and then he and his brothers blinked out of sight, his scent fading with the next breeze.

She turned back to the dragon's mouth, but Clarissa's hand landed on her arm before she could move inside.

"Are you sure that's a good idea?" Her blue gaze traced around the jagged teeth above and below them. "This thing is hundreds of years old. I don't trust it."

Avery, too, balked at the cavernous entrance.

"You and Avery can stay here." Raven removed the carrier and handed her daughter to Avery. "Watch Charlie. I'll get the book. If something happens, you two can get me out."

Avery strapped on the carrier while Charlie patted her cheek affectionately. "Come to your favorite aunt."

"Hey!" Clarissa looked positively offended.

"Clarissa's right, Raven. I don't think it's safe either," Avery said.

But Leena held up a hand. "Elf metalwork is extremely reliable. I highly doubt you have anything to worry about."

Raven drew her wand, the tip casting a purple glow down the throat of the machine. "The book is down there, and there's only one way to get it." With one last glance toward the other women, she stepped into the mouth of the dragon and was surprised when Leena followed her.

"Where do you think you're going?" she asked the scribe.

"I go where the scroll goes." The woman's strange violet eyes glanced at the scroll Raven was holding from when they'd worked out the key.

"I need it in case there's another riddle inside," Raven said. "It might hold more clues."

Leena gestured toward the dark interior of the cave. "If

there is more to work out inside, chances are it, like the key, will require a translator who reads ancient Elvish. You could use a translation spell, but it would be far easier and less draining to simply allow me to do it."

Raven sighed. The scribe made sense, and she wasn't overly excited about going into the dark cavern alone. "Okay, then. Here. You might as well carry this, then." She handed her the scroll. "If we run into trouble, I'll need both hands."

Leena took the precious scroll and carefully rerolled it before tucking it into her satchel. "Lead the way."

Raising her wand, Raven floated a ball of light high in front of them. The glow revealed a set of stone stairs that led down, underground. Her heart pounded as she descended. As soon as she stepped on the third step, torches lit along the walls, and everything inside blazed to life, shone gold. The tomb was filled with treasure.

"Oh my god," Raven mumbled when her eyes caught on a large yellow diamond resting on top of the pile of coins and jewels. It twinkled in the torchlight.

"Is that what I think it is?" Leena's chest rose and fell like she'd sprinted a mile. That was fear in her purple eyes.

Raven knew what it was. She'd held one just like it in her hands once, only it was an emerald, not a diamond. Gabriel's heart. "It's a dragon's heart. I'm guessing Tavyss's."

"It has to be," Leena said. "I read about him just yesterday, and this gem is the same color as the ring described in the text."

A lump formed in Raven's throat. Medea had led her to the burial chamber of her beloved Tavyss.

"Where's the grimoire?" Leena asked. "Why would Medea lead you to the heart and not the book?"

Tentatively, Raven lifted the gem and held it up to the torchlight. It wasn't just reflecting the light but putting off its own. At first, her thoughts flashed to Gabriel's heart, to how the emerald once held the light of his soul. But she didn't feel another presence in the room or sense that Tavyss's soul was still bound to this gem. What she did feel was the hot rush of power like a pulse in the air around her. Her breath caught.

"It's here," she said excitedly. "Inside the stone! Medea stored the grimoire inside Tavyss's heart."

Leena's eyes sparked. "What? Why would she do such a thing?"

Raven smiled. "Because she was truly brilliant. A witch's magic dies with her, but a dragon's magic is inherent to their body. It's why Circe asked the first dragon for her scale in exchange for the ability to shift. That scale could turn anyone who used it invisible... forever. And this heart has magic... magic that fueled the encryption on that scroll and the protective magic of the orbs."

"Brilliant, yes. But how do we get the book out to use it?"

"I'm not sure. Let me think," Raven said.

Leena looked around the tomb, hugging herself and rubbing her shoulders. "This place scares me, Raven. I have a strange feeling of foreboding. I don't think we should linger here."

Raven adjusted the heart, turning it in her hand and holding it closer to the torchlight. If she held it just right, she could see writing. "I can see it. The pages of the grimoire are open to a spell. I'm guessing it's the one to extract the book from the gem, but it's not in English."

"Do you need me to try to read it? I know many languages."

"No need," Raven said with a smile. "I only need to know it exists." As Leena looked on in confusion, Raven reached out with her magic, the same magic that had allowed her to absorb hundreds of books in every human language from Gabriel's magical library, long before she knew she could do it. Metaphysical ribbons extended into the dragon heart, probing the facets to find the book within, feeling the magic and absorbing it off the page.

"What's happening?" Leena asked.

"It's part of who I am... my special power. I can absorb the magic even if I can't read the words."

"Like you did with the scroll," Leena said.

"Mmm-hmm." Raven continued to analyze the magic. "I think it's fascinating how my magic and my sisters' complement one another. Avery neutralizes magic. I take it in and transform it. It becomes part of me. As long as I practice the spells once I have them, they will always be mine. And Clarissa, she makes magic with her voice. Creates it from scratch. From nothing."

"When you put it that way, I can see why the legends say you'd be unstoppable."

Raven turned the gem, and the pages in the book started to flip. "We're not unstoppable. Not yet. But we're learning." She absorbed each spell, feeling the gold light bleed into her, transfusing her with ancient power. So much magic. Her head swam with spells. Her body pulsed with it.

"Raven... Oh my goddess, your skin!" Leena gasped.

Raven looked down at herself. Symbols glowed through her flesh, and she remembered her first days in Gabriel's library. This only used to happen when Gabriel touched her, before she'd understood how to process the magic she absorbed. She stared at the heart in her hands and dropped it onto the pile of treasure, sending a clatter of gold coins to the floor. The symbols faded.

"They're gone. Are you all right?"

"Fine."

"Shouldn't we take it with us? We can't leave it for someone else to find. It's too powerful." Leena frowned at the gem.

Raven laughed. "We're not going to leave the book." Unlike when she'd resurrected Gabriel, there was no soul left in Tavyss's heart. The dragon had moved on to wherever dragons went after they died. The only thing in this golden jewel was the book, and she knew how to get it out.

She drew her wand again, waved it in the air in the shape of the symbol that appeared in her head. A triangle glowed to life, hovered over the treasure, and released rays of golden light that rained down on the heart. The tomb became as bright as day.

Leena stumbled back into the wall, pressing herself against the stone.

Crack. The yellow diamond split in two. Treasure scattered across the room. A book as large as her torso appeared in front of her with a cover of solid gold etched with the image of a peacock.

"Goddess save us all," Leena cried. "My skin is buzzing. I can feel the power all the way over here."

"This is pure celestial magic. I've never experienced anything like it. No wonder Hera wants it back." Raven tucked her wand away and lifted the book into her arms. "Let's go."

She didn't have to ask Leena twice. The elf bounded up the stairs and out of the dragon's mouth. Raven smiled at her sisters as she emerged into the sun with the book on her hip. Avery and Clarissa approached her excitedly, Charlie reaching for her. She shifted the book into one arm and accepted her daughter in the other.

"I found the spell we need," Raven said to them. "I know how to stop Eleanor."

But Avery's face fell, her eyes scanning Raven from head to toe. "What's happening?"

Raven did feel strange, like every cell in her body tingled with static electricity. Clarissa opened her mouth and sang a defensive note, but whatever it was meant to do, it didn't work. Raven felt herself fading.

Charlie! She tried to throw her toward Avery, but the babe was bound to her. She couldn't even move her arms as they both faded away. Just before Raven vanished, she witnessed Leena leaping into the air. The elf collided with her, wrapping arms and legs around her and Charlie. Then a wave of blackness swallowed them all. The next thing she knew, all three of them toppled out of the darkness and onto an obsidian floor.

Raven landed on her stomach. The book flew from her arms, as did Charlie, who wailed as she was thrown across the room. Beside her, Leena landed facedown, her limbs splayed.

"The strength of a magical contract truly is amazing," a familiar voice rang out above her.

Raven tore her eyes away from Charlie and tried to force breath back into her lungs. On her hands and knees, she let her line of sight follow leather boots to black lace tights, then the handkerchief hem of a dark skirt, and finally, a red bustier. Above it all, Crimson Vanderholt stared down at her with a wicked smile, her matted blond curls swinging with each smug shake of her head. "I'm calling in our bargain, Raven. That baby is mine."

COLIN FLEW TO THE TOMB WHEN HE HEARD AVERY AND Clarissa scream. Gabriel, Nathaniel, and Xavier arrived behind him to total chaos. Clarissa's voice was reverberating around them, a living thing that swept his sides and seemed to dig into the earth itself.

"They're gone!" Avery yelled, her sword in hand. She circled, pointing its sharp tip at the air around her.

"Who's gone?" Colin looked into the gaping mouth of the dragon. Surely Raven, Charlie, and Leena would emerge at any moment.

Clarissa stopped singing, her eyes wild with panic. "Nothing is here. No one is here," she babbled.

Gabriel swept into the sculpture's mouth and emerged as panicked as Clarissa. "Her scent ends here, but she's gone."

For the first time, Colin engaged his own senses, a chill icing his blood when he caught Leena's fading sent. "What happened?"

Avery sheathed her sword, her gaze finding the safety of Xavier's before she answered. "Raven found the book. She came out with the golden grimoire in her arms. As soon as I handed her the baby, she started to... to fade. It was like she was fading out of existence. And then Leena..."

"What happened to Leena?" Colin's voice dropped two octaves, his dragon raging inside him.

"She leaped onto Raven. Wrapped her arms and legs around her and the baby," Clarissa said. "I think Leena was trying to stop it, but whatever took Raven took her with it."

Colin's wings punched out, his blood surging in his veins. His gaze darted around the sculpture. "Nathaniel, what type of magic is responsible for this? Are they invisible or gone?"

Nathaniel packed a new bit of tobacco and fired it up. He inhaled deeply and blew a puff of purple smoke over the area in front of the sculpture. Colors flashed, and then symbols Colin didn't know formed in the air. "Gone," Nathaniel said. "This reeks of Mother and her blood magic. My smoke is picking up her unique signature but also something else, something...odd."

"What do you see, Nathaniel?" Gabriel growled, ready to come out of his skin.

Nathaniel looked toward Gabriel. "It's voodoo."

Colin's stomach turned as Gabriel stopped breathing and collapsed to his knees. The pain he was feeling from Leena's loss must be a shadow of Gabriel's pain. A mate and a child—no wonder his brother looked like someone was peeling his scales off his body one by one.

"We have to get them back. Eleanor's been after Charlie from the start. She wants her dead." Gabriel's beast seethed, his skin bubbling with his need to shift and his eyes glowing green with rage. His older brother dug his fingers in the dirt, his eyes burning.

Colin felt it too. His dragon burned with the need to get Leena back. His heart pounded relentlessly, and his skin felt too tight. His wings arched over his shoulders with his rage. He'd gut his mother with his own talons if she hurt a single hair on Leena's head.

Through the panic and the pain, a voice like silver bells rang through Colin's head. *You'll help me find the grimoire, won't you?* Queen Penelope would do anything to get that book. The Defenders of the Goddess had three kingdoms ready to go to war.

"We're going to get them back," he said. He was the

leader of the resistance. All he had to do was pull the trigger.

Gabriel, Xavier, and the witches stared at him expectantly.

"How?" Avery asked.

"We go to war with Paragon. *Now.*"

CHAPTER TWENTY-THREE

"You stay away from her!" Raven screamed at Crimson. She clawed forward on the obsidian, scrambling to get her feet under her.

Crimson reached for Charlie, but her hands never connected with the child. Her body buckled in half as if something hard socked her in the stomach. The witch crumpled to the floor. Raven found the source of the blow in Leena, who was sneering at Crimson, her arms holding an invisible bow and arrow.

From the shadows, magic pulsed. Leena went flying, her back slapping the far wall hard enough that when she dropped to the floor, she didn't get back up. Bright-red blood darkened her temple.

"Leena!" Raven cried.

Like something out of Raven's darkest nightmares, Empress Eleanor stepped from the shadows and hovered over Crimson's fallen body. She reached into Crimson's gut, her hand passing right through her skin and bones, and withdrew whatever poison Leena had rooted there. The black veins that had branched out across Crimson's flesh followed as if Eleanor had plucked them out, a weed by the roots. Leena's poison arrow sizzled away in the palm of the empress's bony hand.

Eleanor turned her full attention on Raven, pointing a long nail at Crimson, who was brushing off the remnants of elf magic from her torso, her teeth bared. "You forged a witch's contract with this woman for your firstborn. She's calling it in."

Raven reached her arms out for Charlie. Crimson stepped between them and lifted the baby from the cold obsidian. Her little girl looked scared and confused in the stranger's arms and started to wail.

"Put her down. You're scaring her!"

"She's mine now, Raven. We had an agreement."

Raven's mind couldn't fathom what was happening. Crimson was here? Alive? All she could manage through the thickening lump in her throat was "How?"

Eleanor grinned. "You of all people should know that sometimes the dead don't stay dead, Raven. After all, as I understand it, you resurrected my son once."

Behind Eleanor, a peregrine falcon perched on the back of her throne and flapped its wings.

"You had it follow me to Earth?" Raven started putting it together. She'd seen that same bird in the tree on the beach in Aeaea and its silhouette outside the window at Blakemore's. Eleanor must have used the falcon to learn about Crimson and then resurrected her with dark magic.

Raven's heart pounded, panic gripping her. She reached for the first spell that came to mind. Forming a triangle with her fingers, she twisted it to the right and uttered, "*Diaíresi.*" The spell, meant to shred Eleanor, dissipated with a wave of the empress's hand. Another fling of Eleanor's wrist and Raven was bound in yellow lightning. She'd grown stronger. Much stronger. They were doomed.

The empress stared down her nose at her. "Give it up, Raven. Your heart rate is much too high, and you are far too unfocused to manage even a basic spell. And now I have this." She bent down and picked up the golden grimoire. "Ransom!"

The captain of the guard manifested in the room, panting, hair matted in sweat. Wings spread, he gripped a sword in both hands. He sounded exasperated when he said, "Empress, Rogos and Darnuith have attacked. They've crossed the border into Hobble Glen! The Obsidian Guard is on the defensive. You must put me back."

"Never mind that, Ransom. Once I use this child's blood to complete my spell, I will turn them all to dust. Take these two to the dungeon."

There was nothing Raven could do but scream as Ransom cuffed her and dragged her and an unconscious Leena away.

RAVEN HATED THE OBSIDIAN DUNGEON. SHE'D SPENT weeks here once, a pawn in Eleanor's scheme to bring Gabriel into her twisted plan. The empress hadn't succeeded, and Raven had sworn she'd never set foot here again. Yet here she was, and despite being exponentially more powerful than before, whatever enchantment was in the walls of this particular cell was strong enough to leave her magically impotent while Crimson held her baby upstairs.

She sat beside Leena's unconscious body and cried, wept with the sort of despair she'd never felt before, not even when she was dying of cancer. This was far worse. Eleanor had the book, Crimson had Charlie, and the empress was going to win.

"Ow." Leena woke and rubbed the back of her head. "Goddess, that woman is a demon in dragon skin."

"You're far more polite than I am."

Leena looked her over and frowned. "She has Charlie, doesn't she?"

"And the book."

"Goddess help us." Leena looked around her, gaining her bearings. "And I thought last night was the worst thing that could happen to me."

"What happened last night?" Raven studied the scribe. She didn't know the woman well, but it was certainly valiant what she'd done to try to help her. When Leena didn't answer her question, she said, "Thank you for trying to save me. It was brave of you, both when you tried to keep me in Rogos with your physical body and when you shot Crimson with your elfin magic the way you did."

Leena shrugged. "I go where the scroll goes." She flashed a weak smile.

Raven pointed to the satchel on her hip. "You had the scroll."

"So I did. I guess I must have been brave, then. Brave or crazy."

"I'm leaning toward crazy."

Leena looked down at the bag that held Medea's scroll on her hip. She started to laugh. "Wait... They threw us in here but left me my satchel? They locked us in the Obsidian Dungeon but didn't take my bag?"

Raven wiped under her eyes and nodded. "The dragon who brought us down here was in quite a hurry. It seems Rogos and Darnuith have attacked. He was anxious to get back to the battle."

A laugh bubbled up Leena's throat, this one stronger than before. "What an idiot."

"There's no way out. The walls drain your magic." Raven shook her head. "I doubt anything written in your scrolls is going to help us now."

"Oh, we're getting out," Leena said through a smile. She started digging in her bag. "And not because of anything written in these scrolls."

The scribe was clearly in denial. Raven's throat felt thick as she said, "I can't do the simplest of spells. We're stuck. We're going to die in here."

"No..." Leena shot her a look like she was positively offended. "We're not. Stupid dragons." She pulled out one of her metalwork quills and started taking it apart. Magic ink spilled on the black stone floor.

"Leena, am I missing something? You seem far too happy about being locked in this dungeon." The scribe reached forward and plucked a metal button off Raven's jacket. "What are you doing?"

"Do you know anything about my people?" Leena asked. "Anything about elves?"

Raven frowned. "You're from Rogos. You worship the goddess the same as Paragonians. You record the history of Ouros. Oh, and you can shoot invisible arrows at your enemies, although I didn't actually know that until I saw you do it to Crimson."

Leena pulled a pin from her braid and a thin metal buckle from her bag. She gave Raven a giant smile. "Oh, come on, Raven, you know more than that. You walked into one of our masterpieces just today."

Her brows rose. "Oh, and you're excellent at working metal."

"We are creators. It's not a magical skill but a mechanical one. We are born able to build things—wonderful things. And with our magic, we can even animate such a thing. But we don't need magic to build. That skill, we are born with." Silver flashed between Leena's nimble fingers. "Dragons know nothing of elves. For centuries, they've ignored us, taken it for granted that we'd remain neutral. Eleanor hasn't spent any time learning about us or our strengths. If she had, she never would have locked an elf inside a dungeon with any tools at all."

Raven gaped as Leena finished her bending and held up a rudimentary skeleton key. The scribe stood, walked to the bars, and jiggled her creation into the lock.

"Few adjustments." She pulled it out and bent a few silver parts, then slipped it into the lock again.

The mechanism clicked, and the door swung open.

"Holy shit." Raven gaped. "You're incredible."

Leena took an elaborate bow.

Scrambling to her feet, Raven retrieved Leena's bag from the floor and held it out to her as she passed out of the cell. By the time they reached the door that led to the stairwell, her magic had come back to her, burning hot and ready in her torso. Leena used her key to unlock the dungeon. There was no guard. Likely every soldier had been called into battle.

"Do you still think we're going to die?" Leena asked her, looking up the stairs and no doubt remembering the two nightmarish women who'd brought them here.

Raven shook her head, dark thoughts brewing inside her. "Oh no. We're not going to die. They are." She grabbed Leena by the arm, twisted into a column of smoke, and blew through the palace, a dark wind hell-bent on getting her daughter back.

CHAPTER TWENTY-FOUR

It was time to kill the Mountain.

Eleanor opened the golden grimoire on her ritual table, the book's celestial energy pulsing against her fingertips. Everything she'd ever wanted, the power that had lingered just beyond her reach for so long, would be hers with the right spell. Light radiated from the pages, poured over her, buzzed against her skin. It was no surprise Hera wanted this. The book was the most potent magical object she'd ever encountered.

"Show me how to kill the goddess of the mountain," she ordered the tome.

The pages flipped, increasing in speed until they came to the spell she desired. The parchment settled with a gust of wind that blew back her hair and then dusted across her fingers, fading with the light.

The grimoire was written in the language of the gods, but with a twist of her ring and a practiced translation spell, the symbols arranged themselves into something she could read. "It's easier than I thought. We spill the child's blood over the heir's heart and direct the reaction into the Mountain like a celestial spear. It will open up a channel where I can absorb the goddess's power and leave her with none. She won't actually be dead, sadly, but drained to the point she cannot wake. And with her power, I will ascend."

Crimson shot her a look. "How will you get Gabriel's heart?"

"I don't need Gabriel's heart. I have Marius's." She palmed the giant diamond. She'd resurrected the witch only hours ago, and under better circumstances, Eleanor would have had time to rest before performing this spell. But there was no time. Even now, she could hear the barbarians at the gate, pounding on the wards around the palace with nothing but her destruction on their minds.

The blond witch scoffed. "I'm not familiar with your magic, but in my world, the heart has to be fresh. There's no magic in a dead heart."

Eleanor lifted a corner of her mouth. She was glad to have this woman here to appreciate the genius of what she was about to do. No one really understood her. No one appreciated the power she'd so artfully cultivated. Maybe this resurrected human witch would.

"Ah, but this heart isn't dead." She held up the diamond between her talons. "See the silver flame inside the facets? It's his soul. I've enchanted it to stay right where it is. More powerful that way. I can reuse it again and again. It's how I resurrected you. That and a child's blood."

Crimson whistled. "That's a dark bit of magic." She poked her tongue into her cheek. The smile she shot her next was too big. It showed all her teeth and even more of her ambition. Yes, this woman did understand. "That's why I wanted Raven and Gabriel's brat. I knew I could use it to make myself immortal."

Eleanor snarled. "And it will. Once I use the child's

blood to kill the goddess, you can have what's left of her to extend your otherwise short human life. I won't have use for the babe after this." A blast shook the mountain, and she staggered forward, pulling the diamond closer to her chest.

"What the fuck was that?" Crimson clutched at her bodice.

Another blast rumbled in the distance. Eleanor frowned. "Darnuith and Rogos. If they haven't made it through the wards yet, they will soon." Her gaze cast to the window. "And when the suns set, Nochtbend and its vampires will be joining the party."

"Vampires?" Crimson's brow rose in intrigue.

"Bring the babe," Eleanor commanded. "We must hurry."

Crimson unlocked the iron cage where they'd shoved the screaming child after they'd rid themselves of her mother. But when Crimson reached inside for her, Charlie snapped.

"Ouch! The little shit bit me!" She yanked her hands back, and Eleanor growled as the child fluttered its strange, feathery wings and flew to the highest shelf in her ritual room. Charlie grinned down from above, her cherubic face framed in flaxen curls.

"Come here, child," Eleanor said in her sweetest tone. She motioned with her hand.

Charlie kicked her feet over the side of the shelf and giggled.

"Retrieve her now," Eleanor demanded of Crimson.

The blond sorceress scoffed. "The contract allowed me to call her to me once. Now that she's mine, I have no more control than you." She glanced at the bite on her hand. "Besides, I'm injured, and you're the one with all the power."

Eleanor sneered. The bite was jagged and bleeding. She couldn't underestimate the spawn of a witch and a dragon. This was no helpless child. Eleanor whirled as another blast shook the palace. She didn't have time for this.

Thumbing her ring, she drew a symbol in the air. Power snapped out, a yellow lasso of lightning that snagged the whelp. The babe's head whipped back as Eleanor yanked her off the shelf. Charlie wailed and dropped. Eleanor caught her, the empress's talons digging into the babe's soft skin. Charlie screamed in pain.

"Hmm. Not the hide of a dragon. Soft. Easy to bleed. That's convenient." Ignoring Charlie's cries, Eleanor wrangled the thrashing child into her pentagram. She placed Marius's heart on the floor at the center of the symbol and braced the babe over her knee with a firm hand, then extended one talon toward her throat.

"Take your hands off my daughter!"

Eleanor had a split second to recognize Raven, and then a blast of pure power knocked her out of the symbol and into the shelves at the head of her ritual room. Magical objects rained down upon her head, the shelves cracking and splitting. From the darkened pile of rubble, Eleanor watched the skeleton of a baby dragon she'd kept on the highest shelf tip forward and back on its perch before giving way.

The last thing she saw before the lights went out was its skull dropping toward her.

RAVEN CAUGHT CHARLIE IN HER ARMS, ONE EYE trained on the rubble. Eleanor wasn't dead. There was no way that was enough to kill a dragon. But the pile of debris didn't move.

"Where's Crimson?" Leena asked from behind her.

Raven's eyes searched the room, ice forming in her stomach when she couldn't find the other witch. A dark cloud manifested behind the scribe. The elf screamed. Crimson pressed a curved blade to Leena's throat and leveled her gaze on Raven. "Hand over the kid or your friend dies, little witch."

Crimson's knife pressed into Leena's neck, drawing a bead of blood that trickled along the edge. The hate Raven felt for the former mambo was all-consuming. She clutched Charlie to her, knowing that as long as Crimson lived, Charlie was technically hers. She'd agreed to it. She'd shaken the witch's hand and sealed the contract before she ever knew she could conceive, when she'd thought that after years of chemotherapy, she was barren.

That was before she respected the boundaries of magic.

Leena blinked wide, fearful eyes at her. She was a scribe. She was supposed to record what happened in this world, not participate in it, and here she was with a knife pressed to her throat. Raven clenched her teeth. She'd have to kill Crimson. Nothing less would break the contract. Raven wasn't a murderer, but she already knew she could do it. She *would* do it.

"Give me the babe or she dies," Crimson said again. She pointed her chin toward the pile of shelving, books, and magical accoutrements that buried Eleanor. "She might not be able to use her anymore, but I certainly can."

"She has a name, Crimson. It's Charlie. She's a person!" Raven wasn't trying to convince the evil woman, just buy time while she considered what to do. She had an almost limitless arsenal of spells at her disposal, but Eleanor was right before—she couldn't wield any spell properly when her heart was galloping and her every instinct kept her clinging to her daughter.

Crimson scoffed. "I don't care what she is, sweetheart. I only care that she has a heart in her chest that can make me immortal."

Raven kissed her daughter's cheek. She couldn't hand her over. Wouldn't.

"No," Leena whispered. "Don't you even think about it, Raven."

"Shut up, bitch." Crimson dug the blade deeper into her skin. Raven watched more blood bubble where the blade bit in.

Something warm and wet dripped on Raven's fingers. She pulled her hand away from Charlie and stared at the bright red staining them in confusion. How was Leena's blood on her fingers? No, this was Charlie's blood. She saw it now, red oozing from her back to stain her beautiful white feathers. Charlie whimpered in her arms.

"Now, Raven!" Crimson said.

"She's hurt. I have to heal her, or she'll be no good to you." It was a lie. Likely Charlie's injury wouldn't have an effect on Crimson's spell at all, but it was a perfect excuse to delay handing her over. "It's going to be okay," Raven whispered, as much to herself as to the baby. With a soft incantation under her breath, her hands began to glow, and she pressed them to Charlie's wounds. "Mommy's going to make it better."

"You're testing my patience, Raven. I don't care about the blood," Crimson said through her teeth.

The wounds stitched themselves together, her daughter's whimpers becoming less intense and then subsiding. By the time the wound was a pale pink, Charlie cuddled into the side of Raven's neck, wiping her wet cheeks on her shirt.

Leena's mouth gaped like a fish. "Raven, the blood—"

Whatever she was trying to say was cut off by Crimson's digging blade. The scribe tucked in her chin, more blood carving a trail from her neck, flowing faster between her breasts, staining her robes. Raven couldn't allow Leena to die for her mistake. She'd get Charlie back. Somehow...

"Enough! Do it now!" Crimson reached for her.

Throat thick, Raven shifted Charlie in her arms and then handed her over.

CHAPTER TWENTY-FIVE

Colin stabbed a sword through the heart of the dragon in front of him, then landed a foot in his gut and kicked him off his blade. The soldier crumpled at his feet. He moved on to the next, punching and slashing, careful not to decapitate them if he could avoid it. These guards were practically children. Eleanor and Ransom had recruited younger and younger dragons into the Obsidian Guard to replace older men who were too wise to continue serving. He doubted most even understood what they were fighting for. He would do everything in his power to avoid killing them.

Beside him, Xavier and Gabriel plowed through the soldiers like machines. The three had slipped through the wards at the gate using a seal of the palace—a magical talisman that Sylas had stolen off one of the guardsman's horses when he and Dianthe had rescued Aborella. It only worked on the gate, a small area near the guardhouse where riders needed it to file in and out of the palace. The seal allowed only one rebel warrior through at a time, but it was a foothold. That was all they needed.

Above him, Nathaniel was using that magic smoke of his to unlock the heavier wards that rose like a dome over the palace. Dozens of witches hovered in the sky behind his brother, waiting in formation for the wards to drop. Wands glowing like stars in the full light of day, their black robes flowed over the backs of their brooms and their lips mumbled spells Colin could not hear. It was an intimidating sight, and he was instantly glad Darnuith was on their side.

If Nathaniel succeeded in opening a small passageway, not only could the witches mount an aerial attack, they could use their magic to unravel the rest of the wards like a knitted sweater with a loose string. Already their dark power pounded warning blows, loud enough he was sure Eleanor could hear them inside.

If the witch army successfully breached the wards, he'd readied the elves to complete the second wave. The tears of the goddess were fused to their arrows in stone capsules, enough to strike fear in any dragon. In fact, Hobble Glen had fallen as soon as the first arrow burned through a dragon in the street. They'd all surrendered, even the Highborns, or locked themselves away in their houses.

And that was before the animus arrived. Rogos had constructed ten giants out of metal and animated them with elven magic. One faceless mass of gears and metal had followed him through the gate and was beating back the Obsidian guards with a massive club.

The uprising was happening all over Ouros. Sylas and Dianthe were leading a battalion of fairies against Paragon sympathizers in Everfield. Sabrina and Tobias were waiting for the suns to set in Nochtbend to lead the vampires into the fray.

"Colin! To yer left!" Xavier cried.

He blocked a strike with his sword, then collided with a

dragon half his age and snapped his neck in two breaths. The boy's body dropped like a stone. *Fuck.* Did that soldier even try?

"They're through," Gabriel called as witches swarmed over them like dark locusts. "I'm going after Raven."

Once Gabriel waved Nathaniel forward, together they soared to the veranda and into the palace. Through a spray of blood and clashing metal, Colin noted that one guardsman paused to take notice and then pulled a Paragonian grenade from his belt.

Ransom. Colin dove forward as the grenade left his hand. He had to stop it from reaching Gabriel. He was too far away, but if he threw his weapon...

Magic rattled down his body. He'd stopped the grenade from reaching Gabriel and Nathaniel, but it had detonated when his sword had collided with it. Colin landed on his back on the ground, his muscles twitching.

Ransom swaggered to his side, a shit-eating grin on his face. He flicked Colin's fallen sword away with the toe of his boot. "You won't be needing that."

Colin couldn't see where he'd kicked the weapon, couldn't turn his head, but considering Ransom's dragon strength, it was likely clear across the field of battle. That's what he'd have done if things were reversed. How he wished things were reversed.

Paragonian grenades scrambled the nervous system. Colin's breath halted in his throat, and his eyelids froze open. He was completely at the younger dragon's mercy.

Sneering down at him, Ransom delivered a kick to his side. Bones crunched. Pain rocketed through him. "Fucking brat. Why couldn't you just fall in line?"

So, this is how it ends, Colin thought, surprised his mind was clear despite his body disobeying his every command.

Ransom lifted his sword, his aim focused on Colin's neck. There would be no mercy from the captain of the guard.

The strangest part was that Colin was ready. Maybe it was even a blessing, considering he was a dragon rejected by his mate. His only regret was that he would not be the one to save Leena. He'd have to leave her protection to Gabriel. It would be all right if his blood spilled out on this field. An honorable death.

Metal flashed behind Ransom, and if Colin could have smiled, he would have. The massive club of a faceless metal machine, an animus from Rogos, connected with Ransom's gut. Colin heard an "oomph" escape Ransom's lungs, and then the captain and his sword went flying.

Unable to move, Colin watched as the metal giant stepped right over him. The whir and clank of working gears filling his ears for one tense moment, and then the machine was gone

Gaaaasp. Air filled his lungs in a rush. The effects of the grenade were finally wearing off. He rolled over, got to his feet, and assessed his surroundings. The good news was the animus had cleared the general vicinity of any would-be attackers. The bad news was, as he'd expected, his sword was gone, and Ransom had recovered from the blow and was flying into the veranda, no doubt going after Gabriel and Nathaniel.

Colin's wings snapped out, and he took to the sky, putting every ounce of his significant weight behind his forward momentum. He became a freight train, or as powerful as one anyway, and slammed Ransom from behind. Their bodies tumbled over the shattered mosaic on the veranda and crashed through the doors to the great mountain hall, sending wood and stone flying.

"You and the others will never succeed," Ransom said.

Colin was relieved to see the other male had lost his sword when the animus hit him, but dragons didn't need weapons to be deadly.

Ransom's wings snapped out, their terrible hooked claws high above his shoulders, ready to draw blood. "You have no idea how powerful she is."

"And you overestimate her," Colin snapped. "Look at the palace grounds! Half of Paragon is attacking the other half. Rogos and Darnuith are closing in. If the elves and witches don't secure this palace before nightfall, Nocht-bend will be at your door. We are winning this war."

Dark thoughts transformed Ransom's normally hand-some features into something truly ugly. "Eleanor will turn you all to dust."

"I don't want to have to kill you, Ransom," Colin said, sinking into a fighting stance. "She's used you. She's got her hooks in you still. But if you surrender now, I promise you I'll do my best to give you a chance at a better life. You'll have a fair trial. You might have a future."

He scoffed. "I have no future without Eleanor." The way he said it held a note of darkness, as if he were some kind of windup toy that only Eleanor could crank.

"What have you done to yourself?" Colin mumbled.

Through bared teeth, the younger dragon hissed. "Made myself into something that can kill you."

He attacked head on, those talons at the highpoint of his wings locking on to Colin's. Ransom connected with his right. Colin kneed him in the gut and tore through the other dragon's chest, drawing blood. He blocked Ransom's coun-terattack.

Ransom was younger and faster, but he'd had less expe-rience in the pits. Which was why Colin was surprised when the dragon landed a stabbing blow in Colin's side.

Colin buckled but managed to stagger back, tearing Ransom's talons from his flesh and putting space between them.

"Surprising, isn't it?" Ransom laughed. "You and your brothers always underestimated me. Do you even remember fighting me in the pits? All of us were forced to lose to you pampered idiots. Not anymore. She's made me faster. Made me stronger. She'll make me king."

Colin laughed, dodging Ransom's blows to give the wound in his side time to heal. He didn't remember Ransom from back then, but those years in the pits had been a blur of bloody noses, blackened eyes, and broken bones. Still, it was clear that Ransom remembered Colin, and maybe that was the key.

"Sure, I remember you. You were the one with the tiny dick," Colin said through a sneer.

"Big enough to fuck your mother." Ransom hissed and attacked.

Colin faked a punch, dropped like a rock, and delivered a cross jab, talons sprouting from his knuckles. He sliced under Ransom's ribs and used the dragon's momentum to throw him over his head. Ransom somersaulted, his blood spilling on the obsidian.

Ransom didn't wait for his wound to heal as Colin had but attacked immediately. Rookie mistake. Colin took advantage of the younger dragon's instincts to guard the wound, blocking his uppercut and connecting with an elbow under Ransom's chin. Using his wings to lever his body, Colin brought both fists down on the back of Ransom's neck like a hammer, eliciting a curse from the younger dragon.

Ransom skidded on his stomach along the obsidian, his path lubricated with his own blood.

"Seems like Mummy forgot to give you advanced healing abilities along with the speed and strength. You're good, Ransom, but dumb. Just like you always were. All those years you cursed having to lose to us, you never stopped to think that we were victims of the same system that held you in your place. And now you're fighting to keep things exactly how you hated them." Colin stepped closer, just out of reach, expecting the next blow.

Ransom's eyes were wild. He stumbled onto his feet and turned a seething growl on Colin. The wound on his side was almost healed. If he waited a moment longer—

"I'm going to enjoy ripping your head from your shoulders." Ransom surged forward, teeth gnashing and talons out. Colin had to hand it to the boy—he was faster and stronger than any dragon Colin had ever faced. But it was true what they said: the bigger they are, the harder they fall. With a thrust of his wings, Colin jumped.

Ransom had poured all his strength into his forward momentum and sacrificed his agility in the process. He couldn't adjust in time to stop Colin from leaping over him. By the time he used his wings to change direction, Colin was already there, grabbing him by the throat and slamming his head into the stone with everything he had in him.

Ransom's skull cracked on the jagged remains of the mural. Blood flowed over the jeweled depiction of the dragon and dribbled into the hole Sylas had left when he'd pried the golden orb from its place in the picture.

Blood sprayed across Colin's cheek.

"If you kill me, she will punish you. And she'll bring me back. I'll watch you die screaming," Ransom said through his teeth.

"I'm not surprised you believe that." Colin's voice was

grit and embers, his dragon close to the surface. "But it's exactly why you're too dangerous to let live."

He sprouted talons in the hand around Ransom's throat, dug them into the back of his neck, and pulled, cleaving his skull from his spine with a sickening pop. Ransom's head rolled from his shoulders, and then his body exploded into dust under Colin's knee. His gray spinel heart clinked across the floor, skidding to a rest near the stone wall.

Colin rose and wiped his hands off on his shirt. Ransom's heart was cracked, black imperfections marring the jewel. How long had Eleanor been poisoning him to cause that kind of damage?

"You fucking idiot." He kicked the heart aside.

He raised his nose to the air. He had to find Leena. There. Her blackcurrant-and-wild-primrose scent came from the direction of the library. He changed course just in time to hear her scream.

CHAPTER TWENTY-SIX

R aven gritted her teeth and held Charlie out to Crimson, knowing she had no choice. If she didn't hand her over, not only would Crimson kill Leena, but she'd take Charlie anyway. Raven owed Crimson. A contract was a contract. And a magical contract could not be broken except by death.

A dark wind like an icy hurricane flowed through the room, knocking Charlie back into Raven's arms. Crimson was gone. Raven whirled to find Gabriel on top of the blond witch, his hands wrapped around her throat.

"Thank the goddess!"

The knife Crimson had held to Leena's throat now protruded from Gabriel's chest, but Raven wasn't worried. Nothing less than decapitation could truly kill a dragon. He'd heal from that wound within minutes.

"Gabriel," Raven pleaded.

He met her gaze. He knew what he had to do.

"Raven, I need your help. Leena's hurt," Nathaniel said.

When had he arrived? But then, he was the one who'd

have had to unlock the ward around this room. Gabriel could not.

It took Raven a second for what Nathaniel was saying to sink in. Leena staggered backward and collapsed. Blood poured from the wound at her neck. Crimson must have sliced her throat when Gabriel pulled her away. Raven clutched Charlie to her body and rushed to Leena's side, muttering the spell she'd used earlier on her daughter. She pressed her glowing hand to Leena's wound.

The blood slowed, but Leena was frightfully pale. Unlike Charlie, Leena wasn't half dragon. She was mortal. Fragile. She'd take longer to heal. Raven kept her glowing hand on the elf's wounds but glanced back toward Gabriel.

Crimson smiled wickedly up at him while his hands tightened around her neck. "I knew this was your fantasy," she said. "You always did want me under you."

Raven's stomach turned at the thought. The mambo had always wanted Gabriel. She'd never been able to take no for an answer. It's what had started all this.

Gabriel smiled at Crimson in a way that chilled Raven to the bone. It was like the man had melted away and there was nothing left but dragon. Fire burned in his eyes—dark, murderous, and merciless.

"Eat your heart out," Gabriel growled. He released her neck and stabbed his talons through her rib cage. Crimson's mouth opened in a silent scream. Gabriel's hand twisted, and Raven could picture his talons shredding whatever dark material throbbed where a human's heart should be. She wasn't sure Crimson actually had one.

The light faded from Crimson's eyes, and Raven knew that she was, at last, dead. She hugged Charlie tighter and hissed out a breath. She turned back to Leena. The bleeding had stopped, but the scribe was unconscious, barely breathing.

"I can try to revive her, but my tobacco isn't designed for elf anatomy," Nathaniel said.

"What happened to her?" Colin stumbled into the room, covered in blood, and darted to Leena's side.

"What happened to *you*?" Raven asked.

Colin cradled Leena in his arms. "Ransom is dead. What's wrong with her?"

"She's lost a lot of blood." Raven turned worried eyes back to the elf. "I healed her wound, but she's going to be weak until she replaces what she lost."

The growl that emanated from Colin's throat had Gabriel across the room and between them in the blink of an eye. He held his hand out toward Raven, and she took a step back from where Colin held Leena. Raven had no idea what was going on, but it was clear Gabriel suddenly saw Colin as a threat.

"When?" Gabriel asked his brother.

Colin cradled the scribe to his chest, looking like his heart was being ripped out through his fingernails. "Last night."

"When, *what*?" Raven asked.

Gabriel didn't have a chance to answer. Something crashed across the room—the collapsed shelves—and Eleanor stood in the center of the symbol painted on the floor of her ritual room, Marius's heart in her hand.

"You and I are more alike than you'd care to admit, Gabriel," the empress said, eyeing Crimson's body.

When had she revived? When had she picked up the diamond? She smeared blood from her talons onto the gem. Raven stopped breathing. That was Charlie's blood!

"*Kaló*," Raven yelled.

Marius's heart shot out of Eleanor's hand and landed in her own.

"Too late," Eleanor said. "It is done."

Wind swirled. Glass shattered, toppled from the few remaining shelves in the gusts. A thin column of blinding light shot up through the center of the symbol, a giant glowing spear. The empress grabbed it in both hands, tendrils of her dark hair twisting in the building magic.

"No!" Raven screamed.

Eleanor grasped and lifted the light, then thrust it through the floor toward the heart of the mountain with such force it made her grunt.

Sparks flew up from around the circle, fireworks that stank of brimstone. And then something else was there. Someone ancient and blond in a toga that seemed to give off its own light.

"Hera!" Eleanor dropped to her knees.

All was lost. If the queen of the gods was standing in Paragon, the goddess of the mountain was truly dead, and Zeus's promised protection gone with her. Raven's heart squinched into a tight ball of dread. How could she fix this? Was this even fixable?

Hera snatched the golden grimoire from the place Eleanor had left it on her workbench, her lips twisting into a wicked, vengeful smile. "It is done," she boomed. "Rise, Eleanor, goddess of the mountain."

Raven stumbled back into Gabriel's arms as Hera disappeared with the book and Eleanor transformed, growing in size from just under six feet to seven to eight to twelve. Raven cursed. She steadied her breath. Eleanor was goddess of the mountain? They were all doomed.

Marius's heart winked in her hand, it's internal light flickering as power surged through the room. The diamond was still smudged with Charlie's blood. Raven's brows lifted. Eleanor may be a goddess, but she'd just proved a goddess could be killed.

"Bow before your new goddess of the mountain," Eleanor boomed. A lightning bolt formed in her hand, her sneer betraying her intention to destroy them all.

"Fuck the hell off, bitch!" Raven circled her hand over her head, and everything turned to black smoke.

Her next breath, she landed on her knees in front of a giant mural of Aitna, the true goddess of the mountain. Gabriel landed on his back beside her. Colin tumbled onto the cave floor with Leena still unconscious in his arms.

Nathaniel landed on his feet and smoothed the front of his tunic. "That was unpleasant."

"Why have you brought us to the cradle?" Gabriel asked.

"Because this is where we undo the spell Eleanor just did. This is where we resurrect Aitna."

"But the grimoire is gone. Hera took it."

Tapping her temple, she met his gaze, allowing the ancient Greek characters to glow through her skin. "I absorbed it, all the spells, before Eleanor took us from the crypt. I have a copy of the golden grimoire... inside me."

❧

ELEANOR HISSED WHEN RAVEN AND THE OTHERS disappeared just as her lightning bolt electrocuted the room. She stepped out of the symbol on bare feet, her dress torn from her increased size, and frowned at the remains of Crimson Vanderholt. She'd make them pay. Before the twin suns set on Paragon, she'd send Raven to Hades after the other woman.

The mountain shook, chunks of stone raining down from above her. Wherever Raven had gone to hide, she'd have to wait. Right now, Eleanor had to finish what her armies had started. In a rage, she raced to the veranda overlooking Paragon.

She drew up short when she saw the blood that stained the mural. A thick layer of ash swirled in the wind around her ankles and across the shiny obsidian. Ransom's scent was undeniable. There, in the shadows, his heart winked at her in the dying twilight. She growled and gnashed her teeth as she swept it from the floor, but there was no light inside this heart. She had not prepared Ransom for death like she had Marius, Brynhoff, and Killian. His soul was gone, moved on to wherever dragons went after they died. Even as the goddess, that place was unknown to her.

Fury seized her, and she crushed his gray heart in her hand and tossed the shards aside. The hate flowed through her like never before. Now it was a goddess's rage. A mountain's rage.

They would pay. They would all pay.

Stepping to the edge of the veranda, she looked out upon the battle. The skies of Paragon were darkened with witches. Her dragon army fought them valiantly, but they were outnumbered. She watched an orange dragon rain fire down upon a witch, who blocked the attack with a shielding spell. Below her, dragons burned and writhed, elven arrows, slick with Aitna's tears, sizzling in their flesh.

And then there were her children. She spotted Sylas first. His garnet scales flashed as he tore through her aerial legion with practiced intensity. Rowan, no princess in battle, fought mercilessly by his side. On the ground, Eleanor spotted Alexander wielding a sword as if he were born with it in his hands, Tobias backing him up.

The suns inched below the horizon, and she could hear them coming. The vampires of Nochtbend surged across the river. Her guard would never survive. Already the enemy was too close to her door.

A growl rumbled deep within her, her inner dragon feeding on her new magic. But how to wield it? Lightning wasn't enough. A single spell wasn't enough. She needed a way to end this now, to save her dragons and only her dragons.

And then she realized she was now the goddess of the mountain. She *was* the mountain. Her lips twitched into a dark and deadly smile. There was one thing that dragons were impervious to that all other creatures of Ouros feared.

Fire.

She raised her hands, tapping into the pure power at the heart of this mountain. The earth quaked. A mighty rumble echoed across the palace grounds.

Witches stopped in the sky, staring openmouthed from their brooms. The elf captains took one look in her direction and screamed, "Retreat!"

"Burn, baby, burn!" Her voice boomed as only a goddess's could.

The rumbling grew more intense, and then the volcano erupted. Molten rock spewed into the sky, raining hellfire from the palace all the way to Hobble Glen. Lava flowed like blood.

A chorus of screams filled the night.

She laughed as witches fell burning from their brooms. Elves and their animuses were swallowed in liquid magma. Arms spread wide, she grinned at the blood, the gore, the glory.

"On your knees! Worship your new Goddess of the Mountain!"

CHAPTER TWENTY-SEVEN

L eena opened her eyes to the world crumbling around her. Colin was there, holding her, and he looked worried.

"I have it!" Nathaniel yelled.

She couldn't see what he had or what he was doing, but his and Raven's anxious murmurs filled the air. She was in a cave, some strange stone chamber that was so hot she thought her skin would peel from her flesh.

"What's going on?" she asked Colin. Her head throbbed. So hot.

"Leena, I want to give you my bond. I know you won't mate with me, but if you take my tooth—"

"Why? What's happening?" She tried to sit up, but she was too weak.

"We're in the palace, in a place we call the cradle," Colin said. "This is where the queen normally incubates her eggs. Raven says she knows a spell to resurrect the goddess of the mountain so that she can fight Eleanor, but the volcano is erupting. Nathaniel and Raven have used magic to protect us, but neither knows how long it will last.

It's not safe for you here, and I can't get you out. All I can do is give you my tooth. I can give you immortality."

"Your bond." She had to yell over the rumble of the mountain.

"Nothing will change." His eyes searched hers. "I don't expect you to honor the mating bond."

"You don't expect me to honor it, but it will exist," she said, picking up on the nuance in his choice of words.

He held her gaze. "It already does for me, Leena. It's not something I can control. I think my dragon claimed you after that first kiss. But that doesn't mean you have to reciprocate. You have your life, your obligations. I understand."

Leena closed her eyes, tried to find that centering force inside herself she used when she gazed into the tears of the goddess. She wanted a vision, a sign, something to tell her what to do. So she prayed... until something occurred to her. "The goddess is dead?"

Colin blinked. "Yes. But Raven is going to resurrect her."

The goddess was *dead*. She'd almost prayed to a being that was no more.

Leena took a moment to wrap her mind around that truth. Her entire life as a scribe had been lived in worship of a celestial being who was ...gone. Immortals, it seemed, didn't always live forever. What did that mean for her? Her vow? Was she bound to a being who no longer existed? If Raven succeeded in bringing the goddess back, would she be bound again?

She swallowed hard before speaking. "Upstairs, when Crimson had her knife to my throat and I thought I would die, I closed my eyes. I knew I should pray to the goddess to care for my soul. But there was only one face I could see, Colin. And it *wasn't* hers. When my life flashed before my eyes, all the scenes were of you. When I thought about what I'd regret—" Tears trailed down her cheeks.

"You regret our night together?"

She shook her head. "I regretted that there was only one night. All the scrolls I've written, all the years I spent recording what happened to other people, I wouldn't miss any of that. I didn't even think of it. I thought of you."

Colin's tentative smile twitched at the corners. The mountain rumbled again. Behind him, Raven was circling her wand. One by one, Colin's brothers and sisters appeared in the cave along with Avery and Clarissa. The witch was calling for Colin to join them. They needed him, which meant Leena had to make a decision. It was so hot. Her brain boiled in her skull, and her body ached.

"I won't hold you," Colin said again. "I just want to protect you."

"Give me your tooth." Leena met his gaze and raised her hand to his cheek. "And give me your bond."

His eyes widened until she could see the whites. "The vow I made died with the goddess. I want you, Colin. I want a life with you for as long as I have left." She didn't add that at the moment, that life was looking quite short.

He reached into his mouth and turned his head away from her. When he turned back, there was blood on his lip and a sharp, jagged tooth pinched between his fingers. He held it in his palm. His ring glowed red, his dragon magic transforming the tooth into a slender white pill. He offered it to her.

She picked it up, pausing for only a moment to appreciate it in the red glow of the cave, and then she swallowed it down. It seemed to wriggle in her throat, and when it hit her stomach, it radiated its magic through her core, her limbs. Immediately the heat became bearable, and the exhaustion she'd felt a moment before bled from her.

What was left in its place was an intense need for him, one she'd have to wait to act on.

"Colin, we need you," Gabriel called.

He pressed a soft kiss to her lips and helped her to her feet before joining his siblings. She watched him go, thinking that happily ever after couldn't start until they survived to see tomorrow.

RAVEN GESTURED TOWARD THE CRADLE. "EACH OF YOU stand in the crater where your egg would have been,"

Xavier tossed up his hands. "Are ye mad, woman? How in the name of Hades are we to know where our egg once was?"

But Rowan spread her wings in excitement. "I do! I know this! The queen always lays her eggs counterclockwise." She pointed to the first indentation to her left. "Starting there. See how it's more worn than the others? That's from centuries of use. This one looks relatively new, right?" She gestured to the end of the ring. "Mother probably had to make these last two. Nine eggs were unheard of."

The mountain rumbled around them, and Avery wavered on her feet. "Raven, the heat."

Raven looked at her sister. She was a sweaty mess, her shirt darkened down the front and at her pits. Her hair stuck to her head. Avery was the only one of them who couldn't take her mate's tooth—her magic neutralized it, which meant, for all intents and purposes, she was human.

"Fuck, hold on." With a wave of her wand and a whispered incantation, Raven made it snow. White flakes drifted over them as if they were sealed inside a snow globe.

"Thanks."

Her lips pressed flat. "I don't know how long it will last once we start the resurrection spell." She placed the bloody diamond she'd been holding in the first cradle.

Tobias's eyes locked on to it. "What is that, Raven?" His voice was low, solemn. He knew. On some level, she thought they all did.

"Marius. Eleanor spelled the heart to keep his soul trapped inside. As sick as it was, it's a good thing for us that she did. We need him for this spell."

Clarissa tightened her blond ponytail. "What now?"

Raven reached for her sisters' hands. "This is where we come in. Dragons were born in the mountain. Aitna made the first one from the fabric of the universe, and centuries later, Circe gave them the ability to transform. Eleanor has stolen Aitna's power. Aitna's dead, but she's not gone."

"So, what do we do?" Avery asked.

"We need to resuscitate her. The grimoire said this room is as close as we can come to Aitna's heart. We're going to draw power from the nine heirs and send it into Aitna. We're going to shock her back to life."

Tobias laughed. "Are you saying we're going to defibrillate the goddess?"

"More or less," Raven said.

The mountain rumbled again, and Sylas growled as chunks of stone bounced off the dome of Raven's magic, which was protecting them all. "Quickly, or things are going to get a lot more complicated."

Raven gave the dragon a sideways glance but ignored his comment. It was too much pressure. She couldn't think about what came next after the spell. Would they be able to escape? She shook it off.

Colin said what she was thinking. "Shut the fuck up, brother. She's doing her best."

Still, all the dragons got into position, standing in the divot that signified their birth order. Raven took a deep breath and blew it out slowly.

"Clarissa, this is what you need to sing." Raven copied the music from the grimoire—from her memory—into the dirt over the stone floor.

"Got it!" Clarissa positioned herself so she could see the music and studied the notes.

"Avery, I'm going to draw on your latent magic. Just hold our hands and don't fight the spell."

"Do nothing. My specialty." Avery saluted.

"What about Charlie?" Leena asked.

Raven had been so wrapped up in all the details of the spell she'd forgotten about her daughter, asleep in Gabriel's arms. She carefully pulled her out of her mate's grip and handed her to Leena. "Please hold the baby." She glanced at Marius's heart, still smeared with Charlie's blood. "We already have what we need from her."

Leena gave Raven a reassuring nod and cuddled the child to her shoulder.

Raven shot one last look toward Gabriel and his siblings standing in a ring in front of the giant mural of the goddess and the altar where Raven had once sacrificed her most beloved possession at the time, her emerald wedding ring. It was still there, she noted, as were the stilettos Rowan had left behind.

She took her sisters' hands. Immediately a charge rose in the room, crackling and snapping between them. She started muttering the incantation she'd read in the grimoire. Ancient Greek. The only reason she could read, understand, or pronounce it was her magic, this strange ability she had to absorb spells from the page and to understand magic immediately through touch. She repeated the words again and again. And then she nodded to Clarissa.

Her sister sang the notes drawn in the dirt. The music started off low, challenging her range, but then increased in pace and octave as it progressed.

"It's working," Leena said.

Raven hazarded a glance toward her mate and saw what Leena saw. The dragon siblings were glowing. Light shafted from floor to ceiling, illuminating the cavern like it was high noon in the desert. The pull of magic threatened to tear her in two. Her sisters must have felt it too, because Avery winced, and Clarissa took more frequent breaths as she continued her song.

They both squeezed her hands as another wave of magic blew out from them. Leena shielded Charlie's eyes and turned her head away from the increasing glow. Raven tried to check on Gabriel, tried to make sure he was weathering the spell, but the light was too bright. She had to look away.

And then it all became too much. Avery squeezed her hand. "Raven, I can't... I caaaan't!"

A loud crack accompanied an explosive force that blew them apart. Avery's and Clarissa's fingers slipped from hers. Her back slammed into hard stone, knocking her breath from her lungs. Something inside her crunched, and a sharp pain cut through her torso.

The torches around the cavern extinguished.

For a moment, she lay absolutely still, afraid to move, afraid to make the pain worse. Then the familiar tingle of

Gabriel's tooth kicked in. Its healing properties branched within her, carving out a path in her veins, invigorating her.

She grunted as she pushed herself up to sitting and blinked her eyes open. The cave had gone dark and eerily quiet. She couldn't see anything but the mural. Aitna's image glowed red, the light the painting was putting off illuminating the altar in front of her. A crack now ran down the middle, the two halves of the stone fallen to each side.

And the mural was changing, the wall behind it falling away. No, Raven realized, the image was moving forward, becoming three-dimensional, smoothing. She muffled a curse as her hand rose to her lips. Aitna stood before her, dressed in liquid fire, her dark hair flowing in a wind that wasn't there.

She looked straight at Raven with black, glittering eyes and said something in a language she didn't understand. Raven shook her head.

There was a pause, and then the goddess said in perfect English, "Who is responsible?"

It was clear to Raven by her tone she meant responsible for her death, not her resurrection. Raven lifted one hand and pointed up what used to be the stairs. She answered with one word and one word only. "Eleanor."

Aitna's black eyes roved upward. She bent her knees and leaped straight into the rock. And then she was gone and so was the light.

Raven blinked away the spots swimming in her vision from the quick change in illumination. A groan came from her right. She pulled her wand from her sleeve and ignited the tip, casting light across the cavern. She pointed it at the nearest torch. *"Fotiá."* Flames ignited within.

"Fuck me," Clarissa said, rubbing the back of her head. "That hurt like hell."

She reached over to shake Avery by the shoulder. She roused and groaned.

"Leena? Charlie?"

Leena stepped out from under the remains of the stairs. "We're fine. I sheltered in the crevice there when I felt the pressure build." She handed Charlie to Raven. The babe was awake now, and Leena gave her a kiss on her platinum curls before letting go.

"Gabriel?" Raven approached the cradle with Charlie in her arms. The area had become a giant mass of oddly piled dragons. They were all stacked on top of one another, bent over the grooves and mounds of the cave floor in various states of consciousness. Raven shifted Charlie to her hip to help Colin up, followed by Sylas. Nathaniel shoved Xavier off him after getting an unintentional look up his kilt, then stood and smoothed a hand through his hair. Leena helped Alexander, who removed his leather jacket and beat it with his hand before putting it on again.

Rowan grunted and dusted off her dress. There was a tear at the hem. "Damn it! This was couture!"

Tobias and Gabriel helped each other up, and Gabriel was at her side in a heartbeat. Raven kissed and embraced him.

"We did it," Gabriel said.

She nodded, but her eyes were drawn back to the cradle, where one more body lay. A body where no body should be. With ghost-white hair, his naked, pale skin carved with symbols, the man wore a ring with a central diamond.

"Gabriel?" Raven's throat tightened.

Gabriel followed her line of sight, as did the other siblings. The cavern went eerily quiet.

"Who is that?" Alexander asked, and Gabriel gave him

a wild look. "It can't be. He had black hair, and where did the tattoos come from?"

Clarissa gasped. "We did a resurrection spell."

They all crept forward, surrounding the dragon whose white wings were splayed awkwardly across the stone. Raven thought he matched his ring, a diamond brought to life, a ghost, a wraith, an animated corpse.

The dragon opened his eyes, and there was a collective inhale at his silver irises. Gabriel softened beside her, collecting himself.

"Marius," he said. "Welcome back, brother."

CHAPTER TWENTY-EIGHT

C olin moved to Leena's side, his body seeking hers out even as his eyes were locked on to Marius. She slid her hand into his and squeezed.

"Breathe, Colin."

"I watched him die," he whispered.

She stroked her fingers along the side of his arm, a simple touch to let him know she was there. "I know."

Gabriel sat Marius up and shook him by the shoulders. "Marius? Brother?"

The dragon's strange silver eyes roved to Gabriel's, but he said nothing. He seemed aware to Colin but unable to respond.

"He's in shock," Tobias said. "I've got to believe being dead for three hundred years or so and then being yanked back among the living will do that to you."

Thunder came from above, and stone rained down around them. Raven's shielding spell shimmered as it buckled at the edges. Colin's wings shot out protectively over Leena.

"I can't hold it," Raven said. "We've got to get out of

here—now."

Sylas pointed to a tunnel behind him. "That one leads to the garden... if it's not flooded with lava."

Raven shook her head. "Too late. The volcano is erupting. I've been holding it back. That passage is toast."

"Why isn't it working? I thought the spell was supposed to wake Aitna and that she'd take care of the rest?" Avery asked. She was bleeding from the side of her head and hung on to Xavier as if he were the only thing holding her up.

Raven stroked Charlie's hair back from her eyes. "The spell did work. I saw Aitna rise. They must be fighting it out up there." She pointed to the palace and the source of the loudest rumble.

Clarissa dug in Nathaniel's pocket and handed him his pipe. "This would be a great time for some teleporting, Nate."

Nathaniel lit the tobacco and took a few puffs. "I'm afraid that isn't an option. Not with our large number. May I suggest we use our wings and the door above the stairs?" He pointed toward the remains of the flight that led to the main level.

"Great. It would figure the only way out is up, where we face Mommy dearest," Alexander said through his teeth.

Xavier lifted Avery into his arms. Her injuries weren't healing as quickly as her sister's, and Colin remembered her magic made it impossible for her to swallow a dragon's tooth. They needed to get her out of here. She probably needed a healer.

Gabriel hauled Marius to his feet. The eldest dragon looked wrong, hollow somehow, like the shell of a fruit that had been eaten from the inside out. But Colin followed Gabriel's lead and swept Leena into his arms. Together, they ascended and burst into the palace proper.

"The veranda!" Sylas yelled over the rumble of shaking earth and cracking stone. "We've got to get off this mountain before it comes down around us." But when they reached the aerial entrance to the palace, they pulled up short and took cover behind whatever debris they could find. Colin tucked Leena more tightly into his side.

What once was the palace veranda was now a war zone. The entire first floor had been destroyed, leaving nothing but partial walls, heaps of debris, and cracked stone to indicate where rooms once stood. Even part of the ceiling was missing. A portion of the mountain had crumbled and was melting into lava that flowed over what used to be the palace gardens. The only recognizable thing still standing was Eleanor's red velvet throne, its ornate but blocky frame cracked and missing part of one armrest but still there.

Eleanor now towered over them, at least twelve feet tall and wielding a lightning whip that crackled through the night air toward Aitna. The true goddess repelled the electric magic with a flaming red sword that gave off an acrid sulfur scent. The red glow of flowing lava and the two full moons backlit their battle. Eleanor thrashed. Aitna slapped the magic away with her sword and thrust forward, slicing into Eleanor's cheek. The wound healed almost instantly.

"We have to find a way to help Aitna," Raven said. "There has to be a way to give her the advantage."

Colin whirled. "I don't understand. How are there two goddesses? Shouldn't Eleanor lose her power now that Aitna is back?"

"There are no rules for this. Hera ascended Eleanor. We revived Aitna with energy we siphoned from all of you. The two goddesses are equally matched. They'll fight until all of Ouros burns if we don't do something." Raven studied her daughter and then Gabriel. "I think I know what has to happen. Gabriel, I need your help." She turned to Avery, but seeing her pale and injured in Xavier's arms, she turned next to Leena. "Can you take Charlie? It's too dangerous."

"Of course." Leena bravely jaunted out from Colin's wing and lifted Charlie from her mother's arms.

Colin watched his mate take the child tenderly and swelled with pride at her bravery. Raven led Gabriel deeper into the palace.

Leena cast him a worried glance. The only thing that separated them from the warring goddesses was the tattered remains of a wall. "Where do you think she's going that is more dangerous than this?"

Colin shook his head. "I have no idea."

***

IT DIDN'T TAKE LONG FOR RAVEN TO RETURN AND PULL Colin into her plan. Leena remained huddled behind the piece of wall with Charlie in her lap. She was surprised to find she still had her satchel with her, the scrolls safely inside. She had done what she said she would do. She'd guarded the scrolls with her life, and although she planned to leave the order and fully become Colin's mate if she survived this ordeal, as of today, she remained a scribe.

"It's okay, Charlie. We're going to hide right here, and you are going to help me write down everything that happens so that future generations remember." She dug her spare quill and a blank scroll from her bag, thankful they were both enchanted, the quill to never run out of ink and the parchment to never run out of room. Who knew how long this would go on? With Charlie's back against her chest and one arm holding her gently in place, Leena positioned her satchel under the parchment on her legs and began to write.

✺

Obsidian Palace
Paragon
Year of the Goddess: ,βιθ, Capricorn 6th

I, LEENA OF NIVEN, SCRIBE OF THE ORDER OF THE SACRED Pools, record the unprecedented war between goddesses as it unfolds at the entrance of the Obsidian Palace. Eleanor, empress of Paragon, having used the blood of the child of Raven and Gabriel, drained the power from the true goddess, Aitna, to the point her celestial energy ceased to exist. Hera then ascended Eleanor, making her a goddess of equal power and strength. Eleanor used her newfound power to rain hell-fire down on Paragon, turning the tide of the war in favor of the dragons, who can withstand the volcanic heat.

Under the leadership of Raven, the three sisters were able to revive Aitna using the combined magical energy of the Treasure of Paragon. Each of the heirs and the diamond heart of Marius were placed in a circle at the heart of the mountain. The three sisters used their extraordinary power to funnel their energy into Aitna's remains.

Although the spell worked, Aitna is not strong enough to regain control. Now the two goddesses fight for the mountain. The battle appears to be a stalemate, and the heirs, along with the three sisters, have a plan to tip the scales in Aitna's favor.

The witch, Raven, has taken charge, giving each of the heirs a part to play in the attack she has orchestrated. Her efforts can't come soon enough. Eleanor has succeeded in lassoing Aitna in her magic, and the true goddess has fallen to her knees, her fire extinguished wherever Eleanor's electric whip touches it.

The plan starts with Rowan. She distracts the empress with a story from her youth, how she lost her virginity to a stable boy at sixteen. It doesn't succeed in breaking Eleanor's attack on Aitna, but it keeps her from noticing what's happening behind her.

Alexander draws a large symbol on the obsidian floor behind his mother. Given his work as an artist, this is suited to his abilities. It's a triangle of Nathaniel's design with ancient runes at its three points.

Raven motions to Colin. Something is happening. The twins are attacking. While Eleanor struggles to contain Aitna, Sylas and Colin dive and stab at her like biting flies. Eleanor's attention slips for a moment, and Aitna breaks free, her fiery fist landing a scorching punch to Eleanor's face. The true goddess has one foot under her. She rises off her knee.

Eleanor's snapping magic connects with Sylas, and he goes down, but Xavier and Tobias are there to take his place, broadswords swinging. Xavier blocks her magic with an iron blade—his mate's blade, Fairy Killer. The iron is specially enchanted against some forms of magic.

Gabriel loops a length of chain around Eleanor's neck and pulls her backward toward the symbol. Alexander joins in the tug-of-war while Nathaniel uses smoke from his pipe to weaken her. Aitna stands, tries to push Eleanor. But the empress is strong. She holds her ground.

Rowan calls Eleanor's name. She has Marius, resurrected during the same spell as Aitna, propped in the empress's throne, Eleanor's yellow citrine crown balanced on his head. This psychological jab seems to affect the goddess more than any other. Her dark eyes turn to pits of rage, and *she abandons Aitna to redirect all her wrath and magic at Marius. She never has a chance to release the blow. Aitna pushes and the heirs pull, and Eleanor's feet land in the center of the triangle.*

Clarissa sings a high note, and the outline of the symbol ignites in purple light. Gabriel and Alexander drop the chain. Sylas recovers and joins Colin, Tobias, and Xavier at her side.

Eleanor raises both hands, but when she unleashes her dark power, it is unable to penetrate the containment of the symbol. The three sisters are chanting, locking Eleanor in and draining her, feeding her energy to Aitna. The true goddess grows stronger as Eleanor shrinks, twelve feet, to ten, to six, until she drops to her knees, looking no stronger than before she ascended.

Raven breaks from her sisters and reaches for her daughter, Charlie, plucks a feather from her white wings, and takes it to Eleanor. "You murdered Medea and Tavyss to keep their unborn child from being born, not because the baby was a danger to Paragon but because it was a danger to you." She drops the feather into the triangle.

Eleanor gags, holds her throat like she can't breathe, and then she starts to age. The heirs circle around the symbol. Eleanor's hair goes gray, her eyes rheumy, and she collapses. With a wave of Raven's hands, the glow around the symbol dissipates. Raven stands over Eleanor, her sisters behind her. Eleanor's skin puckers to her bones.

She reaches her hand out toward Nathaniel. "Help me."

Of all the heirs, Nathaniel seems the most distraught about watching his mother fade, but he shakes his head once and turns his back on her.

"You don't know what you have done, witch," Eleanor hisses at Raven. "You will never have peace. You will never

have unity. Ouros will never accept a dragon mated to a witch!"

Her eyes sink into her head. Her hair and teeth fall out. And then her body crumbles to dust. A loud clink echoes in the empty space when her citrine heart, damaged and hazy, falls to the stone. Gabriel crushes it underfoot.

Aitna grows, towers over the mountain, her light illuminating Paragon all the way to Hobble Glen. With a turn of her wrist, she calms the volcano. The lava stops flowing and cools.

A row of lights shines in the distance. Soldiers from all five kingdoms watch in wonder. She reaches down and plucks the crown from Marius's head and places it on Gabriel's. As she does so, the gems in the setting change, morphing from citrine to emerald. Then the goddess forges another in her palm with fiery magic and places it, still smoking, upon Raven's dark head.

Marius doesn't move. Doesn't protest. He stares unblinking at the lightening sky.

Gabriel and Raven are left speechless. The goddess becomes normal-sized again and places her hand on Charlie's head, casts a smile in Raven's direction, and then she is gone.

The two suns break over the horizon, shining light on the effects of war. Paragon is carved in rivers of steaming lava, the palace is destroyed, and Eleanor has been reduced to ash. Pieces of her blow away on the wind.

I, Leena of Niven, have witnessed the end of Empress Eleanor and the beginning of something entirely different. Entirely new. Perhaps the folktales of old were true. The child of a dragon and a witch did bring about Paragon's destruction, as did the three sisters, but they also saved it. Now a new day dawns on a new kingdom.

CHAPTER TWENTY-NINE

R aven's bones ached. The power she'd used to hold Eleanor and drain her immortality was unprecedented. She'd depleted herself down to her essence. If it weren't for Gabriel's steadying hand on her back, she wasn't sure she could remain standing.

She stood on the edge of the veranda, staring out over a palace in tatters, a garden destroyed, a kingdom in pieces. From the mountain to Hobble Glen was nothing but smoke and stone. There was no ceiling left above them, just a hole in the side of the mountain. The ornately carved wooden doors that used to separate this area from the great hall had been torn free and probably burned in the magma which had now cooled below them.

The walls were gone, save for a few random pieces that jutted up between fallen stone and smoldering furniture. Raven had a clear view of Marius, who still sat on the throne at the far end of what used to be the great hall, staring at the sky and its rising suns. She was too tired to consider what his resurrection might mean for Paragon.

Behind him was nothing but rubble. She thought of the

golden grimoire. Hera had it now. That was for the best. She hoped the queen of the gods would rest, her vendetta finally appeased.

Raven glanced over at Gabriel, at the crown on his head, and felt the full weight of the crown on her own. It was clear what the goddess wanted, but that didn't mean their roles as king and queen would be accepted by the people. After thousands of years of brother and sister ruling side by side, would Paragonians accept mated monarchs?

What about Charlie? She glanced at her daughter, still in Leena's arms, and worried she wouldn't be accepted either. Maybe it was her exhaustion, but despite Eleanor's death, she felt defeated, felt like she was at the bottom of an uphill battle. She closed her eyes. She couldn't think of this now. Later, after she rested.

Gabriel turned to her, a smile stretching across his face. "Do you hear it?"

"Hear what?"

"Listen closely." He took her hand and held it above their heads.

Raven silenced her breath and listened. Her eyes focused in the direction of Hobble Glen, of the people in the streets and what remained of the gardens. They were cheering.

"I can't see that far, Gabriel."

"But they can see you. They're cheering for us, Raven. They're dancing in the streets."

Warmth started in the general vicinity of her heart and spread out across her body. Hope. She reached for Charlie, and Leena delivered her into her arms. The cheers grew louder.

"Oh, Gabriel..." She was overwhelmed. What did it all

mean? Where would they even begin rebuilding this kingdom?

He kissed the side of Charlie's head. "I know."

"Come, everyone!" Raven gestured to the others. "You have to see. You have to hear this."

Colin and Leena hugged each other beside her. Rowan beamed next to them, adjusting her dress and her hair as she smiled at the crowd. Sylas, Alexander, Nathaniel, and Tobias stepped to the edge on the other side of Gabriel; Clarissa joined them, tucking herself into Nathaniel's side.

"Where's Xavier and Avery?" Raven asked.

"Avery?" Xavier's growl rumbled behind them. "Whit's happening to ya?"

When Raven looked back, Xavier's face was bloodless, and Avery was draped across his arms, unconscious.

"She just collapsed!" He squeezed her jaw. "Come on, *mo ghaol*, open yer eyes!"

Raven let go of Gabriel and rushed to her sister's side, where the others had gathered. Xavier pulled her hair back to reveal a bloody gash in the side of her head.

"When did that happen?" Raven tried to think back but the night was a blur.

At her side, Tobias swallowed hard and addressed Xavier. "May I examine her? She's human. I'm a human doctor."

Xavier nodded. Tobias helped him lower her to the ground and began assessing her. When he lifted her tunic to press on her abdomen, he made a low grunt. Her left side was purple and swollen down the back of her hip. Tobias's fingers felt along her bones, evaluating the damage. He dropped his ear to her chest.

Raven was impressed at Xavier's restraint. As a mated

dragon, his instincts must be tempting him to take off Tobias's head at the moment.

"Her heart is failing," Tobias said softly, his voice cracking. "Her hip is most certainly broken, and she's likely been bleeding internally."

"How? Why?" Raven blurted.

Clarissa spoke up. "The resurrection spell. We were all thrown against the walls of the cradle. You and I healed but—"

Raven made a sound like a gag. "She can't take Xavier's tooth."

"Wh-why didna she say anythin'?" Xavier asked, in obvious torment.

"She always puts others first. It's who she is," Raven muttered. Goddess, Avery. She should have known this could happen to her sweet sister. How could she be so stupid?

"Maiara and Nick stayed at the palace in Rogos," Rowan said, "to help heal injured soldiers in the infirmary there. Alexander or I can retrieve her and her healing amulet."

Alexander ran his fingers through his wild dark hair. "I can be there and back in less than an hour."

Gathering her strength, Raven shook her head. "Don't bother. I've got this."

Xavier's pleading eyes met hers. "You can heal her?"

"Yes, I can. The same way I healed Leena." Raven mumbled the incantation. Her palms glowed purple. But as she lowered them toward Avery, a soft breath passed over her sister's lips. Her hands connected but the magic fizzled.

Avery didn't breathe again.

CHAPTER THIRTY

Franticly, Raven pressed her glowing hands to Avery's chest again and again. It was like touching stone. Like her magic had nowhere to go. She jerked her hands back.

"No..." Ice filled her veins. "Tobias, do something!"

Tobias placed his hands over Avery's heart and started CPR.

"Whit are ye doin' to her?" This time there was a warning in Xavier's voice. Even Raven could hear that he'd been pushed to the brink.

"Trying to save her life." Tobias tipped back her head but hesitated. "Xavier, you need to blow two breaths into your mate. Human breaths."

To his credit, Xavier did as he was asked. Raven pressed her healing magic into Avery again, but as the minutes ticked by, Tobias's face became more and more grave. Avery's skin was gray. He stopped chest compressions, placed two fingers on the side of her neck, and then fell back on his heels. He slumped in on himself. "I'm... sorry."

Raven trembled in Gabriel's arms. "Sorry? What do you mean, you're sorry?"

Tobias's gaze locked on to Xavier, who was still trying to breathe for his mate. "There's nothing you can do. She's dead."

Across their sister's body, Raven met Clarissa's gaze and held it. Could she feel what Raven was feeling? Like a vacuum of space had been torn between their souls?

Clarissa shook her head like she couldn't accept it. "No... She can't be dead. Don't say she's dead!"

Raven searched Gabriel's face for the truth. Her mate would fix this. Somehow, someone had to fix this.

But Gabriel was weeping, as was Tobias. Raven cried out and clutched at the base of her throat. Her soul was cleaving in two. Clarissa wept inconsolably in Nathaniel's arms. Alexander moved toward Xavier, no doubt reliving his own loss in Avery's death, but the dragon had gathered Avery up and was rocking and growling like things were going to get ugly if anyone touched him or her.

"It's not your fault, Xavier," Gabriel mumbled. "She couldn't take your tooth. Her magic wouldn't allow it."

Xavier bared his teeth and growled so loudly Gabriel turned Raven to put his body between her and his brother.

Raven collapsed onto her knees and dry heaved toward the obsidian. She'd overused her magic. The grief and exhaustion were unbearable. She couldn't even process it. Nothing would be right. Nothing would ever be right without Avery. They were the three sisters. Three. Without her, Raven would never feel whole again.

Long, tapered fingers landed on Raven's shoulder. Through blurry eyes, she saw it was Leena.

"The scrolls said that Isis and Circe raised Medea from the dead."

Raven blinked at the scribe as if she were speaking a different language.

"You have their wands," Leena said. "You have their power. You have the spells from the grimoire."

Clarissa stopped shaking and staggered toward her, stopping on the other side of Avery. Her eyes roved wildly from Raven to Leena and back again. "We have to try."

Raven tried to stand and failed. Tried again with Gabriel's help. Her whole body started to shake, and she landed on her knees again. Tears carved down her cheeks. When she looked back up at Clarissa, she couldn't stop herself from raising her voice.

"I have nothing left!" A sob ripped from her throat. "I held back the mountain. I raised Marius and the goddess from the dead and used everything that I had left to kill Eleanor. I've tried to heal Avery with the last of my power. I'm so hungry my stomach is eating itself and my mouth feels like a desert. I don't think I can do it, Clarissa."

She hugged her knees into her chest and buried her eyes in her hands. Everything in her was glass, and she was shattering, shattering into a million tiny pieces.

Gabriel's scent surrounded her, and he hugged her shoulders and whispered encouraging words in her ear, but he didn't understand. She could not do it. Not this time.

"Do you know the spell?" Nathaniel's voice was harsh, demanding.

Raven nodded. "It's a variation of the same one we did downstairs, only we direct our magic on Avery rather than throwing our energy into the cradle."

"Alexander, the symbol. Draw it here, around where she lies." Nathaniel barked the order, and Alexander immediately plucked his charcoal from inside his jacket and started to sketch on the uneven floor.

"Give me your wand." Nathaniel held out his hand expectantly.

Raven stared up at him. "I- I should be the one—"

"Stop!" Nathaniel growled and glared at her with such intensity Gabriel's wings snapped out defensively. Nathaniel shot him a look of annoyance. "Give me your wand."

"Nathaniel, ease the hell up," Colin chimed in.

"No, I will not, as you say, ease up." Nathaniel focused fully on Raven, raising his finger in her direction. "You are a woman who has been blessed with significant power. Will you choose to be like my late mother and insist on isolating yourself, never trusting anyone to truly help you? Will you, like her, put all your energy into amassing more and more magic because you think you are the only one capable of wielding it? Or will you wake the hell up and see that your gifts are just one of many tools available to aid you in a just and fair rule? That you are surrounded with those who love you and who can help, if only you will ask?"

Raven lowered her head, ashamed. "Please help, Nathaniel," she sobbed. "Save my sister."

"Give. Me. Your. Wand."

Raven placed it in his hand and sobbed anew at how pathetic she was.

But Nathaniel bowed to her as if her actions were deserving of respect. He motioned to Sylas and Tobias. Together, they pried Avery from Xavier's grip and physically forced him from the symbol. Nathaniel placed Avery's wand on her sternum, then reached back to clasp Clarissa's hand. "Ready?"

Raven's skin tingled. The three wands had forged a connection, charging the air between them. Nathaniel pointed Raven's wand at Avery's. Clarissa did the same with her own wand. The air crackled, growing thick and heady. Clarissa was clearly exhausted, but when Nathaniel nodded, she sang as clear and true as she had in the cradle, her voice charged with mystical energy. Raven's heart ached at the pure love in every note.

Nathaniel fed Clarissa energy, gritting his teeth as he poured magic into Avery's body as well. As fast as his lips would move, he uttered the incantation. How long could he keep this up?

"Breathe, Avery," Raven murmured. "Please breathe." It was taking too long. Maybe the spell wouldn't work without her. She pounded her fists against the obsidian. "Oh goddess, it needs her blood!"

Raven staggered to her feet and took Charlie from Leena, then nodded at Gabriel. He sprouted a talon and pricked her heel. One ruby drop fell toward Avery, into the spell.

The entire symbol glowed with intense yellow light, but Avery didn't move. Raven looked up when the sound of a fist hitting a jaw met her ears. Tobias's body slapped the obsidian, and Xavier thrust past Sylas.

He reached through the symbol and grabbed Avery's head with both hands. "Breathe, wife! Your husband has spoken!" He kissed her hard then, in a way that Raven thought might leave a bruise if she were alive.

Avery's hand flinched. Raven blinked twice and held her breath. Her sister's fingers moved again. And then that hand wrapped around the hilt of the sword at Xavier's side. Avery's sword. Fairy Killer.

"Get the hell off me, Xavier. Goddess, you weigh a ton!" Avery barked.

He pulled back, and she dragged the sword from his belt, hugging it to her chest. "And give me my damned sword."

Xavier's smile lit up the room. "That's my lassie."

Absently, Avery scratched her forearm through the sleeve of her tunic. She tried to sit up, but Tobias shot across the veranda to her and motioned for her to stay where she was. He checked her head and her hip. "Healed."

Raven pulled Avery into her arms. "Thank the goddess."

"I love you too, sister, but you're choking me. Jesus. Battle's over. Eleanor is dead. Get a grip." She got to her feet and fitted her sword into the sheath she wore on her back.

Raven gaped at her. "Avery, you were dead!"

Avery glared at her, the corners of her mouth twitching as if she thought Raven might be joking.

"You were just dead!" Raven pointed both hands at the symbol.

Avery staggered back, and Xavier steadied her. Mouth gapping, she seemed to notice his tears for the first time.

Clarissa's hand clamped over her mouth.

Clearly confused, Avery scratched the inside of her arm again. "God, it's burning." She rolled up her sleeve and stared down at a red-and-black symbol burned into the underside of her arm. It was the size of a quarter, a red spiral adorned with nine black dots. Her skin was seared around its edges as if she'd been branded. "Fuck, what in Hades is that?"

Raven's eyes widened, and she looked from Avery to Marius, who hadn't moved from the throne. His torso was covered in similar markings. Some small and some large. They peeked out of the neck of his tunic.

"I don't know what it is," Raven said.

Tobias cleared his throat. "We can figure it out another day. Right now, we all need to eat and rest. Especially Avery and Marius."

Leena rocked Charlie as the baby started to fuss in her

arms. "Well, you can't go back to Aeaea. Asfolk will welcome all of you. I'm sure of it. And the healers there can help."

Raven nodded and took the baby from her as Gabriel swept her into his arms. Sylas went back for Marius. And soon, they were all in flight, traveling over a kingdom both saved and destroyed. Their kingdom.

With Charlie in her arms, Raven realized the lore was partly true. Her daughter's blood had held the power to create and to destroy. Eleanor had used it to become what she did. Crimson had thought her heart was powerful enough to make her immortal. Raven had used a single feather to take Eleanor's immortality.

"You're not a monster," she whispered to her daughter. "But you are powerful. We both are. And we both will learn to use that power to build, not to destroy. We'll ask for help, and we'll thank the people around us when we get it. I won't become like Eleanor, sweetheart, and neither will you."

CHAPTER THIRTY-ONE

No sooner had Colin landed at Asfolk with Leena in his arms than he discovered she was right about the high lord welcoming them in. They were met with applause and screams of freedom. All of them were surrounded by servants and whisked away to rooms across the palace.

He was more than a little disappointed when his new mate was shuffled from his arms to her own room, but then, she was still a scribe, still dressed in the robes of her order, still with scrolls in the satchel at her hip. He allowed her to go without a fight on his part. He could be patient.

Still, his thoughts lingered on her as hot water magically filled the claw-foot tub in his room and a banquet fit for an entire family of dragons was left on the table in his chambers. When he made to eat, he noticed he was covered in blood, most of it that of the soldiers he'd had to wound or kill to get to Leena. He decided the bath would come first.

"Is the water too hot, sir?" a small elf asked, dipping his wrinkled finger in.

Colin realized he was frowning at the tub, still standing

fully dressed beside it. "Er, no. It's perfect. I just would prefer to be alone now if you don't mind."

The little man bounced on his toes. "Oh yes, of course. I'll be right outside if you need anything." He bowed low and backed away, the door to the suite clicking shut behind him.

Colin stripped out of his clothing and melted into the bath. Blood swirled off his skin, turning the water red. All the time he'd spent training in the pits, all his schooling as a warrior, it hadn't prepared him for the deaths. He'd had to kill his own people. Dragons. He'd had to end immortal lives.

He sank under the water, running his fingers through his hair. When he broke the surface again, he pushed those dark thoughts aside. What he'd done yesterday had saved their world. Eleanor was gone. There would be true peace in Ouros.

It was what he'd worked centuries for. Why he'd led the Defenders of the Goddess. And now it was done. He was a dragon without a purpose. But maybe that was okay. For now, for today, he would just be.

After a scrub down and a long soak, he crawled from the tub and dressed in the clean tunic the elves had left for him. He thought he'd have to call the little man to service the bathroom, but when he turned back around, the tub had drained itself and stood sparkling clean, as if he'd never used it. Elven magic, he realized. Brilliant.

He ate quickly and then stretched out on the massive bed, drifting off into a cool and rejuvenating darkness, at peace with his role in the war and accepting that that role was well and truly over.

COLIN WAS HAVING A VERY ENJOYABLE DREAM. IT MUST be a dream, because it felt like Leena was there in his room, tucked into his side with her head resting on his chest. Everything was dark, but he could smell her—blackcurrant and wild primrose.

His hand met bare skin, and he stroked along her spine until his fingers tangled in her hair. She shifted, and then a soft kiss pressed against his mouth.

"I hope this is okay," she whispered.

He blinked his eyes open. "Lights," he commanded. "Dim." The elven magic ignited two of the sconces on the wall, filling the room with a soft, warm glow.

"I didn't mean to wake you."

"Are you real?" he asked. "Or am I dreaming?"

She laughed, one eyebrow arching with her smile. "Yes, I'm real. I can't get any more real than this." She glanced down at herself, rolling enough that he could make out the curve of one deliciously full breast.

He licked his lips, his inner dragon waking and taking a good stretch. Beneath the covers, his body was ready for her. He was always ready for her. His mouth went dry.

"Turns out my Quanling is here, at the palace, along with the rest of the scribes. She was called in to help in the infirmary when a number of archers were burned in the eruption. I told her everything that happened and about my choice to be your mate."

"I know that had to be hard for you."

"Actually, Marjory made it easy. She said she could see the attraction between us immediately. Something about the carriage ride and being able to cut the sexual tension with a knife. She wasn't surprised, only disappointed she'd have to find someone else to take her position before she retires."

"I always liked Marjory."

"So... I returned my quill and scrolls, which means I am currently homeless with no means to support myself." She smiled as if the idea wasn't as harrowing as it sounded.

"That makes two of us. With the war won, I don't even have a job. The Defenders of the Goddess has no further need to exist, and with Gabriel and Raven ruling, I don't have an official role in the new kingdom, nor do I expect one."

"I guess that leaves us with each other."

He inhaled deeply and reached up to cradle her face, just inches from his. "That's enough for me."

"Me too."

"Say you're mine, Leena." His throat felt raw, and the words came out all grit and cinder.

"I'm yours, Colin. Always." Her warm breath caressed his lips, sending tiny shivers along his skin. His dragon was practically panting for her.

He tried to shift her under him, but she pressed him back against the mattress and straddled him just behind his erect cock. "I've already tasted what it's like to have you over me. I think I'll try something new."

She took his cock in her hand and stroked him hard from balls to tip, twisting her hand over the slick head before plunging her tight grip to the base again.

"Goddess, Leena, you're going to make me come before we've even begun." He reached toward her breast, but she leaned back, just out of his reach.

"Watch. Don't touch." She brushed his hand away. "I read about this in a scroll."

"Oh?" He grinned. Okay, if she wanted to play it that way, he'd be accommodating. He threaded his fingers behind his head and leaned against the pillow.

Leena stroked his cock again, but this time, she rose higher on her knees, her free hand feeling along her stomach to the apex of her thighs. A rush of sensation flowed through him when he saw her touch herself there, her finger circling before dipping inside.

He watched her, his heart pounding, his dragon's need to claim intense. "Leena."

Eyes locked on to his, she lowered her head and sucked him deep into her mouth. Pure ecstasy. He closed his eyes, the sharp edge of desire whipping his dragon into a frenzy. His mating trill rumbled out of his chest, loud enough he was afraid the servants outside the door could hear it.

"Leena, by the Mountain, let me in you. I need to be inside you. Please."

"Your wish is my command, my *mate*." She positioned him at her opening and came down hard, taking him at once inside her slick heat. He sat up, his wings flaring. His mating instinct drove him deeper into her, and he wrapped her in his embrace, claiming her mouth with his.

Her fingers teased along the base of his wings, stroking the webbing. The pleasure was equally exquisite and unbearable. He held her face in his hands.

"Colin..."

"Mine!" He thrust hard and deep.

She made a sound between a moan and a scream and tipped her head back, her mouth open, panting.

"Mine."

"Yours," she said. "I'm all yours."

In his arms, she arched, breathless. He unleashed himself, thrusting into her in a wild frenzy until her body clenched around his cock, her inner muscles milking him. His own release followed hers, filling her, pumping into her.

It was a long time before he was able to come back into

himself from whatever heaven they'd escaped to together. Still coupled, he nuzzled the side of her face. "I love you, Leena. Thank you for choosing me."

"I didn't."

Confused, he pulled back to get a better look at her.

"I didn't choose you. I chose me." She took his face in her hands, her eyes filling with tears. "Once I'd experienced having a life of my own, I knew I'd never be content recording the lives of others. And I wanted you. I wanted you so much."

"There's more I want to show you. You have so much more living to do."

She slid her nose along his before whispering in his ear. "Then show me."

He flipped her onto her back, already growing hard for her again, and landed with his elbows on either side of her head. "First, there is this bed."

She grinned up at him. "Haven't I experienced this already?"

"Yes, once. But we've never tested how many times I can pleasure you in a row in it."

"Oh," she said breathlessly. "It's a worthy question that needs an answer."

He dropped his lips to her neck. "Then let's find out."

CHAPTER THIRTY-TWO

After a day and night of nothing but sleeping, making love, and enjoying the hospitality of the elves from the comfort of their suite of rooms, Raven and Gabriel were invited to dine with the high lord and Queen Penelope to discuss the future of Paragon. Raven's bones still ached from her confrontation with Eleanor. All she could think about was how much magic and manpower it would take to rebuild the palace and repair the kingdom after Eleanor's path of destruction. But being king and queen of Paragon meant taking political relationships seriously. So, she left Charlie with Avery and Xavier, dressed in the gown the palace staff provided, and arrived in Niall's private dining room with a poise she had to dredge up from the deepest part of herself.

"I hope you know the kingdom of Rogos is supportive of your rule," High Lord Niall said to Gabriel. "You were chosen by the goddess herself. We want to see you succeed."

"I am relieved to hear that," Gabriel said. "A strong and independent Rogos and Darnuith are important to us and the ongoing peace in Ouros. We consider you a valuable ally." He smoothed the front of his tunic.

Niall frowned. "I wonder, though, if Marius's resurrection poses a problem for both our kingdoms. He is the rightful heir based on Paragonian tradition, and to be frank, he never had a soft spot for Rogos."

At his side, Queen Penelope scoffed. "No Paragonian ever had a soft spot for Darnuith. We are quite simply in uncharted territory. Relations between our two kingdoms must start anew."

Raven cleared her throat. "Then you must be excited to have one of your own on the Paragonian throne."

Queen Penelope gave her a quizzical look. "You may be a witch, but you are not a citizen of Darnuith."

"Medea was mated to Tavyss. It is Tavyss who appears at the center of Gabriel's family crest. That crest was designed by her, a past queen of Darnuith. While it has been centuries since your people and his have been allies, you do celebrate a shared history, and my sisters and I descend from her sister Circe. We are Medea's only living family, and I have nothing but warmth in my heart for the kingdom of my ancestors."

Queen Penelope studied her carefully. The air around Raven thickened. She could feel the queen's magic licking her, testing her. Tendrils of it swept around her ankles. *Rude.* She stared at Penelope, allowing a hint of the power she'd taken from the golden grimoire to show in her eyes.

"Keep your magic to yourself, please, unless you'd like me to probe you in return," Raven said.

Queen Penelope blinked, growing flustered, and looked away. The feel of her magic was gone. Raven was too tired and hungry to dwell on the witch's assessment of her. It had been less than forty-eight hours since she'd brought about

Eleanor's end. She wasn't ready for another battle and certainly wasn't inciting one.

Gabriel leaned back in his chair and wisely changed the subject. "Has Marius spoken since we arrived here?"

Niall rubbed his chin. "I fear not. Our best healers are working with him, and I am told he has taken food and drink. But so far, he does not speak and spends his hours staring aimlessly."

"Then I think we can safely say that as of now he isn't fit to rule. But should he challenge me for the throne in the future, I promise you, Raven and I will do what is best for Ouros. As you've pointed out, the goddess of the mountain herself placed these crowns upon our heads." He motioned to the matching emerald crowns they were wearing. The green stones put off their own light, imbued with the magic of the mountain. "Leave Marius to me."

"As long as we have an understanding," Niall said. "Whatever happens in the future, we will expect Paragon to remember the generosity of Rogos."

Gabriel gave him a deliberate and reassuring nod.

Raven took another bite of the scrumptious meal they'd been served in the high lord's private dining room as the table plunged into silence. It was some type of poultry, she decided, going off the chicken-like wing on her plate. Only, unlike a chicken, the creature had four legs instead of two. She decided not to ask what it was. It was too delicious, and she was too hungry to spoil it with some story about it being a flying swamp rat or something even more hideous. Such a stomach-turning disappointment had happened before to her in Ouros.

Niall sipped his wine without ever taking his eyes off Gabriel. There was more, something he wanted but wasn't saying. And then with a slight narrowing of his eyes, he added, "As your ally, I'd like to contribute the time of a few of our finest metalworkers to help rebuild the Obsidian Palace."

Smiling, Gabriel bowed slightly over his plate. "You honor me with your generosity."

Under the table, he squeezed her hand. They both understood that this offer came with strings attached. Anything built by elves would likely be accessible by them, a trap door into their kingdom should Niall ever need it. But Gabriel had done the only thing he could do in accepting the offer. Not only did Paragon need the help, but they were also building something here, something that would have to be repeated with the newly elected Chancellor of Everfield and Master Demidicus of Nochtbend. Every move they made laid the groundwork for the future, one they wanted to be marked by a long and abundant peace.

"What of the Highborn Council? Most of the representatives who still stood with Eleanor were killed in the uprising, but not all," Queen Penelope said. "In Darnuith, we have imprisoned any surviving supporters of Eleanor. They will stand trial, and justice will be served. But we cannot control what happens in the other kingdoms."

Raven raised her chin. "There is no place for supporters of the past regime in the future governance of Paragon. However, each kingdom should decide on their own what to do with their past representatives. Certainly, many supported Eleanor in name only. Stripping them of the title would seem enough to us. Gabriel and I plan to reestablish the Council of Elders as it existed before Eleanor and Brynhoff's rise to power."

"I thought Eleanor slaughtered the entire council, including her own parents," Niall said.

"She did." Gabriel nodded. "But according to traditional Paragonian law, when a council member dies, they are to be replaced by their eldest child. Many of those children are still alive, and what openings remain on the council, we intend to fill with representatives from the other kingdoms. Rogos will have a place, as will Darnuith."

That made Niall's smile grow broader, and he tapped his glass against Gabriel's. "Already a true king."

Gabriel cleared his throat. "We would love to answer more of your questions, but many things are still to be decided. Raven and I have barely healed from our ordeal and will need time to rebuild the kingdom. Many changes will be made once the council is in place, and of course, there is the matter of our official coronation. The people of Paragon need to be united behind us, or all of our intentions are meaningless."

"Of course. You need time." Niall sipped his wine again. "I've been rude pressing you as I have."

But Queen Penelope sniffed as if she wasn't quite done being rude. Her ice-blue eyes shifted to Raven. "What about the book?"

"What book?" Raven gave her a guileless look, but of course Penelope was speaking of the golden grimoire. Colin had told her the witch had asked about it and used her influence to try to woo him into obtaining it for her. But Raven wanted Penelope to address it directly with her. She had to start the way she wanted to continue. Paragon and Darnuith had a long, unfortunate history of being at odds with each other. It was time to usher in an era of cooperation.

"The golden grimoire. Colin told me you'd obtained it. I assume that's what Eleanor was after when she summoned you to her. What became of it?"

"Eleanor used it to kill the goddess and take her place.

The goddess Hera helped her ascend in exchange for the grimoire. Eleanor succeeded. What she hadn't counted on was that we would succeed in undoing her ascension."

"The grimoire was once Medea's, our queen. It belongs in Darnuith. It is a cultural artifact." Penelope's eyes flashed.

Raven schooled her features. She'd suspected this would be an issue. "Unfortunately, the grimoire was taken by Hera before Eleanor's ascension. It's gone for good."

"You didn't use it to awaken Aitna?" Penelope shot her an incredulous look.

Raven shook her head. It wasn't a lie. She hadn't used the book itself, only a spell she'd absorbed from its pages. "I didn't need it, which was a good thing because I never got it back from Eleanor. My sisters and I performed the spell together to raise the goddess—without the grimoire. I do not believe it remains on Ouros. Hera seemed anxious to leave with it."

Queen Penelope gave her a dark look, and Raven wondered if she sensed the book's power within her. The witch most certainly understood now that Raven was her equal. She smiled sweetly. "I hope I can trust that if the book is ever found, you will deliver it to me at once."

Those words dripped with honey. Raven placed a hand on her chest, completely immune to the witch's influence, and gave Penelope her most authentic smile. "I will always hold a special place in my heart for your kingdom, Penelope. Our rule and my mating with Gabriel is a new beginning for our people. My daughter, after all, is both dragon and witch. I want Charlie to have more witches in her life. I want us to be friends."

Penelope reached for her glass, wearier now but seemingly resigned. "I'd like that too."

THE INFIRMARY REMINDED RAVEN OF THE HOSPITAL where she'd first met Gabriel, white-walled and with an herbal smell that might have been antiseptic in her human world. More sterile than she expected. Elves used magic to heal as much as witches did, but her understanding of their specific type of magic was limited. When Leena had created the key that had freed them from the dungeon, she'd used science and engineering, not magic. Perhaps the healers here fixed bodies the same way, almost like human doctors. Tobias would find it fascinating. She must show him later.

Marius had a separate room off the main hall, far from the other patients. There were plenty in need of healing. Any of Rogos's soldiers who had been on palace grounds when the volcano erupted had either died or suffered terrible burns. Every cot was taken, and beds had been moved in to fill the entire ward. With so little room here, Raven wasn't sure if Marius's isolation had to do with his former royal status as the heir apparent or with his condition. Even elves, it seemed, were unsettled by the resurrection of the dead.

She found Marius propped up in bed, staring at a painting of the Mystic Wood. He didn't turn to look at her when she walked into the room. She studied the painting that held his attention. In it, a snake dangled from one of the tree branches, and Raven couldn't help but be reminded of the Garden of Eden, although the people here wouldn't understand that reference. A unicorn pointed its horn at the serpent, its white coat gleaming in a ray of sun.

"It's called *The Reckoning*," Marius said in a deep voice lined with grit.

Raven's head snapped around to find him looking at her, his strange silver eyes clear. "You're speaking!"

He pointed to the painting. "It's an elven myth. As the story goes, when elves first walked Ouros, they were powerless until they encountered a tree worm who bit one of the females and infected her with venom that gave her the abilities elves have today. Only, as the story goes, the power made her evil. She enslaved those who weren't like her until the unicorn, the worm's only natural enemy, stabbed her with its horn. Unlike the worm who gave her power, the unicorn gave her empathy, and that is why the elves have always leaned toward peace, fairness, and neutrality. This painting depicts the two beasts facing off against each other from the perspective of the woman."

"I've never heard that story before."

"It was something I learned growing up, when it was assumed I would be king."

The room plunged into silence. After a few moments, she realized she'd never introduced herself. "I'm Raven, by the way. I'm Gabriel's mate."

His eyes flicked to the doorway. "And where is my brother?"

"Taking care of some official business. He knows I'm here. I came to see if I could help you recover." Raven took a step closer to the bed. "I have a few spells in my arsenal for healing. He thought they might help you, but it seems you don't need help after all."

"You're the witch who brought me back." His strange eyes met hers again, and she could not read his expression. Was he happy about it? Confused?

"Yes. One of the three anyway. My sisters and I. You were a... pleasant surprise when we resurrected the goddess."

His eyes closed for a long blink, and she watched his throat bob on a swallow. "We were in the same place."

A chill spiderwalked up her spine. "You were in the same place as whom?"

"The goddess. She was in the same place as me after she died." He rubbed his forehead as if it hurt. "When you pulled her back, I came too. It felt as if I were tied to her somehow."

Raven licked her lips. "It was the spell. The magic required all nine hearts. I linked all of you to the goddess. Since Eleanor had bound your soul to your heart, it brought you back as well." She didn't mention the part about Charlie's blood being a catalyst. He didn't need to know the details. "Do you know where you were... Before, I mean?"

"I was... in between." He toyed with the edge of his blanket. "The goddess is a true immortal. She cannot die, only be forced into the place where I was—that in-between place. Everything there is black-and-white. No color at all unless someone from here accesses it by magic. Your spell was as red as blood." He held a strand of his hair between his fingers, frowning at the white color. "It used to be dark, you know? Almost black."

"Your brother told me."

"Now I look like a ghost. Maybe I am. This is not the life I left behind."

Raven rubbed her mouth, wondering how much she should say. He seemed lucid, but the trauma of what he'd been through was astronomical. She had so many questions.

"No. It's not the life you left behind," she said softly. "Now that you're back, there are things we—Gabriel and I—want to discuss with you."

He turned his head so he was looking at her straight on. "You want to know if I plan to challenge Gabriel for the throne. Try to force the old law." He scoffed. "Trap Rowan into ruling by my side."

Raven frowned. "You could, I suppose. Try it, I mean. Although the goddess made it clear what she wanted, and so has Rowan. She plans to return to New York with her mate, Nick. Royal life isn't for her."

"She never wished to rule, even as a child." A great sigh left his lungs. "And I find I have no desire to pick up where I left off."

Tension Raven hadn't even known was there seeped from her shoulders.

Marius rested his hands across his stomach. "The goddess made it clear to me what she wants, and unlike my mother, I have no desire to go against her wishes. But I would like a life here, a role." His gaze drifted to the painting again. "I find myself in need of a purpose for being here."

"Of course, Marius. Gabriel and I want you to serve as our adviser to the Council of Elders. We're reestablishing it to replace the Highborn Court."

He licked his lips. "I can do that. I *will* do that, on one condition."

Raven braced herself. "What condition is that?"

He pulled up the sleeve of his pajamas, showing her the red symbols on his body. "Tell me what these mean."

Frowning, she stepped closer to the bed to get a better look, and when he indicated it was okay, took his arm in her hands. "The truth is, I don't know. I can feel the magic in them, but it's foreign to me. Do they... bother you?"

His throat bobbed. "I have dreams." He frowned, his face suddenly becoming drawn. "All in black and white and red. Horrible dreams. I'm back there in the in-between.

When I wake, the symbols itch." He pulled the sleeve down. "This body does not feel like my own."

Raven grimaced. She joined her hand with his and gripped it firmly. "I'm not sure what the dreams mean or the symbols, but I will help you. We will figure it out, I promise you."

He met her gaze and squeezed her hand. "Then I am yours, my queen. Tell my brother congratulations on his rise to power and that I hope his coronation goes more smoothly than mine."

CHAPTER THIRTY-THREE

"Colin? Open up—I need to talk to you." Gabriel's gruff voice and harried knock sent Leena flying out of bed. She reached for the purple dress the elves had gifted to her. It was the only clothing she owned. When she'd resigned as a scribe, she'd had to leave all her robes and other possessions behind. They belonged to the temple. Technically, she did have the robes she'd been wearing when she informed the Quanling of her decision—Marjory did not take the clothes off her back—but it would be wrong to wear the uniform of her past calling. She preferred this simple dress. It might have been a gift, but it was the only thing in her life that was hers and hers alone. The only thing aside from Colin.

"Keep your dragon in your skin," Colin called.

He didn't look happy about the interruption. His hungry male gaze raked over her body before she covered it in the dress. How he could still look at her like that after they'd made love so many times was beyond her. Her most sensitive flesh ached with overuse every time she moved. Then again, that look he was giving her made her blood run hot enough she would do it again if there weren't someone at the door.

As much as Leena was not ashamed of her mating to Colin, she didn't welcome Gabriel's judgment. She pressed her back against the wall, out of sight, while Colin slid the small panel built into the door aside and made eye contact with his brother.

"This isn't a good time."

Leena's eyes widened. It had to be important if the new king of Paragon was seeking them out. It was not wise to deny the king entry even if Colin was his brother.

"I'm sorry to bother you," Gabriel said. "But I have something important to speak with you about. Tell Leena she can come out from behind the wall. I can smell her all over you."

Heat burned in Leena's cheeks and neck, but Colin grunted for him to wait a second and slid the peephole door closed. He dressed quickly but paused and looked her way before he opened the door. She nodded. She wasn't going to get any more ready than this. He flipped the latch and let his brother in.

Gabriel strode through the door and gave Leena a shallow bow before gesturing toward the small table in the room. "If you don't mind, I'd like to sit for this. Niall has been running me all over Asfolk today, and I'm still recovering from our confrontation with Eleanor."

Colin nodded and pulled out a chair for her, but Leena went to the pitcher on the side table and poured them all glasses of water before she sat. Her mouth already dry as a stone. She was going to need it, and it seemed rude not to serve the two dragons. They both mumbled a thank-you at the gesture.

For as long as she'd known Gabriel, he'd always made

her nervous. There was his size to contend with—he was as large as Colin but with a deadly sort of cadence to his movements that reminded her of a wild cat... some kind of predator. And his eyes—she always wondered how Raven could stand looking into those eyes. They were dark but always burning, red flecks dancing like sparks deep within. Colin was every bit of a warrior as Gabriel, but her familiarity with him, his gray eyes that always softened when he saw her, put her at ease. With Gabriel... Facing him felt like staring darkness itself head on. Like facing death.

Gabriel sipped his water and looked between Colin and Leena. "Am I mistaken, or are congratulations in order?"

Leena's eyes darted to Colin, whose cheeks had taken on a red tinge. Was it possible that Gabriel could tell what they'd done?

"I don't mean to embarrass either of you." He glanced at Leena. "It's a dragon thing. His mating scent is all over you and this room. And you're no longer wearing your temple robes, so I can draw some conclusions."

Now her face burned again. She pressed her cool palms against her hot cheeks.

"We are mated, yes," Colin said. "Leena is mine. She will not be returning to the temple."

A warm feeling came over her at the way Colin claimed her. She was not a woman who had ever longed to be possessed, but this mark of ownership was mutual. It was not a claim that threatened her freedom. Her mating was not a chain at all, but maybe a long elastic band. She could go from him as far as she wished, but there would always be that bond, always that subtle tug drawing her back to this dragon who made her feel whole again.

Gabriel nodded. "I thought that might be the case. I'm glad she's here. This discussion concerns both of you."

Now Leena squirmed. Was there to be a punishment for her leaving the temple? Would Colin be cast out, or would they both end up scraping by in the Borough?

"I'd like to offer you the position of Master of the Guard." Gabriel studied Colin, his fingers toying with his glass. "I realize that after leading the rebellion, taking over Scoria's position as captain may not be enough for you, but this new position as master will also serve on the Council of Elders. We need to remake the Obsidian Guard into something to be proud of again. A unit that serves the people in peacetime as well as war."

Colin's throat bobbed, his lower lids lining with silver. Leena couldn't remember ever seeing him so moved, with the exception of the moment in the cradle when he'd wanted her to take his tooth. He glanced toward her, almost as if he was asking for her blessing, and she gave him a swift and certain nod. "It would be my honor to serve Paragon in this capacity. It will take work, but I'm confident the dragons of Paragon are up to the task of remaking their military, one that works for and with our allies."

Gabriel's expression softened for the first time, as if Colin's acceptance was a huge relief to him. Leena glanced at Colin proudly. He was perfect for the job, and maybe she could get work in Paragon too, perhaps in the palace kitchen or in one of the shops in Hobble Glen. She knew several languages, after all, and was no stranger to hard work.

"Which brings us to you," Gabriel said, shifting his focus to Leena.

"To me?" In shock, she was speechless as the full force of his attention turned on her. "I promise you I won't be any trouble—"

"We're going to need a court historian."

Leena froze. Did he say what she thought he said?

"With your being a former scribe, Raven and I thought you would be the perfect choice. You'd be responsible for recording all the meetings of the Council of Elders as well as accurately detailing significant events in Paragonian history. Of course, you won't have the benefit of a pool of tears, so you'll have to be where the action is."

"Yes," she blurted, a smile spreading across her face. Was her skin glowing? The joy she felt inside must be visible on the outside. "I will be your court historian. Oh, Gabriel, thank you! You won't regret giving me this opportunity."

"Good. Then it's settled. You'll both move in to the palace as soon as we can get it rebuilt. Until then, the owner of the Silver Sunset has agreed to lease the inn to us. You'll have a room there."

"We'll be living in the palace?" Leena gaped in surprise.

Colin seemed equally unsure. "Neither Scoria nor Ransom lived in the palace. Even when Ransom was... staying in Eleanor's rooms, he didn't officially live there."

"But *you* will," Gabriel said. "And so will your mate. The kingdom of Paragon owes you dearly for your leadership of the Defenders of the Goddess. You'll both live in the palace, and you will be compensated well for what you do and will have access to the royal staff. I assume, now that you've mated, you'll only be needing one suite of rooms?"

Colin shot her a questioning look, and she poured her agreement into her smile. His eyes sparked with masculine heat.

"Are you sure? It's a lot of change for you," he asked her.

She glanced down at the table, embarrassed to be having this conversation in front of Gabriel. She wasn't ashamed. She just wished they'd spoken about it earlier. "I'm sure," she said. "As sure as I have ever been."

"Yeah, we'll only need one," Colin said, never taking his eyes off her.

"Excellent." Gabriel stood from his chair. "Now, if you'll excuse me, I have a few more job offers to make."

Colin shook his hand firmly. "Thank you, Gabriel."

Leena bowed, heart brimming with appreciation for Gabriel's kindness. "It's a new beginning for both of us."

Gabriel smiled, his eyes glancing heavenward. "For all of us."

CHAPTER THIRTY-FOUR

Kingdom of Paragon
The Obsidian Palace
Year of the Goddess: ,βιθ, Pisces 28ᵗʰ
Six months after the Paragonian revolution

With the help of fifteen witch architects from Darnuith and a dozen engineers from Rogos, King Gabriel and Queen Raven have successfully reconstructed the Obsidian Palace for a new generation. The lava rock that previously carved through the gardens has been removed, and new flowering trees and shrubs have been planted in the scorched soil.

The palace itself has been reconstructed to let in more light with an open and welcoming floor plan. It starts in the veranda, where the family crest has been lovingly restored by Alexander, who is now serving as the royal artist. What once depicted a dragon wrapped around a golden fruit tree now includes his mated witch sitting atop his tail. The crest commemorates the love of Tavyss and Medea, whose brave sacrifice in the fight against Eleanor and Brynhoff laid the groundwork for the new kingdom. Rumor has it that the redesign was in part at the suggestion of his mate, Maiara, who is now serving as the court healer.

Beyond the veranda lies a great hall, also designed by Alexander with the help of engineers and architects from Rogos. Fashioned in a circle rather than a traditional rectangle, the room is constructed with collaboration in mind. King Gabriel's goal is to undo the damage caused by Eleanor's reign. To increase a sense of equality and partnership among the five kingdoms, there is no dais and no thrones as there were under the reign of Eleanor and Brynhoff. The king and queen address their guests from the center of a ring of seats, and when they are done, they sit in common chairs among the others.

All fifteen bedrooms have been reconstructed with en suite bathrooms along with the dining room, library, and a state-of-the-art kitchen. Although their location is undisclosed, there are also treasure rooms for the palace dragons. The Obsidian Dungeon, however, has not been excavated, nor has the rubble beyond the library that once housed Eleanor's ritual room. By royal decree, they will be sealed off from the palace, never to be used again.

With the palace and grounds in operational order, Paragon has once again found its voice in the political landscape of Ouros. The Council of Elders has been reinstated and is now comprised of the living descendants of the original council, along with elected representatives from Darnuith, Rogos, Everfield, and Nochtbend. All council meetings are held after sunset to encourage participation by the vampires, something that has never been done before.

Although the fairy representative on the council would prefer to meet during the day when fairies are at their strongest, the assignment of Sylas and Dianthe as diplomats in the region has smoothed over any political unease at the change. The two consider themselves as much citizens of Everfield as of Paragon and have made it their personal mission to rebuild the Empyrean Wood.

They are receiving help from Nathaniel and Clarissa, Paragon's new royal magicians. Clarissa is using her unusual talent for vocal magic to help the trees in Everfield grow faster, while Nathaniel employs his dragon-powered spellwork to help the fairies design homes safely at a faster pace.

Although Avery and Xavier refused a permanent position in the Paragonian royal court in order to spend part of each year in Xavier's Earthly realm, Avery, as one of the three sisters, is now a trusted adviser to the crown, and Xavier is serving as a temporary officer in the guard, helping Colin train the new warriors.

As for Tobias and Sabrina, although they acted as temporary ambassadors to Nochtbend, they will be returning to Earth, as will Rowan and Nick, after the coronation of Raven and Gabriel. Sabrina has her own coven to run, and Tobias has a full life as her consort. Rowan and Nick are anxious to return to their lives in New York, where they run a community center for underprivileged children.

Which brings us to the beloved event that we celebrate today, the coronation of Gabriel and Raven. I, Leena, royal court historian, am pleased to immortalize this moment by documenting it as the first official event of a new era for Paragon. The great hall is adorned in bursts of white flowers that fill the room with a heady, lightly sweet fragrance. Swags of gold rope, a gift from Nochtbend, hang from the ceiling. The floor is lined with emeralds, the king and queen's official gemstone, enchanted by the witches of Darnuith to glow from within. The walls bear tapestries woven by the artisans of

Everfield, depicting the constellations exactly as they will be on this sacred night. And the most talented musicians from all five kingdoms have come together to play for the standing-room-only crowd.

Raven, dressed in emerald vilt, walks ceremoniously to the center of the room from the south, her daughter Charlie's hand in hers at her side. Charlie, who took her first steps only weeks ago, wears a dress made of the same material as her mother's but with a shorter skirt that shows off a pair of shiny golden shoes. The crowd cheers at her tentative steps and the way her soft white wings adjust for balance. Gabriel arrives down the aisle from the north next, handsomely clad in an emerald-and-black tunic suit adorned with gold cords. Avery and Clarissa carry in the crowns from the west aisle, and Marius, to the surprise of many of the guests, arrives from the east as the officiant.

To murmurs of the crowd, Marius places the crowns upon the heads of the new king and queen, saying, "As the eldest son of the last reigning regent, I hereby declare Gabriel and Raven the true and proper rulers of Paragon and renounce all claims to the throne. I crown you king and queen in the name of the goddess and welcome a new era of peace and justice under your reign." And then, to the absolute delight of the crowd, a small tiara that has been hidden inside Gabriel's crown is nestled in the cherubic curls of the royal couple's daughter. "Charlie, in the name of the goddess, I crown you princess of Paragon."

Applause rings out, deafening in the round room. Guests from every kingdom leap to their feet to congratulate the couple.

When the noise dies down, Gabriel addresses the kingdom. "My dearest Paragonians and distinguished guests. It is my deepest honor to accept this crown from my brother

Marius. For far too long, Ouros has suffered under a cruel and ruthless ruler whose only desire was to amass limitless power. My queen and I are committed to a world that shares power, a kingdom whose deepest concern is the welfare of its people, and a reign that will one day be remembered for being as just and fair as its predecessor was cruel."

After another round of cheers, all the guests are invited to a feast in the adjoining ballroom. The festivities are planned for well into the night. Guests enjoy food and drink from the five kingdoms, including Paragonian tribiscal wine, elder-beast from Darnuith, and crizzle rolls from Everfield. By the time the two suns rise above Paragon and the last guests leave the palace, it is clear that the evening has ushered in a new beginning and a bright future filled with potential.

EPILOGUE

The moment Marius placed the crown on Gabriel's head, he experienced an intense and profound sense of relief. Before everything, before he'd... died... he'd thought he wanted to be king. It was what he was raised to do. Raised to be. But now, after everything, it was all too much. What would be the point of going against what the goddess wanted? What the people wanted?

In some ways, he was the last dragon, the last remnant of a kingdom that was no more. But he would not be like Eleanor. He would not fight for more power or play politics to orchestrate his own advancement. He was done with all that.

Later, in the ballroom, he hung in the shadows, leaning against a cane that had proved necessary in his weakened state. He nursed a glass of tribiscal wine and watched the dancing and merriment with interest. These people were strangers to him and not just because those who'd been allies of Eleanor's were either dead or banished from the palace. To Marius, it felt like he'd been gone for a thousand years. He'd spent ages in that place between, had seen horrors that only the dead see. Only the dead who don't pass on.

All this, this game of kingdoms, seemed trivial now. Who could concern themselves with trade routes and border agreements when they'd been given another chance at life? Why fight to be king when he was just happy to be free of the purgatory that had held him for so long?

"You really gave it up? Just like that?" A woman stood beside him, although he had no recollection of her moving to his corner of the room. Strange. He didn't know her, which made the personal nature of the question all the more intrusive.

He grunted dismissively and sipped his wine. Clearly, she was a member of the aristocracy, a daughter of some wealthy merchant from Hobble Glen, he supposed. Although her wings were tucked away, she had the double crescent mark beside her right eye as all dragons did, as well as the smoky scent of his kind. Her red dress was made of the finest vilt, and her caramel-colored hair shone like silk against the fabric. The rubies and diamonds flashing from her ears, neck, and fingers were easy enough to come by in Paragon, but the gold design that housed them and the magic that lit them from within was not. That was only available to the wealthy. She blinked lovely golden hazel eyes at him, only a few shades lighter than what his used to be before he became this... this... ghost.

"Please forgive me," she said, brows crowding together and cheeks reddening as if she was ashamed. "It was terribly rude of me to ask it so bluntly. To be honest, I feel like I know you, but you couldn't possibly know me. It was far too personal a thing to ask."

"Forget about it." Marius braced himself on his cane with both hands. He'd kept his tone polite but not warm.

He wanted to set her at ease but also discourage further conversation. Hopefully she'd get the hint and leave him alone.

Defying his expectations, she stayed right where she was, sipping her drink in awkward silence.

"Why exactly do you feel like you know me?" he asked, suddenly curious. Even as a prince, he didn't mingle with the general population often, and he certainly didn't remember her. She was beautiful. The old him might have noticed.

She raised an eyebrow, her expression growing wistful. "I used to watch you fight in the pits. You were quite the warrior. I'm embarrassed to say I had your poster hanging in my bedroom. I never missed one of your matches."

Oh, so she was a pit bunny. There was always a small legion of unmarried females watching the matches from the stands, hoping by some miracle their scent would find its way into the ring and they'd be noticed by one of the warriors, perhaps a prince. Sad, really, that she'd carried a torch for him all this time. She must have heard what happened to him, and if she hadn't, he didn't plan to explain it to her. Why couldn't she just leave him alone?

He sipped his wine. "That was a long time ago."

"Of course it was." She lowered her voice. "Before you died... and came back. I have to say, I almost didn't recognize you, but... The changes suit you if you don't mind my saying so."

He shot her a glance, a pang of self-consciousness shooting through him at the thought of his white hair and colorless eyes. Her expression seemed genuine, but the comment left him raw. He'd been considered handsome once. Not now. Now he was a sketch of a man that the artist had forgotten to shade in. "If you'll excuse me, I have to..."

He couldn't think of a single thing he had to do, but he drifted away from her.

"I just wanted to know if you'll be fighting in the pits again," she blurted. "Since you're not challenging Gabriel to... um... rule... you have to do something with your time, right?"

He frowned into his wine and made a show of adjusting his weight on his cane. "Not up for a fight these days, obviously."

"Well, not yet," she said with a soft smile. If he'd sensed a hint of insincerity, he might have torn into her, but her words gave off a genuine hopefulness, as if she truly believed he might fully recover. He didn't have the energy to correct her.

He *would* need to do something with his time, wouldn't he? But considering the coronation aisle was the farthest he'd walked without his cane since his resurrection, the pits were likely not in his future. Raven and Gabriel had invited him to act as an adviser to the Council of Elders, but he had to believe the job wouldn't take all his time. Eventually, he would need a distraction, anything so he wouldn't dwell on the disaster that was his life. Funny that it took this strange woman to make him think of it.

"Who are you, exactly?" he asked.

"Harlow. I'm the doormaker's daughter. I think you've met my parents, Darium and Lemetria?" She bowed her head in greeting.

"I have met your parents." He sipped his wine to keep from betraying his feelings about the couple. Doormaking was an esteemed art in Paragon as each home's door traditionally displayed a unique mosaic of gems that represented the history of the family who lived there. The wealthier the family, the more ornate the door. And Darium was the premier doormaker. But all that wealth had made him and his wife drunk with self-importance—at least, that was how Marius remembered them. Then again, it had been hundreds of years since he'd been in a position to judge.

"I know what you're thinking, but they mellowed out over the years you were away," Harlow said. "Certainly the last few, when Eleanor became a power-hungry tyrant."

Marius raised a brow and ground his teeth. "It's hard for me to picture your father in the resistance."

She laughed. "Oh no, he wasn't. We both know that's not who my father is. But he also distanced himself those last months. I suppose that's what earned us the invitation."

Marius glanced around the room. "Your parents are here tonight?" That surprised him. He hadn't spoken to Gabriel about who was associated with the Highborn Court, but he would have assumed Darium and Lemetria to have been in Eleanor's inner circle as they were when he was a young man. He'd have thought Gabriel would have cast them out entirely.

"No." She gave a shallow smile. "My father was called away to meet with a vendor in Nochtbend. They send their regrets. But I am here, representing my family."

"Hmmm." His glass had run dry, and so had his patience. He looked toward her to make some excuse to abandon her presence, but his eyes locked on a figure that had appeared behind her in the shadows. *Killian.* His father's colorless and translucent presence stood wraithlike behind Harlow, his dark mouth gaping silently in his pale face. A red slash marred his neck where he'd been beheaded. He was saying something, mouthing words that Marius couldn't understand.

Marius's skin chilled. He stopped breathing. Stopped blinking. Tried to make out the word his father mouthed to him from the beyond. The glass dropped from his trembling hand.

And Harlow caught it.

"Is everything all right?" Harlow asked. "Are you unwell?" She turned to look where he was staring, his empty glass cradled in her palm. Killian disappeared like so much smoke. There was nothing there. Just the empty corner of the room.

Marius shook his head and took his glass from her. "Thank you. I'm still recovering," he said. "If you'll excuse me, I think I'm going to retire to my rooms."

"I understand. It is very late. Take care of yourself." She smiled, and he noticed her red lipstick exactly matched her dress. Oddly, he found he was almost sorry to have to cut the conversation short.

"It's been a pleasure, Harlow," he said automatically before bowing and retreating from the room. Halfway into the hall, he was surprised to discover that he actually meant it.

❦

THANK YOU FOR READING THE *DRAGONS OF PARAGON. If you enjoyed this title, please leave a review wherever you buy books.*

MARIUS IS BACK, BABY! BUT HE'S NOT SURE WHO HE IS anymore. So much of his identity is wrapped up in his former destiny to be king. Without a place or purpose in this new kingdom, he feels lost. Worse, he's not sure he *ever* was the person his royal life led him to believe he was.

Can Harlow help him remember his true self? With her

at his side, he might just be brave enough to carve out a new existence, if forces from the past don't come between them.

Find out more in THE LAST DRAGON! Order your copy now.

Or turn the page to read an excerpt.

THE LAST
DRAGON

THE TREASURE OF PARAGON BOOK 9

USA TODAY BESTSELLING AUTHOR
GENEVIEVE JACK

EXCERPT: THE LAST DRAGON
CHAPTER 1

Ash snowed from the sky, sparks of bright red fire lighting up the otherwise endless darkness. An otherworldly growl came from somewhere in the woods beyond the cave—thick, dense woods filled with sharp claws and slashing teeth. When the hunters killed, they stole more than one's life. Life was meaningless here, after all. What those monsters took was far more chilling.

"I'm so hungry. We have to try for the temple." The voice beside Marius was a low whine. If a rat could speak, it would have that voice. But the other man was right. They needed food or they'd become weaker and weaker, unable to die but also unable to move unless some other soul took pity on them and carried them to the sacred place.

"We go together," another voice said, this one lower, more confident. Killian.

Marius couldn't see the other man in the darkness, but he knew his face well, knew that he could trust him. They were connected somehow, from before. How exactly, he couldn't remember. That piece of history had been buried by pain and darkness long ago. So long ago. A lifetime.

Maybe, if he'd had time and enough light to see the man, he'd remember. Not that it mattered. Every day was about survival. There was no room in his mind for anything else.

His hand gripped the hilt of the sword hanging at his side in a black leather scabbard. The other man tapped the heel of his spear on the cave floor.

"I'll help too," the rat man said. But Marius knew that only meant he'd follow behind and keep a safe distance from any violence. That man had never even found a weapon for as long as he'd been in this strange, desolate place, and the only reason he had fighting leathers was because Marius had found him some.

Killian didn't respond. An exploding ember lit the sky beyond the cave. "Now," Killian said.

Marius sprinted toward the temple, weaving in and out of trees at breakneck speed. A screech came from behind them, and he whirled to find Killian facing off against a hunter. The winged beast's skin was gray and leathery, its head covered in rows and rows of eyes, and its lipless mouth unable to close fully due to the length of its many teeth. It slashed a multijointed limb through the darkness.

Marius swung his blade, lopping off the thing's claw before it could reach Killian. He spun, ducked, and thrust. A metal-on-metal screech sounded as his sword slid into the thing's steely flesh.

And then he woke up.

Marius blinked at the thing in front of him. He was warm and well fed, surrounded by shiny obsidian. On the floor in front of him was a suit of armor through which he'd stabbed a sword that was not his own. It wasn't even an actual weapon. He realized in horror that it was part of the sculpture, the sword that the suit of armor had been holding.

"Uncle Marius?"

He spun to find Charlie standing behind him in the hall, her blond hair a tangled mess and a stuffed bear clutched under one elbow. What did Raven call it? A teddy bear. That was it. The girl loved her bear. He couldn't get over how much she'd grown this past year. Her development was rapid, even for a dragon. Then again, she was only half dragon. The other half was witch like her mother Raven. It was still to be seen how the two species would manifest in the child. She'd yet to shift and had no ring as he and his brethren did.

"What are you doing up?" he asked her. He silently thanked the goddess that he hadn't hurt her. He could have. Might have stabbed her in his sleep as he had the suit of armor. "Your mother and father would not like to know you're out of your bed in the middle of the night."

The little girl rubbed her eyes with her tiny fists and ruffled her strange, feathered wings. "I heard you."

Marius looked right then left down the hall. If anyone else had heard what he'd done, they hadn't come to help him. "I'm sorry I woke you, but you should have left it for the guards to sort out. What would you have done if I was something dangerous?" He was, extremely dangerous. Again, his stomach tied itself in knots over the possibility he might have hurt her.

"I knew it was you, Uncle," she said, confused.

"How did you know it was me? Anyone could have made this noise." He gestured to the destroyed suit of armor.

Her little nose wrinkled, and she wiped a hand across her forehead, sweeping platinum curls from her eyes. "That's not what I heard. I heard you screaming, inside my head." She pointed at her temple, and ice formed in his veins. "I came and woke you up so you wouldn't be scared anymore."

He swallowed. "You woke me up?"

She nodded. "I used my zappy zap."

"What's your zappy zap?"

"Mommy said I shouldn't talk about it."

"You can tell me because you used it on me," Marius said. "I already know about it."

Charlie's brow furrowed as she thought about that for a moment. Then she clapped her small hands together. A shock flowed through Marius, making the tiny hairs on his arms and legs stand on end. "That's a fun trick."

"Mommy says I'm not supposed to use it unless I'm in danger."

"You have a very smart mommy." Marius held out his hand to her. "Come. I'll tuck you in."

She slipped her tiny fingers into his, and they padded toward her room. "What was your bad dream about?"

"I don't remember," Marius lied.

"I saw a monster." Charlie's slippers scuffed across the floor.

"You could see what was happening in my head and hear me scream?"

She nodded.

"Does that happen to you often?" Marius asked.

"No. One time with Aunt Avery, but her dream was pretty, all sunshine and blue sky."

Marius sighed. "Great," he mumbled. He'd have to tell Gabriel about this. Charlie clearly had some psychic abilities he and Raven weren't aware of. "I'm sorry my dream scared you, Charlie, but it was just a dream. Nothing real. If it happens again, try to push it out of your mind."

She stopped in front of her room and giggled. "It doesn't

scare me, Uncle Marius. You killed that monster. Killed it dead. You would never let it get me."

He kissed her on her head, noticing how his hair, now completely lacking color, almost matched hers, although her eyes were blue and her skin was a warm gold, perfectly smooth and unmarked. He gave her his most reassuring smile. "I would never let anything get you, Charlie. Not on purpose. But I'm afraid, if I'm having a bad dream, I might bump into you and knock you down. I'd be asleep and not know you were there."

Her young face grew serious. "I'll send my zappy zap through you from far away."

That made him smile. "Okay, little one, into bed." He lifted her into the plush four-poster and pulled the frothy pink blanket over her. She tucked her teddy bear under her chin and closed her eyes.

"Uncle Marius?"

"Yes?"

"Mommy says that bad dreams happen when something isn't going right in your life and your brain tries to work it out."

"Hmm. I'll keep that in mind."

"Maybe if you fight the monsters in your real life, you won't have to fight them in your dreams."

He studied the little girl and placed a kiss on her temple. "Goodnight, Charlie."

MEET GENEVIEVE JACK

Award winning and USA Today bestselling author Genevieve Jack writes wild, witty, and wicked-hot paranormal romance and fantasy. Coffee and wine are her biofuel. The love lives of witches, shifters, and vampires are her favorite topic of conversation. She harbors a passion for old cemeteries and ghost tours, thanks to her years attending a high school rumored to be haunted. Her perfect day involves a heavy dose of nature and one crazy dog. Learn more at GenevieveJack.com.

Do you know Jack? Keep in touch to stay in the know about new releases, sales, and giveaways.

Join my VIP reader group
Sign up for my newsletter

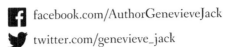

facebook.com/AuthorGenevieveJack

twitter.com/genevieve_jack

instagram.com/authorgenevievejack

bookbub.com/authors/genevieve-jack

(Knight World Novels)

ACKNOWLEDGMENTS

As I close the eighth book in this epic paranormal romance series, I would like to again thank Anne at Victory Editing for her work on this novel. A huge thank you to Lisa Hollett, Silently Correcting Your Grammar, for her editing skills and story bible. Nine dragons plus mates and supporting characters is a lot of moving parts. Lisa kept everyone's hearts and rings the right color and ensured consistency across books. I can't thank her enough.

Another big thank you to Deranged Doctor Designs for the fabulous cover art. They captured the look I was going for with this series perfectly.

And finally, thank you readers for trusting me with the hours you invest in my books. I strive to give you a memorable experience and hope you enjoyed this one.

Made in the USA
Coppell, TX
27 August 2021